THE GOOD PEOPLE AND THE BAD

The Foul and Faustian Misdeeds of Oᴇᴅɪᴘᴜs O'Kᴀɴᴇ Far, Far From His Native Connaught

ORIGINAL TITLE: *TADHG O CÀTHÀN*

a novel of obscene horror by
SHEA LEITRIM

Cover Photograph by Shadow Angelina. Cover & interior designed by Geoff Munsterman.

ISBN-13: 979-8-218-17024-0

FIRST EDITION

10 9 8 7 6 5 4 3 2 1

THE
GOOD PEOPLE
AND THE
BAD

ONE

When Eddie O'Kane woke up, it was 1978 and he was fifteen years old. He blinked at the room around him, at the weathered bureau and the white paint peeling from his windowsill. A dog-eared Creem pinup adorned the wall beside his bed, and for a few seconds he tried in vain to recall the band's name.

Then he rose and stared in the mirror at his hairless chest and stomach. No muscles, no fat. Incredulous, he drew a full breath and held it in lungs that had never tasted a cigarette.

"Let's get up, Eddie, huh?" his father called, and a second later stuck his head through the door. "Oh," he said when he saw Eddie awake.

Eddie said nothing, just gaped at his father.

"Let's get moving, huh?" his father said, and continued downstairs. Eddie studied his own features in the mirror again, pressing his fingers against his temples, squinting to see the face that he knew would emerge during the next decade: his father's.

But that could only hold his interest for so long. He padded downstairs to the kitchen, and nearly laughed out loud at the burnt-orange wallpaper there. Horrid though he remembered it, the glossy floral print looked much worse in person.

"Why aren't you dressed yet, huh?" his father asked him, putting the scotch back in the cabinet.

The old man's antagonism amazed rather than annoyed Eddie. *How can I take this ornery drunk seriously?* And yet he would, for years to come.

The prospect of eating in this hellhole did not appeal to him. He marched upstairs and searched through his clothes. He could not fathom his own piling system, and thus could not tell which pants were supposedly clean. Finally he found the pair with his wallet in the pocket, and inside the wallet his school ID card, which told him he was a sophomore. He had no money.

When he returned to the kitchen, his father had already left, so Eddie set about cooking himself bacon and scrambled eggs. The smell drew his brother, Kevin, to the kitchen, still wearing construction boots, pistol still in its shoulder holster on top of his thermal shirt. Kevin had worked a graveyard shift last night.

"You want some?" Eddie offered.

"What the hell you doing cooking?" Kevin asked.

"I don't feel like eating cereal," Eddie said. "You want any of this?"

"Nah," Kevin said, then added, "All right, I'll have a piece of bacon."

Eddie placed one strip in Kevin's hand and piled everything else onto a plate. Kevin returned to the living room. Eddie sat at the kitchen table, and had eaten two mouthfuls when he heard a bark in the backyard.

For a heartbeat he sat very still, remembering just what day lay before him. Then he rose and went out the back door to see Jabberwocky.

"How you doing, sweetie?" he asked her, rubbing the pointer mutt's short black coat. She licked his hand, and then his face. With his thumb he unclasped the chain from her collar. She followed him into the house.

"Where you taking her?" Kevin asked from the living room as Eddie carried Jabberwocky upstairs. On her own feet the dog would never dare venture beyond the kitchen.

"I'm putting her in my room," Eddie said.

"What for?"

"She's been getting shivers," Eddie improvised. "My lab teacher says to let her spend the daytime indoors."

"She's a watchdog," Kevin said, turning hack to the television. "She belongs outside."

"Look, man, it's *my* room," Eddie said. "Just today, all right? I'll take her for a big walk as soon as I get home."

"If Ma hears her in there, you're out of luck," Kevin reminded him.

"I know that. If Ma asks, tell her I'll put her out as soon as I get home," Eddie said. "Just for today."

After scratching her chest until she lay down, Eddie left Jabberwocky in his room and shut the door. Downstairs he finished eating and said good-bye to Kevin, who had put his gun away.

"You're awful cordial," Kevin observed.

Eddie almost left empty-handed, but realized he needed his schoolbag, and had to hunt around the house for it.

"Hey," his mother greeted him in her bathrobe, her eyes still swollen with last night's drink. "What's that dog doing upstairs?"

"She's in my room."

"Yeah, I see that. How come?"

"She's been sick lately, in the morning," Eddie said. "I asked a vet who talked to my health class, and he said to let her spend a day inside, to adjust."

"Adjust to what?" She wasn't buying it.

"It's to strengthen her immune system," Eddie told her.

"Her *what* system?"

"Today only," Eddie said. "Please? Just let her stay in my room until I get home. Just today."

"If your father sees—"

"I know," Eddie said. "He won't. I'll come home and I'll walk her down the park."

Finally Eddie found his schoolbag tucked beside the china cabinet and left the house. Outside he chose the long route toward the bus stop, so he could see the park.

Three houses away from where he lived, the sight of a vacant lot stopped Eddie in his tracks. Mrs. Denihan's lot, specifically, a wild strip of oak and dogwood and sycamore, an arboretum that would no longer exist by the time he left for college. Today it stood before him, unsullied by bulldozers or cement trucks.

But he had a bus to catch. The lot would wait. He could visit it later, when he came home.

As he walked he decided his schoolbag embarrassed him. *Why carry all this shit? How many books do I need? And I look like a dick wearing earth shoes and corduroys.*

It was late May, and every block threatened summer any minute, from the humid breath of trees to the foliage sprouting in clogged storm drains. Halfway down Pigeon Meadow Road, Eddie realized he was headed toward the wrong bus stop. He didn't have to get the Q65 to the subway, he only had to catch the...whatever bus ran up Roosevelt Avenue to his school.

❧ ❧ ❧

To reach Roosevelt Avenue from where he stood rather than from his parents' house, Eddie needed to cut across the Corridor, an undeveloped span of woodland beneath the flight path to LaGuardia Airport. The Corridor formed the southern border of Queensborough Heights; at the Heights' western limit the Van Wyck Expressway ran perpendicular from the Corridor to the Whitestone Bridge, just as to the east the Clearview led to the Throggs Neck. Both highways met Long Island Sound, the Heights' northern shore, at angles that cut the town into an almost perfect square. Thin fingers of forest served as buffers alongside the roadways.

Though Eddie entered the woods merrily enough, presently he grew uneasy. Morning sun did not heat the dank corners of the Corridor. Among the cool shadows lurked things Eddie had no wish to glimpse.

Through the growth to his left he could see the goalposts and cement bleachers of the soccer field. Then on his right came the Cooperative Farm, a municipal project the city had created to grant garden space to elderly people, since most of the Corridor sat unused anyway. Korean immigrants had taken over the Farm almost immediately to grow produce for the markets down near the Main Street subway terminal.

Between the Farm and the path ran a manmade hill of rubble, eight foot high, dense with weird reddish brambles that bore seed pods a foot long. This land wall protected the ground already cleared for the Farm. *It's small, now. By the time I leave for California, it covers more area than most city parks.*

Here and there across the precisely divided field stood water taps, old living-room chairs, a refrigerator laid on its side, a few small shacks.

Nestled into the Farm's eastern perimeter, a copse of ash trees stood perhaps a dozen strong. The sight of them induced a cramp in Eddie's gut. So he looked away, and walked on.

At last he reached the far side of the Corridor, just in time to cross Roosevelt Avenue and catch the bus before it began to climb the hill. He came aboard self-consciously, embarrassed to have public-school kids see him dressed this way. Nobody paid him any notice, except the bus driver.

"You want to *pay*, young man?" the driver said.

Eddie fished his wallet from his pocket and flashed his pass at the driver, then put it away.

"I said, you want to *pay*?"

The city bus costs a nickel with the pass. Eddie had forgotten. He didn't have any money whatsoever in his pocket.

"I don't have a nickel," Eddie told the driver.

The driver hit the air brakes, opened the door. "Then you can get off," he said.

"Hey, O'Kane," someone said. Eddie turned and saw a guy rise from a seat near the front. "You forget your money?"

"Yeah," Eddie said. He recognized this kid's face, faintly. For his very life he could not match it with a name.

"Here," the guy said, and chucked a nickel into the fare box.

"Thanks, man," Eddie said.

This savior returned to his seat. Since there were no other seats left except at the back, Eddie stood in front of his friend, trying to recall the guy's name.

"You weren't at the dance," this kid said.

"No, I wasn't," Eddie agreed. It was a guess.

"Some nice hummers, you missed it. Last dance this year. Had this one freshman from the Hill. She had some friends, man— you should have been there."

While his companion recounted in detail the hand job this girl had allegedly performed during the dance, Eddie nodded, glancing out the window at the bagel shops and Jewish centers as the bus neared his school.

"So, we're up by the study hall, and I'm making out with her, right?" the guy said. "She goes, 'Frank, I hardly know—'"

"Frank Timpone!" Eddie exclaimed, snapping his fingers in triumph.

"What?" Timpone asked, a little startled.

"No, I," Eddie began, and shook his head.

"You forgot my name?" Timpone asked.

"No," Eddie said. "Never mind."

Timpone laughed. "So, anyway, I'm taking her to a party next Saturday at her friend's house in Forest Hills," he continued. "You want to come with me?"

"Yeah, maybe, that sounds cool," Eddie said. "Listen, do you know what homeroom I'm in?"

Timpone shook his head. "You forget that, too? What, did you get bopped on the head?"

"No, I'm just...wondering if you knew that," Eddie said. "You're in some of my classes, though."

"No, I'm not. What the fuck are you on?" Timpone said. "I'm a *junior*, moron. I only see you at lunch and gym."

"Right, that's what I meant," Eddie said. "When is that?"

For a few seconds Timpone studied Eddie's face, trying to tell whether this line of inquiry were a joke. "We eat at eleven. We have gym on Day Two and Day Four, at ten." He spoke slowly, watching for traps.

"And which Day is it today?"

"Day Three."

As the bus pulled up at their stop, all Eddie's schoolmates rose from their seats. The public-school kids—easily identified by their jeans and concert jerseys, in contrast to the Bishop McCanton students' corduroys and ties—jeered them casually. "Yeah, gotta keep that seat till the last fucking second," one dirtbag said.

Outside on the sidewalk the McCanton kids set off for school in groups of two or three. As he walked with Timpone, Eddie exchanged nods with various classmates, trying to tell which ones he knew well. A few names came to him, mostly those of guys he did not especially like but who made spectacles of themselves. Rocco Sorice, for instance, and Jimmy Mahoney. Nobody smoked pot. Two or three lit cigarettes.

They reached the schoolyard. Eddie scanned the crowd, unable to guess which cliques would welcome him. Where did he hang out? Five or six guys he vaguely recalled stood beside the fence, examining an issue of *Penthouse* page by page.

Farther around the building, near the parking lot, the burnout crew hung listening to Led Zeppelin on a box. Among them Eddie recognized Matherson, a muscular pothead whose name Eddie knew right away because he had always loathed Matherson's loud mouth.

"Hey, O'Kane, you do your homework for Gumby?" an Irish-looking blond guy asked.

"I don't know," Eddie answered. "You're in my class with Gumby?"

"Yeah."

"What period is that?"

"First."

Eddie dropped his schoolbag and rooted through it. He must have done his Gumby homework; few teachers could inspire the same degree of fear as Gumby, formally known as Brother David McCauley. Eddie pulled a looseleaf binder out of his bag and opened it. Inside he found three theorems, each worked out in pencil on a separate sheet of paper.

"Here you go," he said, handing the blond guy his binder.

"I'll give this back to you in class, all right?"

"Yeah, fine," Eddie said. "Listen, what homeroom am I in?"

"How the fuck should I know?" the blond guy said. "Whatever one O'Shea is in."

Follow Brian O'Shea. Eddie hadn't thought of that. Right now he couldn't see O'Shea anywhere.

"Eddie, what's up?"

Eddie turned and found himself looking upward into the face of Desmond Coogan, who smiled innocently while Eddie bristled.

"The fuck do you want?" Eddie asked him.

"Huh?" Desmond asked.

"I asked what the fuck you want," Eddie repeated. "But come to think of it, I don't really give a shit."

The bell rang and Eddie stalked away into the building. Behind him he heard Desmond ask what was the matter. *Figure it out, scumbag.* Not until reaching the second floor of the school did Eddie realize he had started grinding his teeth and could taste acid filling his stomach.

Desmond caught up with him. "Eddie?" he said. "Is something wrong?"

"Yeah, I got this big stupid grease monkey chasing me around, asking what's wrong," Eddie said. "Other than that, everything's fine."

That shut Desmond up and sent him on his way.

Two rows of lockers lined the hallways on each floor of McCanton. It came to Eddie that the upper row belonged to juniors and seniors, and the lower lockers sophs and frosh.

"Hey, man?" he asked a kid locking a lower locker. "You a sophomore?"

The kid nodded.

"What does your last name begin with?"

"J."

Eddie thought he might follow the alphabet to locate his own locker, but time ran out. The bell would ring at 8:30, and the clock said 8:29.

A wave of frustration passed over him. He fought it off. "You know O'Shea?" he asked the J kid.

"Yeah, I do," the kid said.

"What homeroom is he in?"

The J kid thought for a second. "2G or 2H, I think," he said.

"Where's that?" Eddie asked.

"Down there," the kid answered, directing Eddie around a turn in the hall that led to a wing of classrooms.

With barely seconds to spare, Eddie arrived in his homeroom. It felt familiar to him at once. He took his seat at the head of the fourth row, in front of Brian O'Shea.

"How you doing?" O'Shea asked.

"All right," Eddie said.

"You finish *Jude the Obscure*?"

Fuck. "I don't know, why?"

"Today's the test." O'Shea leaned back in his seat and pushed his glasses up to the bridge of his nose. "You forgot?"

Eddie shook his head. "I guess it wasn't that important to me," he said. "What's your locker number?"

"260."

"So I'm 259, right?"

"No, 258," O'Shea told him. "The odd numbers are the upper lockers. You never noticed that?"

Their homeroom teacher, Brother Something-or-other…*Edwin? No, Edmund. We call him Smegmund.* Smegmund read the announcements from a mimeograph sheet. Eddie sat still, and the fidgety quality of the teenagers around him grated on his nerves.

When homeroom ended, Eddie marched downstairs directly to Poobah's office.

"Brother Stephen, sir?" he called inside.

At his desk Poobah turned and held one finger up, for Eddie to wait until he finished this phone call. Eddie stood by patiently. Poobah hung up and said, "What can I do for you, son?"

"My locker doesn't work," Eddie said.

"How do you mean, 'doesn't work'?"

"I dial in my combination and it doesn't open," Eddie explained. "I can't get my books out."

With a sigh Poobah rose from his seat and grabbed a large keyring out of the top drawer of his desk. "What's your locker number?" he asked.

"258, sir," Eddie answered, and followed the principal upstairs.

Poobah opened Eddie's locker for him using an odd black key with a cylindrical stem and a clover bell. On the spot Eddie picked three numbers at random, and Poobah reset the lock to this new combination.

"Thank you, Brother," Eddie said as Poobah left.

Posted inside the door of his locker Eddie found a printout of his class schedule, which told him he was missing Geometry—Gumby's class—right that very second. Later he had English, then Social Studies, then lunch. His schedule even listed the classroom numbers.

Eddie took his Geometry text, locked his schoolbag inside his locker, and walked downstairs to Poobah's office again.

"What now?" Poobah asked.

"I need a..." The proper term escaped him. "When I go to class, I have to show Brother David a note about why I'm late."

"Oh, right. You need a slip."

"That's it, a slip."

Poobah quickly scribbled on a printed sheet of yellow paper and tugged it off the pad. Eddie took the slip, stuffed it into his breast pocket, and set off for Gumby's class on the third floor.

While mounting the stairs, Eddie pulled the slip from his pocket and examined it. Poobah, being Poobah, had not filled in all the blanks printed on the small yellow form. Poobah's signature meant that Gumby would accept this slip without question, that Eddie would not face detention for missing roll call.

Yet the slip did not say what time Poobah had signed it. *How does Gumby know the difference if I show up now, or three minutes before class ends? For that matter, other than for the sake of being a prick, why should Gumby care?*

Each class lasted forty-five minutes. This one had better than half an hour left. Eddie decided to spend his free time parading through the halls, pretending to run an errand. The only people he saw were seniors, since only seniors had free periods. He avoided the study hall, figuring someone in authority would ask why he was there, and headed down toward the library on the first floor.

In the very nick of time, he spotted Poobah coming up the stairs toward him. Eddie turned and ducked into the second-floor bathroom. He held the door open just a slit to watch Poobah pass.

And then it occurred to Eddie that, *If Poobah's up here, no one's guarding Poobah's office.*

Or that key ring in Poobah's desk drawer.

It took Eddie less than ninety seconds to reach Poobah's desk, filch the little black key from the ring, and return to the stairwell. The sheer ease of the operation got him high as a kite.

In an empty stretch of hallway, he picked a locker at random and opened it. An incredible feeling of power washed through him. Any locker in the building, he could open! So long as he kept the key out of sight, no one but the locker's actual owner would spot anything wrong with his rifling through it.

In that first locker he found nothing worth taking. Ditto the one next to it. What Eddie needed was money, after all, and anyone with money would keep it in his pants pocket, to spend at lunch.

Just a second, now.

Matherson would have dope. He wouldn't carry it on his person around school, either.

The clock said Eddie had about twenty minutes before the end of Gumby's class. He raced to his own locker and began to count backwards until he reached the 230s. *These must be M, if not the end of L.* Sure enough, a notebook in locker 232 belonged to Kenneth Maskurski. 234 was Robert Massi 's.

236 was Matthew Matherson's. Eddie didn't even have to check the books; he couldn't mistake Matherson's denim jacket with the crappy *Houses of the Holy* painting on the back.

With a quick glance up and down the hall, Eddie ransacked Matherson's jacket. He found a sandwich bag one-third full of reefer, and slipped it into his hip pocket. He also took two dollar bills folded together.

Then he checked once again for witnesses, and picked up a notebook. On the inside cover, where Matherson had clumsily drawn the Led Zeppelin logo, Eddie wrote FUCK YOU, MATHERSON, YOU PUSSY FART! LED ZEP SUCKS AND YOUR MOTHER BLOWS GOATS!

Eddie replaced the notebook and closed the locker. He strolled purposefully away, grinning at two passing seniors. The clock still gave him another fifteen minutes. Eager to check his haul, he headed into the nearest bathroom and stepped inside a stall.

The baggie held no more than a half-ounce, if that much. Eddie himself would smoke more than that before he could sell it. He racked his brain, trying to recall the names of Matherson's asshole buddies. All he could recall offhand was Andy Meyers. Or was that Meiers? Myers?

Anyway, he knew where to find out. Eddie returned to the hall and opened locker 244: James Mestri. 246 belonged to Andy Meyers, whose pockets were empty. Eddie snaked his fingers down behind the pile of books but uncovered nothing. He lifted the books off the bottom and dropped them one by one. All he saw that interested him was a magazine called *Cheri*. He didn't take it.

Then he slid his index finger inside the lip at the front of the locker.

He pulled out a stoppered glass vial from the chem lab. Inside the vial lay maybe a dozen purple microdots of mescaline.

Eddie slid the vial into his breast pocket and closed 246, congratulating himself on a free period well spent. Before heading to class he stopped by his own locker to drop off his booty, using the hiding spot he had just learned from Meyers.

Gumby glared at him when Eddie opened the door to Geometry.

"Where have you been, O'Kane?" he asked.

"Had to see Brother Stephen, sir," Eddie said, handing over the slip from his breast pocket.

Gumby, whose nickname stemmed from the peculiar slanted shape of his crewcut head, glanced at the form only long enough to see Poobah's signature and flung it into the trash. "Where's your homework?"

Eddie scanned the room and saw his binder sitting atop an empty desk. "It's there in my binder, sir," he said. The blond mick to whom he had lent his homework—Kelly, that was his name—nodded silent thanks to him. Kelly would become a cop after graduation.

❧ ❧ ❧

When the bell rang Eddie went to English and took a test on *Jude the Obscure*. From the phrasing of the multiple-choice questions he gleaned enough to write a decent essay. He snuck a few fill-in answers from someone named McDermott, who sat next to him. Not giving a fuck about his grades made the challenge more fun.

After that came Social Studies. Eddie arrived to discover he sat next to Desmond Coogan.

"Eddie," Desmond said, "are you going to tell me what's wrong, or what?"

"Fuck you, douche," Eddie said, and walked up to the teacher's desk. Then he halted, trying to recall the teacher's name. *It starts with a* C, he was pretty sure.

"Yes?" the teacher asked.

"Mm," Eddie stammered. "I don't feel good. Can I sit by the window, do you think?"

The teacher nodded, and Eddie sat at the back of the last row. He tried to pay attention while Mr. Caravella or Caravello explained how World War II ended, but having Desmond within spitting distance ruined his concentration. At last lunch came.

By now Eddie realized that he normally ate lunch with Desmond, too, so after he spent a buck and a half on a ham sandwich and a large Coke he left the cafeteria. For the first time ever he ate outside, sitting on the loading dock beside the parking lot, where the burnouts hung out.

The sandwich wound up half-eaten in the garbage. He sipped the soda slowly, because they had loaded too much syrup in the Coke machine and he liked it that way.

Gradually, while he sat there, students began to drift out from the cafeteria into the parking lot. No one noticed him. Soon the entire lunchroom would file out here, and then a bell would signal them to return to classes through the front of the building.

For a few minutes Eddie just examined his hands, how young and unscarred they seemed. The hair on his forearms had not thickened into gauze yet.

Then he had to piss. He hopped off the loading dock and stepped behind the dumpster. Only when he had unzipped and begun relieving himself did he pause to wonder whether he should have visited a men's room inside; if any lunch monitors saw him watering the bricks, he would face discipline. They might take it out of proportion.

So he ducked his head lower than the top of the dumpster, wishing he had not drank so much soda. *Come on, come on.* Finally his bladder drained and he zipped himself.

"Fuck that!" he heard someone say.

Eddie peeked over the rim of the dumpster. Beside the loading dock Matherson and Meyers were discussing something urgent: where their dope had gone.

"Andy, man, I trusted you with my share, you should be responsible for it," Matherson said.

"No fucking way! I can't believe you would expect me to fucking take the whole loss!" Meyers spat back. "You got robbed too, man—how can you lay that shit on me like that? That's fucked, man."

Defeated by superior logic, Matherson shut up and glared. Meyers would not back down, so Eddie hid all the way behind the dumpster again, expecting Matherson to shift his stare this way any second.

"You wouldn't even have known quantity was available, if not for me," Meyers said. "You want to go in business with me, you got to share the losses, not just the profits."

"Well, he ain't gonna do it again," Matherson said. "Where am I getting this bread from, out my ass? Richie ain't gonna front. He's so fucking tight, he squeaks."

"If I ask him, he might," Meyers told him. "You never hung out up at Eutectic with him, or at Ozone Park. He knows me different from how he knows you."

"What I want to know is, how come this shit disappears?" Matherson said.

They lowered their voices and lit cigarettes. Eddie's neck began to bother him, so he squatted instead of bending his back. When he peeked again, they had left the loading dock. They walked across the schoolyard to the cafeteria doors.

Eddie followed the pair inside the cafeteria, where he watched them plead with an upperclassman in front of a bunch of longhairs. To these people Eddie was a nonentity. The older guy shaking his head at Matherson, whether he believed that Matherson's dope had disappeared or didn't, would sooner suspect John Travolta of stealing it than Eddie O'Kane.

"If Poobah had your shit, you'd be talking to the cops right now," this Richie said just before Eddie moseyed out of earshot. "Whose dick you think you're pulling?"

From a distance of four tables Eddie monitored their conversation, and glowed with warm satisfaction as Matherson and his buddy sulked away. Then Richie finished eating and joined three other guys leaving for the schoolyard.

Outside, Richie and his friends went to the loading dock. Matherson and Meyers stayed among the crowd. Eddie remained near the cafeteria doors. Frank Timpone breezed by with a grin and a nod.

The mob migrated from the schoolyard to the front doors. Eddie stayed put.

Finally the burnouts joined the exodus. Eddie casually tailed Richie up the walkway and into the school. Ground floor. Second floor. Third floor. Far wing. Locker 371.

After that he had to scramble back to his own locker, and in fact he reached Chemistry on the second floor a minute late. That didn't. matter, though. Mr. Scalia never busted balls.

After perhaps ten minutes, Eddie walked up to Mr. Scalia's desk and said, in a queasy voice, "My lunch didn't agree with me. I think I'm going to get sick."

"What are you standing here for?" Mr. Scalia asked, and pointed to the door.

Eddie left the classroom and booked upstairs. A few seniors milled through the hallway, hands in their pockets. No one paid him any mind as he opened locker 371. RICHARD WEBBER, a notebook said. Eddie's search yielded six bags of reefer identical to the one he had looted from Matherson, all in a bag that also contained twenty dollars, and a vitamin jar with seven microdots.

Once again he charged downstairs to his own locker and deposited the goods. By now his inventory would no longer fit in the slim space where he had hidden this morning's swag, and he stuffed the reefer bags behind his books. No one could open the locker to find the stuff, anyway. Poobah no longer had the key.

On his way back to Chemistry Eddie whistled, and he forgot to act sick when he reappeared before Mr. Scalia. Being fifteen felt much, much better than Eddie remembered. The rest of his day he passed effortlessly, feigning interest in whatever his teachers had to say.

After school Eddie bought rolling papers at a deli and rolled himself a fatty to smoke while he walked his dog. When at last he arrived home, his mother greeted him at the front door, almost drunk but wide-eyed.

"Edward," she said. "Did you see the garage?"

He hadn't seen it, but he knew what had taken place: Mrs. O'Hallahan from across the street had left her four-year-old, Jennifer, in their Gremlin with the engine idling. Waiting for her mother to return, Jennifer had decided to play driver. The game ended when the Gremlin knocked down the rear wall of the O'Kane garage. Both car and child survived, scratchless.

"Oh, Eddie," his mother told him, on the verge of tears, "if you hadn't put Jabberwocky in your room this morning, the poor dog would have gotten crushed."

Eddie knew that, also. Only too well.

TWO

Eddie decided to cut the reefer into nickels. In Richie Webber's packaging, those quarter-ounces would stand out too much to sell to any McCanton burnouts. Then too he had to count on the fact that high-school kids didn't usually buy quarters, they copped dimes and nickels.

Eddie's father repaired climate systems in office buildings. He drove a red-and-white company van outfitted with metal shelves and drawers in the rear cabin to store washers, bolts, wing nuts, screws, copper tubing, thermostats, fuses and thousands of other minute objects whose names Eddie never learned.

Around five-thirty the old man pulled into the driveway and staggered through the side door. Immediately a battle ensued between both Eddie's parents, and Eddie's ears, newly unaccustomed to this nightly abuse, could not withstand it.

"You gave me your *word,* Joe!" Mrs. O'Kane bellowed. "Your word is worth nothing—that means *you're* worth nothing!"

"For Christ's sake, will you stop?" the old man pleaded, though he knew very well she would not. "You're like a broken record."

"*You* broke me!" she screamed.

For refuge Eddie snuck into his father's truck and read the girly magazines his father kept hidden in the metal compartments.

From inside several drawers Eddie also swiped tiny plastic and manila envelopes.

Later, when the warfare subsided faintly for dinner, he bolted down his meatloaf as quickly as possible and fled to the sanctity of the basement, where he turned up a Traffic eight-track to drown out his parents' voices above. Around ten he went to bed.

In the middle of the night he locked himself in the bathroom to cut his ounce-and-a-half into twenty three-joint nicks. He added the Seven hits of mesc from Webber's vitamin jar to Meyers's small vial, which he could hide in his locker more easily. Then he smoked a joint himself, blowing the smoke out the bathroom window, and returned to bed with a warm buzz. His clock radio lulled him to sleep.

The next morning Eddie rushed to his normal Q44 stop early. To reduce crowding on the buses, Queens public schools—Edison and Aviation, in this case—began their class day on the hour. While Catholic schools uniformly began at 8:30, public-school sophomores had to be at school at 7:00, freshmen at 8:00, and juniors at 9:00.

Not realizing this schedule, Eddie only caught the freshmen, a fortunate accident. Edison and Aviation kids did not take McCanton boys seriously. Only the freshmen would contemplate copping from Eddie. Once they smelled the product, he had sixty-nine dollars in his pocket in ten minutes. They bought twelve bags of weed and three microdots.

"I never expected to cop off a Catholic-school kid," one guy said.

"How you know I go to Catholic school?" Eddie asked him.

"Look at how you're dressed, man," he replied.

That made Eddie's mind up for him: *I have to go clothes shopping, pronto.* Even if McCanton wouldn't let him wear jeans or sneakers to school, he had to ditch these outfits his mother bought him. The shirt he wore today, for instance, resembled a tablecloth from a restaurant in Little Italy.

"How can you sell mesc so cheap?" that same kid asked him.

"I got a small pile at a bargain, is all," Eddie said, and shrugged. "Normally you pay, what? Five?"

The kid nodded. "You better hope the Crew don't find out you're underselling them, man, they'll get pissed."

"Who's the Crew?"

As he spoke, the kid glanced over his own shoulder, making sure no one else was listening. "This gang from Sena. Any mesc in Queens, it passed through the Crew's hands. They're pretty fucked up."

"I don't think I've ever even met anyone who goes to Sena," Eddie said. "I don't see why they would hear about me."

"Talk gets around, man." The kid nodded good-bye and left on a bus crowded with his classmates.

Eddie stayed at the stop. More than he had yesterday, he felt ridiculous dressed this way. He smoked a joint to calm down, but put it out halfway through when it made him paranoid.

"What the fuck is that?" Timpone greeted him. "You smoke pot?"

Eddie handed him the half-jay. "Try it," he said.

Timpone shook his head.

"Didn't you lend me money yesterday, by the way?" Eddie said, and handed Timpone a dollar. "Here."

"I didn't lend you mo—wait, you mean when you got on the bus?"

"Yeah," Eddie said.

"Fuck, I gave you a *nickel*," Timpone protested.

"Don't got any change," Eddie said with a smirk. "Take it, man. I had a good morning."

They rode the bus together. At one point when they passed the Corridor, Eddie spotted the ash grove beyond the farm and the soccer field, and cold blood pulsed through the veins in his neck. Even while forcing himself to look away, he could sense the quiet watchful trees, untouched by the tame captivity that parceled the land all around them.

He lost track of what Timpone was saying, not that Timpone's topic ever deviated from sex. Eddie interrupted him and asked, "Sena is on Booth Boulevard, isn't it?"

"What, Sena the high school? Yeah, I think it is," Timpone said. "I know it's near the Expressway, because you can see it from the overpass. That school is all full of fuckups."

True enough. Named for a reform-school delinquent who went on to champion progressive education as borough president, J.A. Sena Regional High received all the incorrigibles from public schools across northern Queens. Kids from Aviation and Edison feared Sena students, whereas McCanton kids feared everyone.

"I know a chick from Sena, actually," Timpone went on. "Real nice hummer. She lives around the block from me."

"But you live in Whitestone, right?"

Timpone nodded. "She got thrown out of the Hill Academy, I think it was. Either there or St. Elizabeth's. She got caught selling dope."

"There you go, Timpone," Eddie said. "I'll give you a joint. Invite her out to get high. You'll probably get in her pants."

Apparently no one had mentioned this drug-sex connection to Timpone before, because it opened his mind at once. He accepted the joint from Eddie with just a few questions about the smell and possible side effects.

When they reached the schoolyard it pleased Eddie to watch Richie Webber push Matherson around. A tormented rabbit's expression came across Matherson's face when Webber spat on him. Briskly Matherson spun on his heel and left the loading dock. Webber, neither finished nor sated, followed him, nearly shouting.

"Meyers wasn't there. *You* were," Webber reminded Matherson. "You saw where I put it. Nobody else knew the shit was there. Plus, I know Andy fucking Meyers a long fucking time. I don't know you for shit, and I never liked you."

Matherson stopped to plead with him, in a voice too low for Eddie to hear at this distance. Webber, on the other hand, spoke even louder now that they once again stood face to face.

All around them sophomores whom Matherson had bullied for the past two years watched avidly. Matherson's jaw moved up and down with that erratic quiver of a teenager fighting tears.

This could not have worked out better. Eddie did not merely smile, he beamed.

"No, pal, you *are* responsible," Webber barked. "*I* say so."

This exchange cheered Eddie enough that even the prospect of Gumby's class could not ruin his mood. He sailed into homeroom, whistling. O'Shea lent him the new *Lampoon* until the bell rang.

In the hall after the end of Social Studies, the future Officer Kelly sought Eddie out and asked, "O'Kane, you know where O'Shea's mother works?"

"In Ridgewood. Why?" Eddie asked. "What's wrong with O'Shea?"

"You know what company?" Kelly asked.

Eddie shook his head.

"Fucking Matherson beat him unconscious," Kelly said. "Me and Ostermann pulled Matherson off, or he would've killed him. Poobah drove O'Shea to the emergency room at Booth Memorial. They didn't even wait for an ambulance. His mother changed jobs since he started school, so the switchboard don't have her work number anymore. They need her permission to do anything."

"I couldn't tell you where she works. I couldn't even tell you who to ask," Eddie said. "What's Matherson got against O'Shea?"

"I think Matherson's on fucking dope. We pin him to the floor, and Poobah comes up, and he goes to Poobah, 'This guy wrote on my book,' like that's a reason to pound someone six inches shorter than you into a coma," Kelly told him.

This revelation landed on Eddie as would a hurled piano. He heard his own mouth repeat, "His book."

"Yeah, Poobah's calling the cops, and Matherson's showing him something somebody wrote about Led Zeppelin in his notebook," Kelly said. "Jimmy Flynn says the notebook just fell out of Matherson's desk and O'Shea chucked it back in for him, and two seconds later Matherson's smashing O'Shea's head on the tiles. That asshole's out of here now, I'll tell you. Once you leave McCanton in a squad car, you're gone."

Kelly said some other stuff, but a bout of dizzy nausea prevented Eddie from listening.

At lunch it seemed to Eddie that everyone in the cafeteria, every cluster of kids at each of the long tables, could talk only about O'Shea's beating. Today's cafeteria pizza (despite the Day 4 schedule, it was Friday, hence no meat) didn't taste anywhere near as bad as yesterday's ham, but Eddie's appetite withered.

He chucked the pizza into a garbage can and went outside to the loading dock. Once again he had the place to himself, so he lit the other half of the joint he'd started at the bus stop that morning.

From the corner of his eye Eddie glimpsed someone approaching, and he jerked the joint behind his back.

No need, though. It was a pothead, one of Richie Webber's crowd, some guy whose Black Sabbath jacket Eddie had seen a million times. The kid smiled at having caught Eddie toking.

"I didn't know you got high," the guy said.

"Sure do," Eddie replied, and passed him the jay.

"You hang out with that douf, Coogan, right?"

"No," Eddie said, shaking his head. "I used to."

They finished the joint together, and the guy introduced himself as Bengler. He was a junior. Bengler began talking about obscure Pink Floyd albums.

"I just know *The Wall*," Eddie said.

"Yeah, I painted that," Bengler boasted, "me and this guy from my homeroom. We came up here on a Saturday night."

"You painted what?"

"The wall. On the handball courts," Bengler said, waving at the public park across the street. "We painted *Dark Side of the Moon* on the handball court. What wall are you talking about?"

Eddie changed the topic. "You know about the Crew, by any chance?" Eddie asked.

"Sure," Bengler said. "My cousin's in the Crew."

"Do they do weed deals?"

Bengler nodded. "Good hemp, too."

"Can you hook me up?"

Bengler said, "Just go to that park behind Sena. Ask them for Dennis Bengler. I'm Timmy Bengler, tell him you know me. They'll treat you all right. Just be cool."

Lunch ended, and Eddie sat through his remaining classes, his thoughts constantly drifting to Brian O'Shea.

School let out and Eddie caught the first bus down Roosevelt. When he got off the Q44, he could transfer to the Q17 or the Q27 for seven blocks, but instead he walked it with a junior named Contos who worked at a hardware store in the neighborhood.

They stopped at a crosswalk on Kissena Boulevard. A face in the window of a passing car seized Eddie's attention, the face of a girl wearing a parochial uniform.

Eddie spun to watch the car speed away up Kissena. His heart shook his chest.

"You know that girl?" Contos asked.

"No," Eddie said. Weirdly true.

"You just have a thing for sixth-graders from St. Kevin's."

"She goes to Mary of Bethlehem, my parish," Eddie said. "She's in eighth grade."

"I thought you didn't know her."

"I don't," Eddie said, wishing he hadn't spoken. "I know *of* her."

"Do you mean you've 'had knowledge' of her?" Contos asked. "In the Biblical sense?"

Shut up, Contos. "Something like that." Eddie grinned and waved good-bye as he turned down Poplar, toward his parents' house.

His mother had started on the wine early today, so without even changing his clothes Eddie left to walk the dog. Jabberwocky came along eagerly. Eight blocks later, when they reached the Corridor, he unleashed her.

Despite sniffing out every rabbit and quail along the way, Jabberwocky stayed close at hand for the whole trip. They did not pass the soccer field or the communal Farm, or those ash trees; this time Eddie crossed the Corridor toward the east. He came out on Booth Boulevard, a block from Sena, whose students filed out its doors while Eddie watched.

A few grinned at Eddie as he and Jabberwocky passed. Most ignored him. He wished he had changed his shirt, at least, but wouldn't let that turn him back. The park behind the school had no real shape to it, so Eddie just followed a trail uphill.

When he reached the summit, he could no longer see cars in any direction. Up here crumbling pavement actually covered portions of the trail. It must have at one time served as some manner of road, but nothing had driven upon it in decades.

The path took him across an overpass, from which he could see the road and sidewalks below. East of him, storm fences surrounded undeveloped lots; west, he saw anonymous 1950s-vintage houses. No clapboard shack could ever seem to Eddie as bleak a hovel as a one-story tudor.

Not long afterward, Eddie reached another overpass, a crumbling brick bridge. This time he saw a lake to the east, with public benches. Teenagers sat there, drinking beer, their tape players blaring.

"Come on," Eddie said to Jabberwocky.

They picked their way downhill toward the lake. They had to cross a street to get there, and as they did Eddie saw a sign that said PIZZINGRILLO PARK. The first few people he reached were couples making out, so he said nothing to them. Finally he spotted five guys and two girls sitting with a cooler at the top of a small rise.

"Hey, man," Eddie greeted them.

Their faces seemed amused that he should want their attention.

"What's up?" said an Italian-looking hood wearing a motor-cycle jacket.

"You guys know the Crew?"

Now everyone stopped talking and listened.

"Yeah, maybe," the Italian answered. "What about the Crew?"

"I'm looking for Dennis Bengler," Eddie said.

"He ain't here," someone else said.

"I know his cousin," Eddie said. "His cousin said the Crew could hook me up with a weed deal."

The Italian cleared his sinuses, spat. "All right," he said. "What kind of piece you looking for?"

"What can you do for fifty?"

"Well, since you know Bengler's cousin," the Italian said, "we can make it pretty sweet. But you got to pay me the fifty up front."

"No problem," Eddie said, tugging nine fives and five ones from his hip pocket. Nervousness made his hand shake as he handed over the money. Jabberwocky regarded him curiously.

The Italian counted it, folded it and stuffed it into the gun pocket of his jacket. "It's a little short," he said. "It's not a whole hundred."

Eddie paused, swallowed. "You said fifty."

"Price just went up. You got a hundred?"

"No," Eddie said.

"Go get the rest, we'll wait here," the Italian said.

Everyone laughed. Eddie tried to smirk, to snap them out of it, to suddenly command their respect. It did not work. He was a fifteen-year-old in a checkerboard shirt and earth shoes.

"Give me the weed, or give me my money back," Eddie said through gritted teeth, his voice adenoidal.

"Watch your tone of voice, son," another guy warned him, a bigger guy with bushy blond hair and a mustache.

"Why don't you do yourself a favor," the Italian suggested, zipping up his jacket, "and step the fuck off?"

The girls turned to smile at him now, as though watching a temperamental child disciplined.

Eddie's whole body shook. He turned on one heel and headed back the way he had come. Jabberwocky followed, cocking her head as if to ask why he had handed his money away. The couples he had avoided on his way in watched with mute amusement as he departed. *I should come back with Kevin's gun.*

He walked under the overpass and turned right so no one in

the park could see him. Then he climbed the hill, back up into the trees.

"Fuck!" he shouted, once no one could hear him. "Goddamn it!"

When Jabberwocky came toward him, he kicked a stick at her. She jumped away, and instantly remorse calmed him.

"I'm sorry," he said, and rubbed her chest. She forgave him. He sat still with her awhile.

How could I fall for that shit? Just because I have my school clothes on? Somehow he had become a genuine fifteen-year-old.

In time he returned to that bridge above the underpass. From there he watched the kids who had just robbed him. They laughed and drank and passed joints, and every so often someone would visit them for a few minutes. Eddie could not tell where these other people entered the park.

Night began to fall. Eddie did not care. He stayed on the decrepit bridge, dislodging loose bricks when he grew bored. He threw some sticks down the dirt road for Jabberwocky to fetch.

Soon he could barely discern that bench on the rise beside the lake.

The girls had left by now, and before too long the Italian himself stood up and shook hands with three of his remaining friends. Then he and the bushy-headed one left. They came toward Eddie.

"*Don't* get in a car, *don't* get in a car, *don't* get in a car, *don't* get in a car," Eddie chanted to himself quietly as he watched them exit Pizzingrillo Park. *Don't don't don't don't don't*

They didn't. Better yet, they parted company; the bushy dirtbag turned to walk in the direction of the school. The Italian shook his hand good-bye and continued toward Eddie. He obviously lived on the other side of this trestle.

In the brief period while he waited for the Italian to pass below so he could tail him, Eddie pictured this kid growing up over to the west there in those pathetic houses. This kid's family probably lacked the money for a bigger house, or a neighborhood like the Heights, where Eddie lived.

It seemed very likely that hanging out in a park, selling dope, would be the high point in this guy's sad-sack life. Ten years from now, he would work in building maintenance somewhere in Manhattan, telling anyone who would listen about *The good old days, me and my friends hanging out, smoking joints, feeling chicks' tits. Jesus, I had it made when I was in high school. I wish it never ended. They used to call us the Crew, we were some badasses, Jack.*

Funniest thing was, one time I took fifty bucks off this Catholic-school dick, didn't even give him a joint!

Rage flooded Eddie.

He picked up one of the bricks he had plucked off the wall. Just as the Italian emerged from beneath the bridge, Eddie released the brick directly onto his head.

The Italian met the sidewalk with almost no sound.

Eddie scrambled down through the trees and undergrowth. When he reached the sidewalk he belatedly thought to check for witnesses, but saw none in either direction.

Quickly, dreading the sound of a car coming, Eddie unzipped his victim's jacket and unsnapped the gun pocket. From inside there he pulled his fifty dollars and then some, as well as a baggie full of tiny rectangles wrapped in foil. Eddie pocketed all of it.

The gravity of what he had just done did not touch Eddie until he checked the drug dealer's face. A huge lump had begun to rise where the brick had struck, and now that he knelt close, Eddie saw an open rupture near the hairline.

Then he moved the guy's head slightly, and found that the brick had bashed open the skull. That lump on the forehead had formed due to an air pocket.

Blood cascaded from this wound. With no streetlamp close by, Eddie had not noticed till now the dark stain pouring across the sidewalk toward the gutter, too large a deluge for the concrete to simply absorb.

"Holy fuck," Eddie said, and stood up. "What..." He could not speak, even to himself—perhaps least of all to himself.

The brick. He could not leave it here; the cops would finger-print it.

He bent down and picked it up.

I should've just followed this scumbag home and robbed his house later. Why didn't this stupid fuck just sell me some fucking dope?

Eddie knelt and checked for a pulse. He detected one, yet that fact gave him no hope whatsoever. Of course the heart still beat; it would continue until it pumped most of the body's blood onto the ground.

Once again Eddie checked in both directions and saw nothing. He raided his victim's hip pocket and found a wallet, which he took.

Eddie scrambled back up to the path, and bolted in the direction of Sena High School. He ran nonstop, too panicked to tire. When at last the school became visible over the brink of the last hill,

Eddie froze, and glanced at the woods around him.

"Jabberwocky?" he called.

No answer.

"Oh, *fuck* me," he cursed, stamping his foot.

For a terrified fifteen-year-old, he had hardly begun to run, and his mad dash back to the bridge made him sweat yet didn't wind him.

Just off the path, at the spot where he had hugged his dog to show her his tantrum had ended, Eddie found her leash. He pocketed it and whistled, called the dog's name.

Nothing responded.

He hung over the edge of the bridge, saw the corpse right where he had left it. No Jabberwocky.

Still carting his lethal brick, Eddie fled anew, barreling headlong down the trail. Ahead in the distance he spotted a middle-aged man walking a dog, and veered off the path. The undergrowth slowed his flight, but he couldn't let this man see him.

Seconds would stretch into millennia if he waited for the dog and owner to reach him. In the brush alongside the path Eddie kept moving, stumbling over logs and stumps. With no warning the dog barked at him so viciously that it startled Eddie into holding still. He raised the brick in his hand, in case the dog should attack him.

From where he stood concealed by foliage, Eddie could see the dog owner's light-colored jacket easily. The man held still, letting the dog flush Eddie from hiding.

"Come on, Buck," the man said, leading the dog away. Eddie

waited, counted to forty and returned to the path.

He encountered no one else as he vaulted downhill, past the school and into the Corridor. In truth these woods were the last place he wanted to visit now, but he had no choice.

At last Eddie arrived on Pigeon Meadow Road. Merely reaching Queensborough Heights calmed him considerably, and he decided to drop the brick down a storm drain.

That done, he sat on the curb and took inventory: He had missed dinner, so his mother would fly into a frenzy when he got home, and he had lost his dog.

And he was a murderer.

That thought triggered his stomach into retching. Luckily he had not eaten much all day, so he only had to deal with spitting up his own bile. The pain bent him over, nonetheless.

For some time he stood there, bent, gagging, aware that a few passing cars might notice him. Finally one did, and pulled over.

"Hey, Eddie," Mr. Coogan said, getting out of a two-door that Eddie had never seen before. "You all right, there?"

Drained, Eddie shook his head.

The Coogans' Impala pulled up behind Mr. Coogan, and Eddie saw Desmond watching him from the driver's seat. Then Eddie remembered that sometimes, when Mr. Coogan had to drop a car off at a customer's house, he let Desmond follow in the Impala to drive him home.

"What's the matter, Eddie? You eat something bad?" Mr. Coogan asked. "Hop in the car with Des, we'll take you home."

Too weak to refuse, he climbed into the Impala's passenger seat, and tried to quell his own trembling.

Desmond started driving again, and made a point of ignoring Eddie.

Fine by me. They went several blocks, then turned onto Kissena. "Where am I taking you?" Desmond asked out of the blue.

Eddie had not thought of that. "Home, I guess," he mumbled. The wrenching in his gut had subsided.

"My father doesn't know we ain't friends anymore, that's why he stopped for you," Desmond told him.

"Look, man," Eddie began, and then all he could do was sigh.

"Yeah? What? What'd I do?"

"You haven't done anything," Eddie said.

"So you're mad at me for nothing?" Desmond said. "You call me a douche in front of people for no reason?"

"I've got my reasons," Eddie said.

"What are they?"

"If I told you, you wouldn't believe me," he said. With a start he spotted blood drying on the cuff of his left sleeve. While Desmond talked he hurriedly rolled it up.

He missed whatever Desmond said, but finally Eddie told him, "Just suppose I had a dream, and in this dream you did something to me that made me feel that I never should have trusted you at all."

"A dream," Desmond repeated. "You had a dream."

"More or less," Eddie said.

At his side Desmond had his father's revolver. He always made a big deal about being responsible for it whenever he had to help his father close the gas station. And Mr. Coogan even had a permit for the gun. Kevin acted much less fussy about his automatic, which he owned illegally; repairing streetlights on the night shift, he had to carry his weapon much more than Mr. Coogan, who only truly needed this .38 while driving his receipts to the bank.

At Laburnum and Kissena, Mr. Coogan parked the other car and brought the keys to someone's front door. Then he came and sat in the back seat behind the two boys.

"So what's your story, there, Ed? Under the weather?" he asked cheerfully.

"No, Mr. Coogan, I'm okay," he said. "I was just out looking for my dog, and I got sick all of a sudden. Didn't eat enough, I think."

"Where'd your dog go?" Mr. Coogan asked.

"If I knew that, I wouldn't be out here looking."

"Ah, dogs always come home when they get hungry," Mr. Coogan said. "You hungry? You want to come eat with us? Come on, Liam hasn't seen you in a while."

By the time Desmond pulled the Impala into his family's driveway and very formally pocketed the revolver, all thoughts of what had happened in and around Pizzingrillo Park had ceased to torment Eddie. Instead he thought about the chaos awaiting him at home.

As soon as they entered the Coogan house, Eddie picked up the kitchen phone and dialed his own number.

"Hello," his mother answered.

"Hi, Mom? It's Eddie."

"Where in the hell did you go?" she hollered, and from there her conversation disintegrated into drunken shrieks. Eddie heard his father's voice in the background, yelling for her to shut up. Then his brother took the phone.

"Yeah, Eddie?" Kevin said.

"Yeah."

"Where the fuck are you? You missed dinner."

"I'm eating over at the Coogans' tonight. I told her that three times, and she forgot," Eddie said, almost believing it himself. "I told her last night, this morning and this afternoon."

"All right, well, she's drunk and didn't remember," Kevin said. "The dog came home without you and started acting weird, and Ma thought you were in trouble someplace. Fucking got me out of bed."

"Yeah, I guess Jabberwocky went home," Eddie said. "Sorry."

After he hung up, Eddie went inside and said hello to Liam, Desmond's older brother.

"Hi, Eddie, you know what?" Liam said, his eyes slightly crossed behind the thick lenses of his glasses. "I'm really glad you came over, you know why? I like you. That shirt's nice, Eddie, it looks good. We have Atari now, Eddie, and you know what? I'll play against you and I'll win. I'm really good. This boy at my school called me a dick, and you know what? He got in trouble. He got in real trouble, and everything. I'm in a play at school, and sometimes you know what time I come home? Seven o'clock." He paused for effect. "My school's all the way in Maspeth, is why."

Liam insisted on sitting next to Eddie while they ate. Eddie didn't mind, especially since Liam never talked while eating. Midway through the meal, Eddie looked over at Desmond and grinned. Desmond grinned back.

Mrs. Coogan looked different from how Eddie remembered her.

He couldn't shake the idea that she must be sick already and not know it. From time to time, she would rub her stomach, and he wondered if she felt pain there, if she had any sign yet that she was dying.

After dinner, Eddie thanked Mr. and Mrs. Coogan and apologized to Liam that he couldn't stay to play Atari. Then he left. Desmond walked him out to the driveway.

Desmond brought it right up again. "So you're not going to tell me what—"

"I'm sorry, okay? Things are happening that I can't discuss with anyone. Just forget about what got me mad, it doesn't make sense," Eddie told him. He discovered a jay in his pocket, and said, "You want to smoke a joint?"

Desmond's eyes lit up. "So *that's* why you're acting weird!" he said. "You're on drugs now?"

"It's a joint, Desmond, it's not drugs."

"It's dope. I'm against it."

"Well, it's not making me act weird," Eddie said. "I just offered it to be social, don't get worked up."

"You just seem different, Eddie," Desmond said.

"I *am* different," Eddie told him.

On his way home, Eddie smoked the joint by himself in Mrs. Denihan's lot. As he got high he scanned the trees around him, making certain none was an ash. *I've got enough creepy shit on my mind.*

Back here he could see Mrs. Denihan's yard, her unused garage and the white wrought-iron benches the Denihans had removed from the lot before Eddie was born. They now served as absurdly ornate patio furniture. Across the yard behind the benches stood the eight-foot redwood fence the McGowans had erected around their whole yard. Then the Germans. Then the O'Kanes.

Eddie crushed out the jay and went home.

His mother lay passed out on the couch, and his father had gone to bed. Kevin sat watching television dourly, awakened too early for work but too late to go back to sleep.

Jabberwocky snarled when Eddie stepped out the back door.

"What's the matter, baby, where'd you go?" he asked her, reaching to scratch her head.

She dodged his hand and ran to the end of her chain. When he cornered her, she snapped at him. So he gave up and went to bed.

He had trouble falling asleep. Eventually he unfolded one of those foil rectangles he had taken from...that thief. Inside the foil Eddie found a dime of hash.

He crumpled some into a joint and exhaled the smoke out his window. *Good hash.* He zoned out studying the skyline, forgetting anything that might have happened that day, thinking only of the queer way those ash trees in the distant Corridor loomed over other trees and houses, loomed over the streetlamps, over the powerlines and churches, over Queensborough Heights, over the earth itself.

THREE

Lying in bed Saturday morning, Eddie made up his mind to avoid reading the newspaper. He would spend the day in the park with Jabberwocky, he decided.

Yet after getting dressed he found Jabberwocky bristled at the sound of his voice, and bared her teeth at him from beside the O'Kanes' wrecked garage.

Murderer, she hissed. *Murderer.*

Fuck you, dog. After breakfast Eddie walked to the Jolly Joint on Roosevelt and bought a hash pipe. In a tiny park beside the public library he smoked the rest of the dime he had started last night. He went to the RKO Keith's and watched *Star Wars.*

The O'Kanes didn't eat dinner together on Saturdays, so he came home around nine that night. His father lay on the couch watching TV. His mother had gone to bed.

"Where you been all day, huh?" his father slurred.

Eddie looked at the old man, at his sullen bloodshot eyes, how his head bobbed and weaved. The urge to say something cruel evaporated. "Been out," Eddie said. "Went to the movies."

"Lets get some work done around here tomorrow, huh?" his father demanded.

"You got it," Eddie told him. He stumbled upstairs to his room, where he smoked another dime and a half of hash before sleeping. He didn't even have to open his window, since the fumes didn't smell like pot.

Sunday morning he woke to the sounds of his parents fighting in the kitchen. At the first lull, he crept downstairs and made himself toast and tea.

"Have you been to Mass?" his mother asked, in her best hungover cop's voice.

"Yep, last night," Eddie said.

"Who said it?"

"Some foreign guy, I couldn't understand a word he said," Eddie told her. "He's from a mission in China, I think."

At that moment Eddie's father exited the bathroom, so she dropped Eddie's interrogation in favor of busting the old man's balls over some derogatory remark he'd made about the priests at Mary's of Bethlehem.

Eddie grabbed the funnies off the kitchen table and headed inside, yet when he reached the dining room his eyes fell upon a different part of that day's paper: the news section.

Murder In Electchester, pg. 3, one headline read.

He ate his toast and read Snoopy. None of the other strips he liked had begun appearing yet.

Murder In Electchester, the paper kept telling him.

Eddie had not known what name he should properly call that area behind Sena. When he finished his toast he opened the news section, surprised at his own calmness but figuring that, after all, he ought to read what the police had to say.

Marc Tcholowitz, the kid's name was—though Eddie had taken his wallet, he had not looked inside it yet. Police found Marc Tcholowitz with his head bashed in not far from Pizzingrillo Park. Tcholowitz's friends had last seen him leaving the park. Marc was a good kid, not involved with anything illegal, according to his family.

The article ended with a number to call for anyone who might have information to help the police.

They have nothing.

A weight lifted from Eddie's mind, if not from his soul.

He spent the rest of the day stoned, reading and listening to the radio. When he thought about Marc Tcholowitz lying brained on the sidewalk, left bleeding to death alone over a paltry fifty dollars, Eddie felt an urge to tremble and scream. So he didn't think about it.

❦ ❦ ❦

Monday morning, Eddie learned he had made a friend for life: Timpone had scored big time, or claimed he had. Not only had this experience made him tolerate drugs, he now wanted to buy some.

"You need a pipe to smoke this, but it's worth it," Eddie said, handing him a dime of hash.

"Yeah, she's got a pipe," Timpone said. As he spoke he turned the hashish around in his hand, examining it. "We smoked some of her pot in it. What do you do, put the whole block in there and burn it?"

"No, you tear little chunks off, and shred them up," Eddie said.

"She'll know what to do with it. You want to try mesc?"

"How is it different?"

Eddie tried to explain. Timpone shrugged and said sure, so long as he could owe Eddie until the weekend. Eddie had no problem with that, and they shared a half-jay on the way from the bus to the schoolyard.

"I had no idea you were into this drug shit," Timpone marveled, tucking his three microdots into his breast pocket as they reached school.

"I'm not," Eddie said. "That's how it has to be. If you hang around with the drug fuckups, Poobah's going to notice that and tell your parents. So forget you know anything about me. If you get caught getting high, tell them Matherson sold you the shit."

"Who?"

"Matherson, he's a sophomore," Eddie said. "He's already in a world of shit, so it won't matter. But if they catch you with dope, any kind of dope, they won't let up till you tell them someone's name. So say Matherson."

Timpone nodded. They parted ways in the crowd, which acted far more reserved than usual. Even Richie Webber's friends around the loading dock seemed subdued.

After the bell rang Eddie's homeroom teacher read the announcements soberly, starting with Poobah's wishes for Brian O'Shea's speedy recovery; his nose and teeth had required surgery over the weekend. Eddie hadn't thought much about it since going home Friday.

Leaving Gumby's class, Eddie fell in alongside Kelly, who said, "You should go see O'Shea in the hospital, man, they'll let you in."

"How did he look to you?" Eddie asked.

"Still kind of stunned, I think," Kelly said. "I don't know him that good, so I just says, 'Hey, you know, keep your chin up' and that. His face really hurts him, it looks like."

Kelly entered his next class and Eddie strolled on toward English.

All around the school a charge hung in the languid air, and during English Eddie learned why: Classes would end on Wednesday. It was nearly summer.

Sitting next to Desmond during Social Studies did not bother him so much. After class they met again in the cafeteria and ate lunch together. Eddie could tell how relieved Desmond felt to forget Eddie's affront to him from last week.

The rest of the day crawled past, and while pretending to pay attention to Mr. Scalia Eddie tried to imagine how to deal with the tedium of living through his junior and senior years. Then again, compared with a full-time job, school might not suck, after all.

It just took money. And as long as he had Poobah's key, and didn't get greedy with it, Eddie could generate capital at will. The kids who had dope virtually advertised the fact by the way they dressed and acted, and all Eddie had to do was locate their lockers and wait.

He carried more money on him now than anyone else in this school, he felt sure of it. He liked that feeling. Yet during the summer months, how would he keep that up? He had to find a connection, and soon.

Step one, of course, was his new wardrobe.

During Religion, last period, Eddie raised his hand. "Brother?"

"Yes?" Brother Declan replied.

"May I be excused?" Eddie asked him. "Something I ate is turning my stomach."

Brother Declan nodded, and Eddie left the class.

Once he turned the corner of the hall, Eddie began watching for witnesses as he strolled. Whenever no one was paying attention, he opened upper lockers with his key at random. But it was late May, he soon recalled; no one wore a denim jacket to school unless they had an album cover painted on it, which would make the jacket too easy to recognize.

He could steal denim jackets next fall, then—that's when most kids would wear them brand-new, to boot. For this summer he might not even need a jacket.

Eddie continued his occasional search anyway, just due to the feeling of power it gave him to spy at whim, and so thoroughly. He could even tell what some guys jerked off over. By chance he opened a locker on the third floor that contained a familiar *Sabbath, Bloody Sabbath* jacket.

The looseleaf binder said TIMOTHY BENGLER in crude ballpoint. "Yeah, thanks for helping me get hooked up," Eddie muttered, digging into Benglers pockets. Inside Bengler's Marlboros, tucked behind the foil, Eddie found at least half of a large joint.

"Thanks, don't mind if I do," Eddie said. He slipped the roach into his wallet and closed locker 327. Then with his hands in his pockets he strutted his way back to Religion, where Brother Declan smiled to see him in better spirits.

That afternoon Eddie rode the Q44 all the way to the part of Roosevelt Avenue where he had purchased his hash pipe on Saturday. First he checked all the T-shirts in Jolly Joint, then he tried the store across the street that sold concert Jerseys. Gradually he caught himself getting lost in the selection process, actually searching out bands he liked, when of course he ought to strive for anonymity.

"Which shirts do you sell the most of?" he asked the redhead behind the counter.

"That Led Zeppelin one," she said, popping her gum as she pointed out the *Led Zeppelin II* shirt behind her. She seemed twenty at the oldest. Probably younger.

"What else?"

"The Sabbath and Pink Floyd."

He bought all three. It crossed his mind that she wanted him. "Why do you buy the top sellers?" she asked as she placed them into a bag and passed them to him. "Why not get whatever group you're into yourself?"

"I don't like any of the Stones shirts you have," he told her.

"Yeah, they ain't been selling, either," she said, nodding. "That live record last year sucked, and I don't like *Black and Blue*. They're probably over with at this point, they're so old and everything."

"Don't bet on it," Eddie said.

For the first time Eddie studied her face up close.

Holy shit, it's "Eileen," he said.

"Yeah?" she asked. "Do I know you?"

Eddie shook his head.

"Then how do you know my name?"

His mind raced for any plausible answer, and lost. "I don't know," he hedged.

"Oh, my God," she said, then spoke more quietly to him. "Are you sensitive? Are you psychic?"

That's right, she's into that shit. "I...guess I must be," he said. "This is the first time anything like this ever happened. I know you, but I don't know how I know you."

"Don't let it frighten you," she told him, her voice and eyes abruptly solemn. "It's perfectly natural. It's a gift."

Twenty-five minutes later, at the payphone outside the T-shirt store, Eddie dialed his own number.

"Hello?" his mother answered.

"Ma? It's Eddie."

"What's wrong?"

"Nothing's wrong," Eddie said. "I have to do a project for school, I'm not going to be home for dinner, okay? I just thought I'd call now and warn you."

"Where are you?" she asked.

"I'm on my way to this guy's house," Eddie said. "Frank Timpone."

She bought it. Dealing with his parents didn't require the endless hassles he recalled. He was smarter than they, after all, and their constant boozing only furthered their disadvantage.

After he hung up, Eddie walked another two blocks toward the RKO Keith's and bought a pair of jeans. He wore them out of the store, along with his new Zep II shirt. Now only the earth shoes had to go, and he didn't have money for boots. That would have to wait a few days.

Some biker with a pit bull on a spiked chain had pedestrians abandoning the sidewalk for the street. Yet when this dog saw Eddie it snarled and pulled to one side, to avoid him. The biker could not understand it.

Eddie walked back to the T-shirt store. Eileen stood waiting for him out front. "You look like a different person," she greeted him.

"I am," he answered. "Sorry I took so long. Where do you want to go smoke this?"

She shrugged with a practiced nonchalance. "My house should be cool. My father won't be home for dinner tonight."

Eileen lived in Whitestone, and wanted to take a bus there. Instead Eddie brought her to the taxi stand and they cabbed it. That impressed her. So did the adult way he carried himself, and the amount of fine dope he had.

The girl's cat freaked out and ran to the basement when Eddie entered the house. Which was fine; Eddie detested cats, anyway.

When Eileen led him into her bedroom he seduced her in a way no one ever had. High-school romeos substitute vigor for finesse; Eddie had plenty of both, and took his time, and even introduced her to her own G-spot. He spent an hour playing before penetrating her.

Around eight she heated lasagna for dinner. It was better than what he could expect at home, certainly. For dessert he helped himself to another piece of her ass. After that he dressed and left.

At ten-thirty Eddie arrived home, nearly aglow. He came in the front door and found his brother in the dining room. Kevin's holster hung over the back of his chair. Kevin had worn it since becoming an A-man in the union. The gun was a regular sight around the O'Kane house by the time Eddie had reached high school. Eddie vaguely recalled taking the pistol out of the hiding space beneath Kevin's dresser a few times.

"Where you been?" Kevin asked without looking up from his breakfast.

"Out, working on something," Eddie replied. "What's up?"

"Nothing," Kevin said. "Met a girl, that's about it."

"Yeah, I did, too," Eddie told him, and walked into the kitchen.

The old man sat at the kitchen table, too drunk to talk, though of course that never stopped him. Eddie surveyed the kitchen, pretending not to notice his father. There was no bread in the breadbox. His mother's leftovers in the refrigerator would disgust the dog.

Speaking of whom.

Eddie opened the back door. Immediately Jabberwocky leaped to her feet and barked at him.

"What's your problem?" he asked.

The dog growled and trembled. Her lips drew back.

Murderer.

Eddie went to his room and smoked some hash. The dog had unnerved him. Turning on music helped a little. Despite the antenna Kevin had rigged for him, Eddie's radio had crappy reception. *That's something I ought to buy,* he told himself, *a stereo. Something loud.*

Then his blood turned icy as he realized he had not done his homework for Gumby's class. Eddie bolted upright, and knew at once that in his present condition he could neither solve nor copy

Geometry. He lay back down. It struck him odd that, now he had become a murderer, he still worried about doing homework.

The hashish did its work, and he slept.

❦   ❦   ❦

The next morning he arrived at the Q44 stop early, to catch the public-school freshmen. They knew him by sight now and copped his hash dimes eagerly, in most cases splitting one between two buyers.

"Fuck, you *have* to be hooked up with the Crew," said that kid who'd first mentioned them. "This is how they deal hash. I mean, exactly. The foil's cut the same way and everything."

"Coincidence, my man," Eddie assured him.

The Edison students scarfed up Eddie's product, and bid him cheery farewells as they boarded the Q44. After not seeing any schoolmate with whom he wished to travel, Eddie almost stepped onto the bus. He stopped himself in midstride, however, and turned around.

There's one day left of school. What can they do, give me detention over the summer? Fuck Gumby's class. Eddie hadn't done the homework, anyway. He would eat breakfast someplace, enjoy himself, and saunter in during second period. In all likelihood, he hadn't had a lateness all semester.

Where Roosevelt met Franklin stood a Greek diner, the kind that served a bowl of pickled cucumbers and tomatoes as appetizers. Eddie sat in a 1950s-style booth and ordered a Western omelette. His waitress flirted with him. While he ate he watched busloads of Aviation and Edison juniors pass the diner on their way up Roosevelt.

After that, McCanton boys took their place. If he saw Timpone out there, Eddie thought, he should fetch him in here and they could get high together as they headed into school late.

"Would you like anything else?" the waitress asked.

"I'd like your phone number, actually," Eddie told her, "but I don't know how to ask for it without sounding like I use pickup lines I learned from my dad's *Playboy* collection."

She laughed.

"Do you have newspapers, by any chance?" he asked her.

"Sure, what one you read?" she rejoined, still giggling.

"How about the *Times*?"

He finished off two cups of coffee while he read the news section, admiring the paper's timeless, stilted writing. Then he paid his bill, got the waitress's phone number, and left to catch the bus with his paper folded under his arm.

Eddie wound up on a bus full of Aviation students. He didn't mind at all; just from the way he carried himself, people no longer perceived him as a child, so no one would treat him as a Catholic-school kid.

He also stayed on the bus two stops later than normal. It made sense to him to lay extra low while smoking pot near school. No point in risking trouble now that he carried quantity on him.

So he wandered through the neighborhood around his school, known as Briarwood. The streets had military names, and most blocks were curved: Burdon Crescent, Pershing Crescent, Montgomery Crescent. On one empty stretch, Eddie loaded his pipe and toked. He did it again, and would have fired up a third bowl had he not seen a woman with a stroller approaching.

He reached school about ten, nervous that his red eyes and reeking breath would give him away. He grabbed the cafeteria door and pulled. They had locked it.

Having never come to school this late, Eddie had no idea how to gain entrance. He tried the front doors, then the ones at either end. Plodding back toward the cafeteria, he peered in through the windows and saw a deserted classroom. Then another.

He paused at the gate, straining his hash-clouded mind for an explanation. *Did classes end already, yesterday instead of tomorrow? They said Wednesday.* He checked the *Times* under his arm: Tuesday.

"What's the problem?" a voice said.

Eddie turned to find Poobah crossing the parking lot toward him, clearly displeased.

"Hello, Brother," Eddie said. "How do I get inside?"

"What, did you forget a book?"

Eddie glanced once more at the empty classrooms, then back at the principal. "There *is* school today, right?"

Poobah's face dropped, subtly. "You didn't hear the announce-ment?"

"I'm just getting here," Eddie explained. With relief he saw that Poobah was pissed about something other than Eddie's lateness. "I had a problem at home, and I couldn't get a bus until just now."

"Well," Poobah said, "we had a student die last night. Classes are canceled for today, probably tomorrow as well."

Automatically Eddie said, "I'm sorry to hear that, Brother."

"You and me both," Poobah told him. "He took some kind of

dope and walked onto the Van Wyck Expressway."

"It wasn't Matherson, was it?" Eddie asked. "Matthew Matherson?"

Poobah shook his head. "A junior," he said. "Frank Timpone."

Eddie's mouth opened. No sound came out.

"Did you know him?"

Slowly Eddie's head moved up and down.

"I'm sorry," Poobah said. "Did you know anything about him taking pills? His girlfriend says he thought it was some kind of LSD. The police say it was angel dust."

Still Eddie couldn't speak.

"How did you know Matherson's name would be involved?" Poobah asked.

"He's," Eddie began, scrambling. "He talks about drugs."

"Well, supposedly he sold Timpone these dust pills. Only Matherson swears he didn't, and he hasn't been at school," Poobah said. An expression of genuine pain lined the man's face. "I don't need this crap. We've never had anything worse at this school than a couple of dopes smoking pot at a dance. Now we're in the *Daily News* today with a drug story. Most of you kids don't even drink."

Drink. Fine idea, that.

Eddie said something hollow and encouraging to Poobah and left. At a deli three blocks away he bought a quart beer. He drank it in a tiny playground, trying to shake the image of Timpone dusted, parading into oncoming traffic.

That quart didn't do the job. Neither did the next one, nor the one after that. When Eddie staggered onto the Q44 sometime around noon, the vision of Timpone's death still tormented him. By now his eyes were red from crying as much as from drinking.

Not until he reached his parents' property did Eddie think of facing his mother with alcohol on his breath. This early in the day, she might not have started herself, so she'd smell him and fly off the handle.

Eddie crept up to the side of the house and peeked. He did not see her in the living room or the hall. So long as she wasn't in the kitchen, then, he could probably slip in without—

Jabberwocky clamped her jaws upon his hand.

"Fuck!" he cried out, and kicked the dog.

She scampered a few feet away, as far as her chain would let her. There she resumed her menacing pose.

"You bit me," he told her, feeling stupid even as the words left his lips. Yes, she had bit him.

She bit me, after I travel back in time to fucking save her life. She bit me and stands there accusing me of murder. Ungrateful little bitch.

Thanks to the building's missing rear wall, it took Eddie all of five seconds to storm into the garage, snatch his father's long-handled spade, and bring its blade down firmly into Jabberwocky's skull.

The dog collapsed. He smashed her a second time, a third, a fourth. With the spade raised in the air Eddie glanced at what he could see of her face. His last blow had enucleated one of her eyes, which now sat on the broken bridge of her snout.

He dropped the shovel, and slouched into the kitchen.

"Who's that?" his mother called from upstairs.

"Me," he replied.

"What are you doing home?"

"They canceled school." Involuntarily his voice dropped as he gave her this information. Telling her about Timpone would only drag her down here to question him, anyway.

"What?"

"We had a half-day," Eddie said.

She said something else. Her words blurred into a drone behind him as he dashed to the bathroom. The beer and breakfast in his stomach burned its way back up his esophagus.

If asked to identify the substance blasting out his mouth and nose, Eddie would have guessed gasoline. That he got most of it into the toilet gave him only the faintest passing satisfaction.

Ages later his heaving subsided. He rinsed his mouth from the faucet and rested against the wall, drawing air into his lungs over and over.

When he felt strong enough, he reached behind the shower and pulled out the wet mop. The few spots where he had spewed stood out on the dirty white tiles, yet once he had cleaned the area around the bowl he had to mop the rest of the floor.

It took him ten minutes, and by the time he finished and entered the kitchen again, he felt better, practically sober. He walked back outside, wanting a breath of fresh air.

He opened the door and found Jabberwocky's battered corpse. Ants had already begun eating her eyeball.

"Oh," he said, feeling as though something unseen had landed a tremendous blow to his abdomen. "Oh, Jesus."

He had killed her. His dog. The only friend he had missed from his entire childhood.

What filled Eddie's heart then was not remorse, not disgust with himself, not even guilt. What caused the blood in Eddie's veins to pound at his temples was terror. For a long moment—just how long, he could not say—Eddie stared at the sky above him, his arms waving slowly, impotent. His jaw moved, yet his mouth formed nothing like words.

Then his eyes fell upon the spade, the murder weapon, and in some manner that sight snapped him back to the work at hand.

Inside the kitchen, under the sink, his mother kept large black garbage bags. Though she complained whenever anyone took one of these, Eddie filched one and carried it outside. He stretched the mouth of the bag wide to fit Jabberwocky's head and front legs into it. Once he could no longer see her poor crushed face, his task became easier.

At first Eddie had no conscious idea where he might bury this parcel. By the time he reached the front sidewalk, however, he knew he meant to go to Mrs. Denihan's lot. The only other possible site would be the Corridor, and he could not walk eight blocks carting a shovel and...*and this bag.*

As he entered the lot past the surveyors' poles, heading back near the fence where he knew the bulldozers would not touch the earth, Eddie recalled playing with Jabberwocky here in the snow one winter, how she zipped from tree to tree while he chased her.

Then he dug a hole and put her in the ground.

§   §   §

After he buried his dog, Eddie replaced his father's spade in the garage, and went for a walk. He needed badly to get high.

With few exceptions, the roads of Queensborough Heights fit a botanical theme. Avenues bore tree names, alphabetically: Ash, Beech, Cherry, and so on. The streets had long since reverted to numbers, but had once had floral names such as Tulip and Violet.

In a neighborhood near the western Corridor, south of the Main Street terminal, the streets formed an odd curving pattern. These had the names Phlox Place and Hydrangea Place. Eddie had always liked this neighborhood, probably because he so seldom visited it. His grandmother had called it the Back Parish; Eddie didn't know why.

He went there now to smoke hash and stare at the old apartment houses as he shuffled along. The foundations had been laid to match the layout of the blocks, so that the buildings curved in the same pattern as the streets.

Eventually he made his way homeward, still dreading the sight of Jabberwocky's chain lying on the grass in his parents' yard. Thus he meandered onto the block where for eight years he had attended St. Mary of Bethlehem elementary school, across the street from the church of that same name.

As he approached, he studied the school with stoned interest. So much smaller than he remembered it. *It could be someone's house.* In his dreams it always towered over the town.

Eddie fell still.

Two lines of uniformed students, one male and one female, followed a woman down the school's front steps; she marched them with the gingery stride of a nun who flouts the habit. Sister Margaret. He'd had her in eighth grade himself.

Near the middle of the girls' line was the girl he had glimpsed in the passenger seat of her mother's passing car on Friday. She carried her books in a knapsack over both shoulders, with her hair in silly-looking pigtails.

Anger consumed any worry or recrimination inside Eddie. He returned home with his teeth grinding.

"Where the hell did you go?" his mother asked as he entered the kitchen again.

"Out," he answered.

"Out where?" she demanded.

"I walked around the park, why?"

"You don't walk out of here without saying anything to me," his mother said. Her breath, thick with cheap wine, made him wince.

"I asked you something and you didn't answer me," she said.

"When, before?"

She nodded. "How come you haven't asked me for carfare?"

Eddie tried to figure out what she meant.

"You haven't asked me for carfare," she repeated. "Where are you getting money from?"

"I have no money."

"Let me see your pockets," she insisted.

For one instant they stood glaring at each other, then Eddie said, "No," and walked away.

Shocked, she watched him leave. While he walked up the stairs to his room, she called out, "Where's that goddamned dog?"

"On my ass, picking daisies," he replied, and went into his room.

FOUR

Summer came. Via some miracle, Eddie passed all his finals except History, which he could scarcely master even under normal circumstances. He had to attend summer school.

So on a hot day toward the end of June, an impersonal bald man named Brother Angus in McCanton's guidance department gave him three choices of locations: the Hill Academy, Edison, or J.A. Sena.

"You live in Queensborough Heights, yes?" Brother Angus asked.

"Yes, Brother."

"Then Sena is closest to your house," Brother Angus said, filling out Eddie's form.

"Uh, I'm not sure—"

The man cut Eddie off with narrowed eyes. "What's the problem?" he asked impatiently.

While his brain reeled, trying to concoct an excuse other than *I killed somebody right near there*, Eddie's mouth hung open.

"I see," Brother Angus said quietly, as if Eddie had spoken. "Edward, I understand why you're hesitant."

Does he?

"This isn't the regular school year," Brother Angus explained. "You won't have to obey a dress code, and you won't be the only kid there from Catholic school. Everyone takes summer school at the closest place to their house. Sena won't be full of regular Sena students, so it won't be any tougher than the Hill Academy, or wherever."

By now, Eddie stopped caring. His reticence at hearing the name Sena was only a reflex; once he had a few seconds to consider the issue, he didn't really believe the place would trouble his conscience. Not enough to make him commute to Edison, anyway.

And of course, the Hill Academy was out of the question, because—*well, because.*

❦ ❦ ❦

Eddie opted for the afternoon session, which meant showing up at two and dismissal at close to five. As it turned out, Kelly from McCanton had to take Geometry again at Sena, so Eddie had a friend. From the first day, the presence of girls made school infinitely more bearable. By the end of class Eddie wanted to transfer here for good.

Outside he found Kelly talking to a blonde with a Farrah haircut.

"'Sup, man?" Kelly greeted him, and then introduced him to the blonde. "This here is Eddie O'Kane. Eddie, this is Lenore."

Eddie momentarily froze. It really *was* Lenore. He had never realized where or how Kelly met her, nor that they had met this early. She didn't look the way Eddie remembered. But this was the '70s, everyone dressed weird.

"Hi, I'm Eddie," he said.

"That's a cool shirt," Lenore told him. "I love Sabbath."

"What you up to?" Kelly asked him. "Hey, you talk to O'Shea?"

"Yeah, he came in during finals. He was all banged up," Eddie said. "His teeth are still broken, they can't fix them until the end of the summer, almost."

Kelly nodded, and Eddie could tell that he had brought the topic up mostly so they would have some reason for adult-sounding dialogue in front of this girl, Kelly's future wife.

"What happened?" Lenore asked. "Your friend was in a car accident?"

"Nope, he got beat up by a real asshole at our school," Kelly informed her. "A real asshole who doesn't go to our school anymore."

"What did it start over?"

"Nothing," Kelly said. "This guy Matherson's notebook fell out of his desk, and O'Shea picked it up and threw it back inside for him, and Matherson freaked out. I think Matherson was on drugs."

"Who isn't?" she quipped, and gave a quick laugh.

Kelly's eyebrows began to raise but held still, from fear of blowing it with this girl.

"Speaking of which," Eddie said, "want to smoke a joint?"

"Sure!" Lenore said.

Kelly's eyes darted from her to Eddie and back.

"Where should we go?" Eddie asked.

"The park," Lenore said. "Can I invite my friend Jan?"

"But of course!" Eddie told her.

Lenore spotted Jan leaving the school and introduced her to the two boys. "Want to go fire one up?" she asked Jan.

"Yeah, dynamite," Jan said. She had a few too many pounds around her middle, but not so much that it didn't resemble baby fat. *This girl ought to wear flannel.*

The four of them walked behind the school, with Lenore leading.

"I bet you really like the Who," Eddie said to Lenore.

She shrugged. "I don't know that much about them," she said.

Give it another year. "Have you heard this new Stones album, it just came out?"

"Oh, with that disco song?" Jan said. "I hate that shit. I can't believe the Stones went disco."

"I'm into Zep," Kelly said.

"Who isn't?" Lenore said. Her big line, apparently.

Not until they reached the gates did Eddie realize exactly where Lenore had steered them: Pizzingrillo Park.

"What's the matter?" Jan asked him. Kelly and Lenore turned to see why Eddie had stopped walking.

"Uh," Eddie said. "This park?"

"Yeah, it's cool. I used to get high here with my boyfriend," Lenore said, then clumsily added, for Eddie's and Kelly's benefit, "My ex-boyfriend."

"Doesn't the Crew hang out here?" Eddie asked.

"Fuck the Crew," Kelly smirked.

"They won't bother us," Jan said. "I know them."

"No, you know what?" Eddie said. "Let's go to the Corridor."

"The what?" Jan asked.

"The Corridor, down the street from the school," he said. "It's cooler than this. I just don't dig this park, is all. Here, we can smoke while we're walking." From his pocket Eddie fished his pipe and a dime of hash. He filled the bowl, lit it, and passed it.

"Nice shit," Jan told him. She was more of a head than Lenore.

"Cool," Lenore said, as she held in her hit and handed the pipe to Kelly.

Kelly hesitated, just barely, then drew too hard on the pipe and broke into a coughing fit.

"Didn't you ever smoke hash before?" Lenore chided him. "The smoke expands in your lungs."

Eddie led them back past the school. In ten minutes they entered the woods along the path that he had used to reach Sena this morning. Midway that path intersected the horse trail, in overgrown disuse since the local stable ended afternoon rentals. Eddie guided his party down this trail till they reached a gully where they all leaned against a graffiti-covered boulder while continuing to pass the pipe. Eddie kept reloading it.

Getting high amplified Kelly's shyness around the girls, a trait Eddie had not remembered but which made Kelly's eventual marriage to his high-school sweetheart logical. In his first life, Eddie had not truly become friends with Kelly until senior year, by which time Kelly and Lenore were "pre-engaged" or something.

In any case, Kelly did not talk much now, and Lenore focused on Eddie instead.

"What did you call this place? The coroner?" Lenore asked him.

"The Corridor. It's a flight corridor," he explained. "When they built LaGuardia Airport, the city forbade anyone to build on the strip of ground where the planes descend to land. This way, if a plane crashes, it won't hit any houses."

With the toe of his brand-new motorcycle boot Eddie drew a map of Queens in the horse trail's sandy clay. "See?" he said as he sketched. "All these parks connect, from Shea Stadium and that park over there to the Botanical Gardens, and when you get to Bayside you've got Peck Park and the golf courses there."

"So what park is this?" Lenore asked. Kelly might as well have been invisible.

"No park," Eddie said. "That's why we just call it the Corridor. Everyone in Queensborough Heights calls it that. Where do you live?"

"Fresh Meadow," she answered.

Kelly quietly said something to Jan, and Jan responded in kind. Neither Eddie nor Lenore paid attention.

"So there's this whole piece of land, and nothing on it?" Lenore asked.

"A few things. Some houses at one spot, which were built before the airport," Eddie said, pointing in the houses' general direction. "They didn't have to move out. And there's a farm, and a soccer field. You want to see?"

She looked at him, a faint grin curling in her dimples. "I guess," she said. Then she turned and interrupted Jan mid-sentence to say, "We're going to go check out this farm. I'll see you later."

"You want to meet here?" Jan asked her.

"No, I'll just have him walk me home," she said. "It's getting late."

Eddie shook Kelly's hand good-bye, and thought he sensed a tiny dislike. *Too bad, sometimes you have to take whichever girl's left.* Eddie and Lenore headed off on their own.

The rush of scoring magnified Eddie's buzz. As he and Lenore trekked down the trail, she made a point of keeping close beside him.

"So you're a senior next year, am I right?" he asked her.

"Yes," she answered.

He gave her a chance to wonder how he knew that. When she didn't ask, he spoke. "I could tell," he said. "You act mature."

"God, look who's talking," she said. "If I didn't go to school with you I would think you couldn't be in high school. You're like grown-up."

They came upon the Farm. It gave her pause, the expanse cleared and plowed and neatly cut into parcels, each small plot sown with a different crop.

"Wow," she said after a beat.

"It's still small. In another four years it will take up five times as much of the Corridor," he said, waving for her to follow him down a narrow row between planted lots.

"What are they growing?" she asked.

"You name it."

They passed a Korean woman in a bright red cloth jacket who grinned and nodded at them as she hoed the soil. A few plots away they peeked inside a six-foot-high shed filled with some kind of produce.

"What's this little house for?" Lenore asked him.

"It's a curing shack," Eddie said. "I think you keep the door closed when you cure in it, and open when you dry something. This stuff's being dried."

"What are they drying? It looks like peas."

"Those are too big to be pea pods," Eddie said. "And they're brown. Doesn't it look like the floor's cement? They even put in a drain." In fact, the floor of the shack was brushed earth.

"We have a fire extinguisher like that in our basement," she said, nodding to a waist-high pump can with a hose attached.

"No, that's a spray can, for watering remote plants," Eddie said.

"Who owns this land?" Lenore asked him, scanning the field on every side of them. Already the Farm had grown larger in area than a city block. Water taps rose knee-high from the ground at forty-foot intervals.

"The city. The Koreans apply for permits," he said. "Originally this was set aside for senior citizens, but old people weren't doing anything with it."

Her sneakers sank in the moist soil of a watermelon patch, which had a fiberglass pond sunk beneath it to trap the water. She had to hold onto Eddie's shoulder so she could untie each shoe and rinse it beneath a faucet in turn.

When she had put her shoes back on, she kept touching him. Then they kissed, and Eddie took her by the hand to lead her back toward the woods.

"Come on," he said.

"Where are we going?"

"I want to show you—" Eddie stopped dead.

Twenty feet in front of him stood a wall of ash trees.

That's got to be a hundred trees. There weren't that many of them, it was only weeks ago. True, Eddie had avoided all thought of the place, but he remembered this grove smaller, much smaller, a tiny patch on the edge of the Farm.

"Show me what?" Lenore said.

Eddie spun and said, "No, it's the other way."

"What is?"

"This place I want to show you," he said.

"Let's just get off the Farm," she said. "The way you were headed, through those trees."

"No, I think those trees are poison oaks." Eddie studied them, one hand rubbing his chin. "Yeah, they sure look like it."

That persuaded her. They left the Farm the same way they had come in, and Eddie led her down the trail into the next clearing, an artificial space behind a metal fence.

"This is a football field," Lenore said as they stepped onto a giant white grid chalked onto the turf.

"Soccer field, actually," he said, leading her onto the turf. "Looks really new, too. I thought they redid this in, like, '74 or '75. Must've been more recent than that." He examined one of the goal posts up close. Its all-weather steel still shone.

The Parks Department had planted an even row of maples around the field's perimeter. A sea of green leaves rose unbroken above the storm fence, at a uniform height taller than a house.

"You feel like smoking more?" she hinted. "I mean, if you got it."

"Tell you what," Eddie said. "On the other side of the field is Roosevelt Avenue. There's a pizzeria called Bella Chica's. Let's go eat, then come back and smoke."

They crossed the field arm in arm. When they got to the pizza shop, he jumped on the bill and insisted that she share a small calzone with him besides having a slice.

They returned to the soccer field half an hour later and sat on the cement bleachers, which stood four rows high and seventy-five feet long, the only unrenovated element of the facility. It had withstood decades. "When I was little," Eddie said while loading his pipe with hash, "I always thought these were stairs for a giant."

"I could see that," Lenore said.

"This used to be abandoned then," he said. He drew off the pipe and handed it to her. "I think it was a football field a long time ago, like before World War Two, but they changed the rulebook and it wasn't big enough. Something like that. This is going to be the main soccer field in Queens by the time I leave for college."

"How do you know so much about what's going to happen?" she asked.

"I live here."

They began kissing, until Eddie stopped. "I have another prediction," he said very seriously.

"What?"

"Sometime in the next minute, I will urinate," he informed her. She laughed. "Yes! I see it clearly! Urination shall become part of my life. Excuse me."

She kept laughing as he got up and strutted down to the bleachers' far end. Over his shoulder he called, "Go ahead, smoke some more while you wait. This could turn into a big project."

At the bleachers' end he hopped off onto the ground, unzipped and began relieving himself underneath them. The builders had not bricked up this side of the bleachers, for some reason, though they had sealed the other end. As a result everyone chucked garbage under here. Why the giant stone bench had been left gaping, a tunnel to a dead end, Eddie could not guess, but—

Something sprang at him.

With a squeak it bolted from the darkness beneath the bleachers. It crossed his feet, and he felt its paws scamper over his boots.

"SHIT!" Eddie cried. "FUCKING SHIT! *DAMN* IT!"

He leaped backward, both hands shielding his penis.

"Son of a bitch," he said, calmer, still fuming.

"What happened?" Lenore asked. She had run down here to help.

"A fucking rat came at me from under there," he said, nodding at the open space.

"This thing's hollow?" she asked. Then she looked at Eddie again. "Are you okay?"

"You asking me or my dick?" he said, smiling in embarrassment and putting it back inside his pants.

Lenore doubled over, hysterical. It lasted until they returned to their spot. "You are the funniest fucking person I ever met," she told him.

"You think you have something to laugh about now," he said, "I almost pissed all over myself."

The maple barricade blocked the waning sunrays, making it dark prematurely where they sat. They smoked most of a dime of hash and made out.

His hands roamed Lenore's body expertly. Her breathing grew heavier, more erratic. When he touched her breast, she pushed his hand away, then guided it back. She nursed on his tongue until she hyperventilated.

"Slow down," she said, pushing him back gently.

"What do you mean?"

"I mean," she explained, drawing a huge breath, "I just met you."

"I'm just kissing you," he said. "Sorry, I didn't think I was getting carried away."

"*I* am." She looked at him balefully.

Eddie retreated, to make her feel comfortable. He searched his mind for a new subject to bring up.

"You should listen to the Who," he said.

"I've heard one song they do, I don't know what it's called," she said.

"You'll love them," Eddie told her. "I know you will. Trust me."

This conversation carried on between kisses, and night steadily overtook the sky above them. Presently they found themselves once more in a tight embrace, and again she begged off.

Eddie soothed her, told her they did not have to do anything she did not want to do. He said only mutual desire mattered, and improvised a *Cosmopolitan* column on sexual etiquette. Finally, pinch-massaging her nipples as the stars awoke overhead, he cajoled her into fucking him.

❦   ❦   ❦

After he had walked Lenore home to Fresh Meadow, which was on the far side of Sena, Eddie went to Desmond's house. First he smoked two bowls of hash down the block, then he entered the Coogans' backyard and peered in the window of the TV room.

Desmond, still wearing work clothes, sat eating a sandwich on the sofa. Eddie tapped on the window, and Desmond opened the back door.

"What's the word, Eddie?" he greeted him.

They sat down and watched *Star Trek.* "Hey, can I use your phone?" Eddie asked.

"Sure, knock yourself out," Desmond said.

Eddie went into the kitchen and dialed his own number.

"Hello?" Eddie's mother answered.

"Hi, it's Eddie," he said. "Listen, I'm going to be later than I thought I would."

"Where the hell are you?" she demanded.

"I'm at Desmond's, right where I told you," he said, indignant. "I've been here all night."

"Desmond's?" Despite slurring, her voice sounded wary.

"Yes, just like I said."

"Oh," she said. "I forgot you told me that. I thought... Well, your brother's going to be angry, I woke him up over it."

"Anyway, I'm going to be here a while yet," he said. "We're watching the Mets. Didn't realize what time it was getting."

Disarmed, his mother muttered something, and then Kevin's voice roared in the background, and she hung up. Eddie did the same, then stretched and yawned. On his way back to the TV room, he passed through Desmond's father's den.

On the wall of the den hung four large frames, each displaying eight or more photographs, most of them group shots: class pictures, family picnics, the little-league team Mr. Coogan's service station sponsored.

In the dim light from the adjacent TV room, Eddie examined the photos one by one. In the middle of the second frame he located a female face. *That's her.* Eddie flicked on Mr. Coogan's desk lamp so he could see her better. *No bout adoubt it.*

"Hi, Eddie, why are you here?" Liam asked.

With a start Eddie said, "Liam, man, you scared me."

"Hi, Eddie, I didn't know you were at my house," Liam said. He was wearing pajamas, tan cotton ones with brown piping. Without his glasses his eyes resembled a mole's. "I was in bed, and you know what? I had to go to the bathroom. I didn't know you were at our house, Eddie."

Desmond entered the den and said sternly, "What are you doing out of bed?"

"Eddie's here," Liam said.

"Yeah, I know Eddie's here," Desmond said. "I asked what are you doing out of bed? It's after eleven o'clock."

"He was just going to the bathroom, and he saw me," Eddie explained.

"Why is this light on?" Desmond asked, pointing at the desk lamp.

"I put that on," Eddie said.

Desmond seemed surprised.

"I'm sorry, I was looking over your family pictures," Eddie said, waving at the wall. "Something caught my eye as I passed."

Liam returned to his room. "Good night," he said.

"Sorry about that," Eddie said.

"No, that's cool, I don't care," Desmond said. "He gets out of bed sometimes in the middle of the night."

"I don't mean to get him riled up," Eddie said, then summoned Desmond's attention to the photo. "Who is this girl?"

"Oh, that's—" Desmond halted and squinted at the face to which Eddie pointed. "I don't know who she is. That's from a picnic, a few years ago. I don't think you were there."

"I'm sure I wasn't."

"She might be Jimmy Cooper's daughter," Desmond said. "Jimmy Cooper's this guy who used to work for my dad. They live on Kalmia Avenue. She's cute, huh?"

"She's a child, perv," Eddie pointed out.

"Old picture, though."

They watched TV. After *The Twilight Zone* ended, Eddie left the Coogans' house through the backyard. Down the block he stopped to smoke some hash, but upon reflection he decided to wait until he got home.

Instead, he walked briskly to the Farm in the Corridor.

As he traveled, Eddie saw a police cruiser pass. Other than that, he saw no one on the road or sidewalk. At last he turned left onto Colden Street and came to the Farm's entrance.

No one would see him here so late at night. The houses across the street from the Corridor sat quiet and decaying, as though no one had lived in them for decades.

Yet Eddie could not force himself to enter past the rusted fence. He would sooner step off a roof. *Those trees.* The skin on his arms crawled.

From right at the fence he squinted into the unlit Corridor, trying to count the ash trees. No question, there were more now than there had been. That grove had never extended this far; a dense growth of ragweed used to separate it from the Farm, except in one spot.

A bat sailed over the crops. Everywhere wind combed the foliage, making branches wave soundlessly in shadow.

"I must be crazy, coming anywhere near here at night," Eddie told himself out loud, and it was true. What he did not add, for he had not considered it, was that he could only come here after nightfall—during daylight, the very sight of the grove repelled him.

I have to go in. I said I would.

The trees waved at him.

What can they do? Come after me?

So he left, walking Colden Street, studying the Corridor as he went. The ash forest continued another block. It seemed wider all around.

As soon as he passed the end of it and the flat weedy ground resumed, Eddie felt great tension leave his body. In its wake, relief poured through him.

At once he felt ravenous. He had not eaten in seven hours. At two places nearby he knew he could eat this late: the pizzeria behind the soccer field, or the diner on Franklin.

Reaching the pizza place meant crossing the Corridor.

Eddie picked the diner. He arrived there just in time to watch the maitre d' eject a trio of drunk college rowdies.

"Fuck you, greaseball, you'll get yours," one of them jeered. The other two laughed.

"Is that right?" the maitre d' said amicably. "You want to come back at six when I get off, we can talk about it then?"

No one offered any retort.

Eddie went inside and took a table facing the window, so he could watch traffic pass on Roosevelt Avenue. Even here cars seemed impossibly scarce. *Was Queensborough Heights really this sleepy while I grew up here?* The diner had only three other booths occupied, one by a fivesome of giggling teenage girls and the others by quiet older people.

The waitress—not one he would flirt with, even in a pinch— brought him French toast and ham with a fried egg on top. Eddie ate every bit, and as he finished he wondered to himself when he had last eaten here.

He answered his own question: *The day I heard Timpone died. The day I killed Jabberwocky.*

The food in Eddie's stomach threatened suddenly to rise.

Firmly he clutched the table, inhaling and exhaling, deep breaths. *No,* he told himself very rapidly, *no no no that was not my fault, I did not know what would happen, how could I? No.*

With great determination he steered his mind away from the memory of his dog with her skull crushed. *She turned on me.* Which was true, certainly. *She turned on me, and I have a temper now that I didn't used to have, I just have to learn to control it, very simple, I don't care how many fucking ash trees grow in the Corridor.*

His nausea passed. Rather than sick he now felt cold.

His tired waitress returned and broke the spell. "You want some more coffee?" she asked.

"Yes, thanks." He held out his cup.

The five girls piled out from their booth, still giggling. One of them immediately noticed Eddie staring at her.

"Hi," Eddie said.

"Hi," she replied. All of them fell quiet. "Do I know you?"

"No," he said. "I mean, yeah, but not really. You go to Mary's of Bethlehem."

"Not anymore," Marypat said.

At this comment the girls again burst into laughter, and three of them cackled their way up front to pay the bill. Marypat and her friend—*Jesus, it's Ruthanne!* He had never seen Ruthanne before she began bleaching her hair.

"You two sing in the folk group together, at nine o'clock mass," he said.

"Ten o'clock mass, you mean," Ruthanne put in.

"Yeah, whichever. So you graduated," Eddie said. He expected to feel uncomfortable talking to Marypat but could not resist.

"Mm-hmm," Marypat said, nodding vigorously.

"You're going to the Hill Academy next year," he told her casually.

"How did you know?" she asked.

Eddie shrugged with dramatic nonchalance. "I just know what I read in the paper," he said. "When a woman's brilliant *and* beautiful, she winds up at the Hill Academy."

Marypat smiled. Ruthanne cracked up.

"You guys are out late," Eddie went on.

"We're supposed to be at *her* house," Ruthanne said, pointing at one of their friends up near the cash register.

"Yeah, her mother's out with her boyfriend," Marypat said.

"Whose boyfriend?" Eddie asked. "Your friend's or her mother's?"

That broke them up again, and Ruthanne left to join the others up front by the register.

"Well, it was nice meeting you again," Marypat said, "even if I don't remember you from Mary's of Bethlehem. You must sit in the back at Mass. Where do you go to school now?"

"McCanton," he told her. "Though right now I'm in summer school at Sena."

"Summer school?"

"Yeah, I'm stupid," he said. Now that he had her alone, away from her hysterical friends, his jokes worked better on her. She smiled, and her eyes glowed. Any hatred he had felt toward her melted. He had never seen her so young.

"I have to go," she said.

"Hope I see you around," he told her, and reached out his hand. "My name is Eddie O'Kane."

Her friends had already stepped outside, drawing her magnetically toward the door, but she shook his hand, and hers felt tiny and soft.

"I'm Marypat Cooper. See you at church," she said, and left.

FIVE

Throughout the early summer, Eddie laid Lenore at least twice every week. In late July she brought him to a basement apartment in Jamaica Estates near the college and introduced him to someone called Hawes, who had straight hair that resembled a whisk broom. Hawes also sported a brutal sunburn.

"This is Eddie, my boyfriend," Lenore told Hawes.

Boyfriend? Eddie blinked, without flinching.

"Cool," Hawes said.

"You can front to him, to get him started," she said. "He knows what he's doing. I'll vouch."

"Cool," Hawes said.

"Give me a quarter-pound, you'll have your money in a week," Eddie promised.

"Okay, cool," Hawes said. He had no desire to fraternize once they finished smoking a joint and discussing business. No, he couldn't hook Eddie up with psychedelics, but he always had downs. "I gotta see," was the most committing statement he made.

Leaving in Lenore's car, Eddie lit a joint and stared out the window.

"Hawes is kind of burnt, huh?" Eddie said.

"Yeah," she snickered, "you could say that."

"How do you know him?"

She shrugged. "He went to grammar school with my brother."

"What's he, older than you?" Eddie asked.

"Uh-huh, can you believe that?" she replied sarcastically. "Older than me, even? Like God's age, I bet?"

"Don't be vain," Eddie warned her.

Lenore drove in silence for half a block before asking, "What do you mean?"

"Don't act that way," Eddie said. "When you look for a reason to take insult instead of just telling me what's bothering you, it only makes what's bothering you worse. Which makes you unattractive."

She exhaled through her nose, then spoke. "You're so fucking *adult*," she said. "You know that? I don't mean it as a compliment."

He smiled out the window at a girl wearing a halter top.

"I think of you like you're older than I am," she said. "You're even older than my brother, that's how you seem to me."

"How about taking Grandpa home for a piece?" Eddie suggested. That didn't make her laugh. Instead she exaggerated her need to concentrate on her driving, and affected a disinterested air. Finally she said, "You're using me for sex, aren't you?"

"We're using each other for sex," he corrected her. "Doesn't mean we can't be friends."

"Why don't you want me to be your girlfriend?"

He sighed. "It's not that."

"It's not what?" she asked. "You *do* want me to be your girlfriend?"

"No. I just know you belong with someone else," he said. "But that doesn't mean we shouldn't be lovers now. I just know it won't lead anywhere."

"But how can you say that?" Suddenly she sounded close to sobbing.

"I know you," he said. "Haven't I been right so far? I told you about the Who and you like the Who, right? And you like that Tom Robbins book I gave you?"

"This is different," she said.

"I care about you," he said. "I'm being honest with you, because when it's time for us to stop fucking, I still want to be your friend."

While she digested that, they rode in silence for several blocks. "I guess it's time for us to stop fucking, then," she said at last. Eddie didn't respond, because he could tell she didn't mean it.

After she dropped him off, he walked to Main Street and met Eileen when she got off work at the T-shirt shop. She cooked him dinner again, ziti this time.

❧   ❧   ❧

No Sena student assigned to summer classes actually attended, so Sena in fact had a dearth of drug dealers at this time, strangely enough. Eddie's operation went into profit his first week.

He no longer needed Lenore to accompany him when he copped from Hawes. Thus, he let her stop seeing him without contest. Eileen took Lenore's place. He began dealing Hawes's downs, too.

Eileen accepted his disappearing act through some mystic explanation she dreamed up on her own. "You're on a journey, and that's the most important aspect of this lifetime for you," she told him. "I can see that very clearly."

Nobody noticed that Eddie began attending church on Sunday mornings. The ten o'clock Folk Mass, no less, which normally he would have avoided even had he believed in God. The "hipper" young audience gave the parish's youngest priest a chance to imitate Alan Alda. A folk group alongside the altar sang "One Tin Soldier" and similar drek. Marypat Cooper and her friend Ruthanne sang. Eddie would lock his gaze on them throughout the entire service.

The first time he went, he talked to her and she told him to call her Marypat, everyone did. They spoke while behind her Manny the bandleader broke down the music stands and packed his nylon-string guitar.

"You get in trouble that night I saw you?" Eddie asked.

With great glee Marypat held a finger before her lips. "Shh," she admonished him in a stage mutter. "No. No one knows. My mother thinks we sleep when I sleep over there."

"Good deal, then," he said, reeling for another idea to introduce, to keep her talking.

"I'll see you next week," she said, just as Manny picked up his guitar case and nodded at her. They left together. On the church steps, out of their sight, Eddie watched them round the corner onto Kalmia Avenue.

❦ ❦ ❦

After Mass the next Sunday Eddie asked Marypat, with a sly nod of his head toward Manny, "So are you and that guy going out?"

She shook her head, studiously making sure Manny couldn't hear her. "No," she whispered. "We used to be."

So that's over already. "Then can I walk you home?"

She said yes and told Manny she'd see him at practice Wednesday night. Manny acted pissed and jealous.

The candy store on Negundo still had its original soda fountain (it would transform into a row of video games within two years), so en route to Marypat's house Eddie invited her there for ice cream.

They sat at the counter and drank egg creams. Marypat had never had one, but Eddie promised her she would like it. She did.

"Are you all Irish?" she asked him.

"You know it," he said. "Mother's Roscommon and Sligo, and my old man's pure Mayo."

"What's that?"

"Those are counties in Ireland," he explained. "Don't you know what county your Irish relatives came from?"

"Uh-uh," she said. "I only know I'm Irish, Italian and Polish."

"Cork," he told her. "Your grandfather came from County Cork."

"How can you tell?"

"I know everything." He finished his egg cream. "I'll tell you something that will freak you out: Go home and ask your mother tonight about your grandmother. She was Hungarian, not Polish."

"My grandmother's Italian."

"No, the one you never met," Eddie said. "Your father's mother. She wasn't Polish."

Marypat stared hard at him. "How could you know that?"

"Just ask your mother. I got a hunch, that's all." Before she could question him, he asked her, "Do you know Desmond Coogan?"

She shook her head.

"You know his father, maybe," Eddie went on. "Sean Coogan."

That struck a bell, but she couldn't place it.

"Owns the gas station, next to the Back Parish."

"Yes!" Marypat exclaimed. "Mister Coogan! My father used to work with him. I know Mister Coogan."

"Well, Desmond's his son," Eddie said. "Big doofy kid with pimples?"

"Nope." She shrugged. "Don't think I know him. I only know Mister Coogan. My father really likes him. I don't know his son."

Eddie nodded and paid attention to his egg cream.

"Why did you ask me that?" she said. "Does he know me?"

"Desmond, like, used to be my best friend. To some degree, years ago," Eddie told her. "The other day I was at his house, and I found a picture of you on his wall."

"A picture of me?" she said. "What, from the play?" She meant *The Sound of Music*; mounted on the inside of her closet door, Eddie knew, Marypat had the front page of *The Mary's of Bethlehem Weekly Tablet* with her photo as Liesle. It would stay there as long as Eddie knew her.

"No, from a picnic."

"And you found me in this picture on your friend's wall?"

"Yes," Eddie said. "Kind of odd you don't remember him at all. He sure knows you."

She blinked as a way to prod him on. When it didn't work, she said, "How do you mean?"

"I don't know, I still act like we're friends, you know? I go over there and hang out with him, maybe once a week now that it's summer," Eddie said. "I don't believe in giving up on a person."

"That's so cool," Marypat said quietly, reverently.

"But he scares me," Eddie added.

Again the goading blink, which he again defied. *I can wait if you can.* He knew her better than she knew herself, after all, knew that forcing her to specifically ask that he go on would prevent her from thinking him a gossip. "Why does he scare you?" she asked.

"He gets crushes on girls, and he acts really weird," Eddie said. "I am afraid he's going to get arrested or something. He's just so weird."

"What's weird about him?"

"He follows girls, spies on them, calls them on the phone," Eddie said. "He tape-records himself saying creepy stuff to them on the phone. He had this one girl crying, and he used to play the tape over and over, laughing about it." With a quick glance to insure their privacy, Eddie lowered his voice and said, "I think he was jerking off to that tape. Can you believe that?"

She searched his face for any trace of humor. He showed none.

"I'm totally serious," Eddie said with supreme gravity. "He beat her father up, after that. Last time I was over there, he said he had a new tape, and the only reason he didn't make me listen to it was that I said I would leave. I don't know what he does to her on this new one."

"And this guy has my picture," Marypat said, sounding numb.

"Yeah," Eddie said. "He's come to see you at Mass a bunch of times, he says. I mean, if he hasn't bothered you, no reason you should give it a second thought."

She would, though. Certainly. For now, they let the topic go. "Have you ever smoked pot?" Eddie asked her.

Marypat shook her head.

"Curious?"

She was. Eddie walked her home, and waited around the corner until she came back out wearing jeans. Then he took her to Memorial Knoll, a patch of the Corridor where in 1921 someone had planted twenty-six pine trees to commemorate dead locals. An engraved boulder at the knoll's edge read IN MEMORY OF THOSE WHO GAVE THEIR LIVES IN THE GREAT WAR. They sat atop this huge marker and smoked a joint.

"So," she said, fighting shyness as the pot sank in. "How's summer school going?"

"It's fucking great, what do you think?" he laughed. "I'm sitting inside every afternoon while you're sunning in the yard. I haven't been to the beach *once* all summer. Summer school sucks."

He knew how to make her comfortable. After they spoke awhile, he led her into the knoll and curled up around her beneath an evergreen, and they wrestled together on the carpet of dry needles. Her body had barely begun to blossom. To his fingers her flesh felt pliant, immortal.

❧ ❧ ❧

Although only Eddie knew, throughout the summer neighborhood history unfolded secretly three houses away from the O'Kane residence. Mrs. Denihan, who had lived in that third house for so long that no one on the block knew her given name, had come outdoors for the first time in Eddie's existence. A car had taken her somewhere and had not brought her back.

The live-in nurse had never exchanged more than a polite greeting with anyone on the block, so no one could ask questions. By kindergarten Eddie had learned exactly three things about Mrs. Denihan: She went deaf before he was born, she was old, and she owned the lot full of trees next to her house, where he wasn't supposed to trespass, ever.

Naturally, as a kid Eddie played there daily, and a few times he glanced upward to find Mrs. Denihan watching him from the window, her hair a thick white mat.

Now that she had gone, different elements would battle for her will, and the family would lose. No one who lived on Poplar would know. The winners in that drama would not step forward until the summer before Eddie left for college, after the property values in the neighborhood had sunk.

As soon as the new houses were built, seven Puerto Rican and South American families would fill them. This carefully orchestrated scare would collect eleven houses in four months for an oily realtor from Maspeth, a man named Clifford Manchesi, married to Mrs. Denihan's nurse.

A four-block strip of Poplar would become a haven of cheap boardinghouses for illegals. By 1985 crack dealers would operate openly on Poplar and 158th Street, and Eddie's parents could only sell their house to Clifford Manchesi.

Seven years from this summer. It started now.

One day most of the trees in Mrs. Denihan's lot disappeared. The next day a bulldozer dug two deep pits there, and by the end of that week cement trucks had poured two foundations. Slowly but steadily these two houses took identical form beside one another.

A watchman in a gold Duster became a nightly fixture in front of the site. The first time the watchman showed up, Eddie remembered that soon Mrs. McGowan would start complaining about *Screw*'s routinely appearing in her trash can; the watchman read girly magazines in his car on company time.

"See how that guy's there Sunday night?" Kevin pointed out a few days after the trees vanished. "That's because they ain't union. Normal job conditions, you don't need a watchman all weekend—you put your materials away until Monday. These guys want their job finished quick before anyone reports them."

"Should we report them?" Eddie asked him.

"Nah, not worth the effort," Kevin said with a shrug.

One late afternoon shortly after the lumber skeletons rose up, Eddie finally brought himself to glance around the site. Behind one of the houses lay the spot where he had buried Jabberwocky. His besotted parents had asked him about the dog whenever they saw him for weeks after he killed her; now a fresh hill of clay covered the dog's grave. The sight wrenched him. So he looked away.

With his conscience rarely affecting him, the summer went well. Eddie did remarkable business and avoided making any friends. Everyone his own age bored him to tears. He hung out late watching TV at Desmond's one night a week, usually embarrassed that the two of them had so little to say to each other. Brian O'Shea called once and left a message with Eddie's mother, but she got trashed that night and afterward could not remember what O'Shea had to say.

Eileen stayed cool. Once in a while she might ask him to tell her he loved her. Nothing difficult.

❧ ❧ ❧

In August, Kelly turned sixteen. He had behaved differently toward Eddie ever since Eddie swiped Lenore from him, so Eddie didn't want or receive an invitation to help Kelly celebrate.

Fine by Eddie. During the summer Kelly had spent some time with Jan, apparently, and discovered a penchant for stupid lawbreaking—thrown liquor bottles, pissing off the overpass onto Expressway traffic—to impress her.

For his birthday he stole a LeMans. The cops caught him and didn't suspect he was a minor. He punched a cop, and they beat the shit out of him. It happened right outside Pizzingrillo Park.

Kelly didn't show up at school the next day. Jan had been in the car but the cops had not arrested her. She copped two dimes off Eddie just before class, by which point he had already heard the story from other eyewitnesses.

"They had him in jail overnight, because he didn't have ID and he was dusted," Jan said. "He doesn't want to talk to anyone now. His father could sue the city, big time."

"Will he?" Eddie asked.

"No," Jan said, rolling her eyes. "His father's this big rah-rah cop, and he thinks the cops are always right."

Eddie studied his shoes.

"You know what pisses him off the most?" Jan said. "That his son can't be a policeman now."

"How is Kelly?"

"Oh, he's still dusted. You smoke good dust, it lasts at least until the second day," Jan said.

"There's no such thing as 'good' angel dust," Eddie said.

Jan smirked at him. "Wanna bet? He stayed so crazy all night that nobody touched him. Being dusted saved his life."

"I don't think you'd know if that's true or not," he said.

From behind them as they entered the school, Lenore ran up and said, "Hi." At first Eddie felt glad someone had come to free him from Jan, whom he found creepy. But then Eddie saw Lenore's face.

"Can I talk to you, Eddie?" she said.

Jesus fucking Christ, this is NOT fucking happening. No. No. No. No. He followed her to a stairwell. *No. This whole fucking thing is a dream, it has to be.* So young, she didn't realize that she had no need to expound, that merely asking to see him in private told him everything save the amount of the gynecologist's bill. *No. No.*

She didn't fall apart while she gave him the news. She saved that for after class, on the steps outside school.

"I just, really—" she gasped, between sobs. "It's, it's not—"

"Calm down," he said and slid an arm around her. "Calm down. We know what has to be done."

"I don't have enough money," she said.

"I'll cover it," he said.

"I can only pay you—"

"Forget it, that's not a problem," he said. "Do you know where you want to go?"

She nodded, facing a blank wall so passersby could not see her cry.

"Do you want me to go with you?"

"You don't have to," she said, automatically.

"I know I don't have to," he said. "Do you want me there? Or you want to be alone? I'm just thinking about you."

He knew all the right things to say.

After summer school let out, they had another two weeks until regular school started. Lenore made her appointment then. They rode in together on the subway. The clinic was in Manhattan, high above Fifty-sixth and Second.

"I'm glad you're here," she said as they rode the elevator.

"No need to thank me, citizen," he said.

Lenore checked in at the desk. Then she and Eddie waited in plastic bucket seats for someone to call her name.

"Stop tapping your foot," he said. "You're making yourself more nervous. Just relax."

She couldn't. "My mother, I..." Very deliberately she swallowed and cleared her throat. "I'm really glad I'm not here alone."

"What? You expect me to turn my back on you?"

"None of my friends would come with me," she said.

"I'm your friend and I'm with you, all right?" he said, rubbing her forearms. "It's not a big deal. You're going to the doctor's and you wanted someone to go with you. Let's talk about something else."

"All right." Lenore sighed. "Like what?"

"You hear about Kelly?"

Lenore shook her head. "Kelly who?"

"Dennis Kelly. The guy you were talking to when you met me," he reminded her.

"Oh, yeah," Lenore said. "Jan's boyfriend."

"He should be *your* boyfriend," Eddie told her.

She thought she had misunderstood. "What?"

"You two belong together."

"I don't touch my friends' boyfriends," she insisted.

"But he's *your* husband." Eddie scanned his brain for a sane lie to explain it to her. None came to him. "I just know."

"That's fucking ridiculous," she said, shaking her head. "You are out of your mind."

"You always say I'm so grown-up," he said. "If you trust my judgment, listen to this: I say you belong with Kelly. You and he would be great together."

"He's going out with my friend," she said. "And he's been in jail. No thanks. My father's a cop, Eddie."

"I cut in on him when you first met him," Eddie said. "Remember that day? I came over and scoped you right out."

She smiled.

"That was the first time he ever smoked pot," Eddie said. "I bet if I hadn't asked in front of you, he never would have. You probably would have stopped getting high to hang out with him."

Nodding her head as if she believed every word of it, she said, "Whatever you're on, I want ten bucks' worth."

"First off, Jan is weird," Eddie reasoned.

"All right, that's true."

"Second, Kelly isn't. I know him, trust me." Eddie nodded several times, trying to concoct a conclusion for his argument.

"So I should steal my friend's boyfriend."

"How about if he makes a play for you?" Eddie said. "Would you just go out with him somewhere for a date?"

"Why should I?" she asked. "So he can marry me?"

"I mean this," Eddie assured her, growing frustrated. "It's the truth. You should just hang out with him and see what he's like. If he comes to speak with you, just be cool and meet him somewhere. Discreetly. For me?"

She laughed loudly.

"For me?" he asked. "To make me happy?"

She rolled her eyes. "I'll think about it."

"Not good enough," Eddie said. "If he comes to see you, you have to say yes. Just to have coffee somewhere or whatever. Somewhere you two can talk."

"Miss Vale?" the woman at the desk called.

Lenore stood up, shaking her head at him. "You got my mind off it," she said, grinning. "Thanks."

She followed a nurse in through the large swinging doors, and Eddie stared out the window at a cable car leaving Manhattan, three blocks away.

❦ ❦ ❦

Forty minutes after Lenore went in, Eddie looked up from the horoscope in *Cosmopolitan* to see the woman from the desk approaching him.

"You were with Lenore?" she asked him.

"'Were'?" Eddie asked.

The woman grimaced at her own faux-pas. "I'm sorry," she said quickly. "Lenore's emergency number doesn't check out. Her last name isn't really Vale, is it?"

"What's the emergency?" Eddie demanded.

"What's your relationship to her?"

"I brought her up here when no one else would, what's the fucking emergency?"

The woman glared at him. "She's hemorrhaging," she said simply.

"Badly?"

"Badly is the only way you can hemorrhage," she said. "We have to get her family here. What's her real last name?"

"Shit," Eddie said. "I don't—I don't know..."

"Is she school age? Where does she go to school?"

Eddie strained to recall. "She just finished summer school at Sena, in Queens," he said. "She goes to Catholic school, I'm pretty sure."

On the desk the phone rang. The woman left to answer it.

"Sullivan!" Eddie cried out. "Her name's Lenore Sullivan!"

The woman spoke on the phone for less than half a minute and then replaced the phone in its cradle.

"She's a senior!" he told her. "Her name's Lenore Sullivan, she's a senior. At St. Elizabeth's. It's in Queens."

"I'm afraid," the woman began, until the look in Eddie's eyes halted her and she had to start anew. "That won't help us now. You're going to have to talk to the police."

Her father's a cop, Eddie told himself. *They'll tell him who I am. He will kill me.*

"Oh, Jesus," Eddie said.

"I'm sorry," the woman said. "I am very sorry. Are you all right?"

Eddie shook his head. "I think I'm going to be sick. Where's the men's room?"

The woman pointed down the hall. Of course, during the past forty minutes Eddie had visited there himself. He knew right where to find the men's room: across the hall from the elevators.

He waited just inside the door of the men's room, listening for the elevator bell. It didn't ring. After a minute that lasted years, he tugged the door open a sliver and studied the three elevators facing him. No signs with illuminating numbers to show which floor the car was passing, only a beacon light.

He peeked outside the doorframe. The receptionist sat speaking earnestly on her phone. Calling the police, no doubt.

In one movement Eddie crossed the hall, pressed the down button and returned to the men's room. The receptionist did not see him.

Soon the lower half of the beacon lit, and one set of doors opened.

Eddie bounded across the hall again, nearly as fast, and leaped into the elevator.

"Hey!" he heard the receptionist cry behind him.

The other passenger in the elevator was a balding man in a suit.

"Wait a minute!" the woman called. "Stop him!"

The bald man looked at Eddie. "Stop who?"

The doors closed. "Huh?" Eddie said.

"Why was that woman yelling, 'Stop him'?"

"Oh," Eddie said, dismissing it. "Some guy up there was harassing people in the waiting room."

The man regarded him carefully.

"I don't even like delivering to these clinics, I'll tell you," Eddie went on. "They're so depressing, and I always expect some kook to bomb the place when I'm here."

They rode silently to the lobby. Eddie left the building and descended to the subway. No one paid any attention to him on his way home.

He hung out at Desmond's that night, constantly thinking of ways for the police to trace him—most obviously, checking schoolmates from J.A. Sena.

But they didn't take yearbook photos for summer school. And if Lenore's death broke her father's heart, it didn't give the man a seer's power to track Eddie down. Eddie, after all, had not done anything illegal. For that matter the people at the clinic had no proof Eddie had even gotten Lenore pregnant.

The next day he went by himself to Jones Beach, but couldn't bring himself to lie down. He rode back to Queens alone on the bus.

A week passed. He smoked pot, hung out in the park. He had no idea where they buried Lenore, nor when, and he wisely kept it that way.

The last few days before school started, Eddie spent hour upon hour watching the workers build the houses on Mrs. Denihan's lot. For some reason they had slowed down work for more than a week, and just now had begun laying bricks.

Classes at McCanton started on a Monday. Juniors had orientation the Friday before school started. After talking to O'Shea, whose upper lip still had scars from his beating last May, Eddie sat through the assembly wondering how he had endured high school the first time. At the very least he had to get out of McCanton and go to school with girls, someplace he could wear jeans.

They got their locker combinations, and formed lines to get their textbooks. On line for Trig he saw Kelly.

"Hey, motherfucker," Kelly said.

"What's up? How you been?"

"All right. Holding the law at bay," Kelly boasted, grinning. "You hear what happened to, what's her name—Lenore?"

Eddie performed a very practiced shrug. "Who?"

"Lenore. You met her. She knew Jan."

"Oh, sure, you introduced me to her," Eddie said. "How is she?"

For an instant, Kelly stared at him, unsure what to say. "She had an abortion, and she didn't live," he said. "You honestly didn't hear nothing about that?"

"Shit, that sucks." Eddie blinked into space several times. "When did this happen?"

"A week ago, or something. Totally fucked up," he said. "She went to get an abortion and she bled to death in her pussy. All by herself, she didn't even tell anyone she was going."

"No one would go with her," Eddie said.

"What?"

Eddie scratched his head. "I don't know," he said.

"Did you say no one would go with her?"

Eddie nodded. "Well, she wasn't feeling so close with her friends, is all. It's just something she said to me," he said. "That one day I met her. Hey, how is Jan? That was the day you two met, right?"

Kelly thought it over, distracted. "Yeah, I guess," he said. "Our anniversary's July third."

They spoke awhile, then Kelly had to change lines for Physics. "I don't think I can stand this place any longer," he said. "I feel so different now, since I'm with Jan."

"What are you, going to transfer?"

"Nah, fuck that," he said. "Just blow school off. She knows people in Oregon, we might just roll out there and work the land. Grow pot and shit. There's great dope in Portland and Eugene."

Kelly wandered off. At least he wasn't mad at Eddie for stealing Lenore from him, since Kelly barely remembered the event.

❦ ❦ ❦

This is not real, Eddie told himself that night as he smoked a joint out his bedroom window, trying to make himself sleepy. *Everything is a dream. I'm dying, somewhere.*

SIX

Saturday afternoon Eddie went to see the Mary's of Bethlehem folk group jam with the youth choir at a synagogue up Roosevelt Avenue, toward McCanton.

While they sang he struggled not to picture Lenore dying alone in a room full of strangers in masks and gloves, Lenore lying cold in the earth somewhere beneath the snow and the rain, Lenore alone forever.

The songs discussed God but avoided the Jesus issue, understandably, and veered toward Paul Simon and James Taylor. Manny the folkie transformed into Manny the ecumenical conductor. Eddie recognized someone on the choir, but could not place him.

Afterward the synagogue threw a curious nonmixer, encouraging teenagers to accept and understand one another's differences, while ruling one another out as potential lifemates. Eddie immediately sought out Marypat, who smiled to see him.

"Hi, Eddie," she said. "You weren't at Mass last Sunday."

"Hung over, sorry," Eddie said. "Last Saturday of the summer." In truth he had spent the previous Saturday night awake, tormented, and couldn't rise on time the next morning.

The tenor Eddie had recognized now chatted up Ruthanne, and Eddie realized who he was: This guy would cop Ruthanne's cherry the same month Eddie copped Marypat's. Yes, this was the same guy.

"Hey, there," the guy said, offering Eddie his hand. "I'm Ben."

"That's right," Eddie said.

They all talked and listened to records awhile, and then Eddie asked Marypat if she wanted to walk home.

"We're on the other side of the Corridor," Marypat said. "It's miles to get home."

"It's a nice walk," he said. "Good day for it."

"You're crazy," she said, shaking her head.

"Tell you what, let's walk to the pizzeria and eat. Then I'll call a cab and we'll taxi it home," he said.

That got her. Manny the bandleader stood officiously discussing music with someone from the choir, and Ruthanne nodded absently at Marypat and Eddie as they left the building.

The instant their shoes touched the sidewalk he had his arm around her. His arm stayed there until they reached the pizzeria, a brick building painted white. Bella Chica's.

Not until they had ordered and sat down did Eddie realize he had made a dire mistake bringing Marypat to this particular place; the last time he had eaten here was with Lenore.

"What's wrong?" Marypat asked him.

He shrugged.

"How come you keep getting quiet like that?"

"Like what?" he asked, failing to avoid the sullen inflection his voice always assumed when he felt ill at ease.

"You're fine one minute, then you look like you're about to come apart," she said. "It happened while we walked over here, too, and right after the concert ended."

"I've got things on my mind," he said, "things I'd rather not have on my mind, so please try to distract me."

She gave him a smile and he returned it.

"So you think your friend Ruthanne will go out with Ben?" he asked. "Think they'll be a couple soon?"

"Who's Ben?"

"That guy we just met, from the choir. Ben. Curly black hair, puberty-looking mustache?"

"'Puberty-looking,'" she repeated, tittering. "Wait, that guy she was talking to when we left?"

"Yeah. She's into him. Give it some time." The cook behind the counter nodded to them, and Eddie rose from his seat to fetch their order.

"No way. She hates guys like that," Marypat called after him.

"Guys like what?" Eddie said as he carried their pizza to their booth and sat down. "Jewish guys? Mustache guys?"

"No. God, you're so mean. She's not prejudiced," Marypat said. "She doesn't like guys with, like...disco guys. She likes rock guys, not disco guys."

Eddie behaved as though he took this distinction as seriously as Marypat did. "How about you?"

"Me? I'm into rock guys, too," she said. "Though there are some foxy disco boys. I went to my graduation dance with Tommy Mallon, and he's disco."

Without rising from his seat Eddie began dancing the Hustle, jabbing one finger in the air over and over. Marypat laughed.

Marypat laughed at every joke he made, as a matter of fact, while they ate and after they left. She didn't have to go home right away, she said.

As they walked, each with an arm around the other's middle this time, Eddie felt himself grow hard in his jeans. She pouted at him. *Totally unself-conscious. She has no idea how fine she is.* Soon her body language would become adult—controlled, calculated. *Any year now. Not yet.*

The thought of getting her pants off kept Eddie from paying attention to where they walked, not that he cared.

"Let's go in there," Marypat said abruptly.

The soccer field. They had reached the quiet part of Roosevelt Avenue, where it crossed the Corridor.

"No," he said. *Oh, no.*

"Why not? It's open." She steered him toward the gate.

"It's not safe," he argued. "If somebody mugged us, we'd have nobody to yell for. No one could hear you in there."

"Mugged?" she asked, too patiently.

"It's not cool, is all," he said. "You can get a trespassing summons being in here."

"I've been here drinking three or four times," Marypat said. "Nobody's ever bothered us."

Eddie drew a deep breath. *The dead are dead,* he reminded himself. *We feel remorse mostly because we believe we're supposed to. It helps nothing.*

"Okay," he said, leading her inside, toward the bleachers. "Want to smoke a joint?"

She did. He rolled one, and taught her to roll one. By now it was dark, especially here inside the enclosure of maples. She did a horrible job. He congratulated her, and sat her on his lap.

First he nibbled her nape. "That feels good," she said. "I like that." He knew. His hands ran up and down her thighs, and slid gradually up to her breasts. She stopped him, held off, gave in. He unbuttoned her shirt, unhooked her bra.

"Oh," she whispered.

Goosebumps covered her breasts. He turned her over in his arms and nursed upon her nipples, gnawed them.

"You turn me on *so* much," she purred. He opened the waist button of her jeans, and got her zipper halfway down before she seized his hand. "Don't," she said. "Please?"

He stared into her eyes. She looked confused. "Fine, whatever you say," he told her. "I'm sorry if I got carried away."

"You know my body better than I do," she sighed. "It's not fair."

That's true. He sat her upright, his lust evaporated.

"Don't be like that," she said, sliding off his lap. "Come on, this is the most I ever did with any guy. I'm not ready to go further. I'm only a freshman, Eddie."

He nodded. "I'm not mad at you. You're right, I shouldn't be trying to get over on you."

"No, you're welcome to try," she said. "You just can't succeed. I mean, I hardly know you. And you know me like a book you read in first gr—*now* what?"

He lost his will to pretend. "Don't say that," he said. "Don't talk about how well I know you, okay? It bothers me."

"Why?"

He inhaled, he exhaled. She waited for an answer.

"Because of *how* I know you so well." He cleared his throat and continued. "I have a secret that'll just freak you out. You probably won't feel comfortable around me if you know."

Her eyes widened. "Are you following me? Like that guy Desmond?"

That gave him a weak laugh. "I made that stuff up," he confessed, picking at his thumbnail as he spoke. "Desmond Coogan isn't obsessed with you. I just wanted you to stay away from him."

The thickening dusk obscured her reaction.

"I figured if I made you scared of him, you'd avoid him later in life when you met him," Eddie said.

"I told you: I don't know him."

"But you're going to meet him, from dating me," Eddie informed her. "When I'm away at college you'll visit him at his mother's wake, and the two of you will fall in love."

They sat in dark silence.

"What are you talking about?" she asked. "You can predict the future?"

"I came from the future," Eddie said. "I'm not making this up."

"How?"

Eddie shrugged. "I don't know the how of it," he said. "One morning I woke up fifteen again. Last May."

"That's crazy."

"You have a biology teacher who walks around peeking into girls' blouses, right?" he asked her.

After a beat, she nodded.

"By next summer, she will have left the school," Eddie said. "This girl in your class, who sits in front of you in lab, is Dominican, yes?"

"I haven't had lab yet," she said.

"When you do, ask the girl in front of you if she's Dominican," Eddie told her. "Her parents are going to settle out of court with your school. The Hill Academy will pay them a quarter-million dollars and you'll never see her again. Next year three graduates will come forward and say this teacher felt them up, too. The judge will tell them to take a hike."

"So you want me to believe you, but the proof will take a year," she said.

"I didn't know you until you were older," he said. "I could convince you more easily if this were then. But this time that will all be different, too. Everything is different, every little thing changes everything else. It's amazing how it works."

"You can't expect me to just believe this, though," she said, fixing her bra and shirt. "How old were you, before you came back?"

"Thirty-one."

"And you don't know why you came back?"

"I didn't say that," he said. "I don't know *how.* I do know why."

"Well?"

Night had risen from the ground all around them. Crickets filled the brief silence before Eddie spoke.

"I made a deal with somebody," Eddie said quietly.

"The devil?" Marypat asked.

Eddie shook his head. "I don't think so," he said. "I hope not."

"What was the deal?"

A heavy sigh wracked him, and then he began speaking as though each fact he dropped relieved him of its weight.

"I killed someone," he said. "I didn't think I would want to live after I did it, but I got away alive, and I didn't want to die."

"That sounds made up," she said.

"All right," he went on. "There's this virus, like a venereal disease, only it hasn't been discovered yet. It's fatal. I got it. This sounds really fucked up to say, but I had this virus and I didn't think I deserved it because I wasn't gay."

"This makes no sense at all," she said.

"Forget that, then," he said. "Pretend I had cancer or whatever. I knew I was going to die, is the important thing. I had this virus for years, and I started to get pneumonia, which is how you die from it.

"So I came back from California to kill a man named Clifford Manchesi. I figured I didn't care if I got caught, because they would just stick me in the hospital on Riker's Island and treat me anyway."

He noticed Marypat's head moving in the shadows, searching for a hole in his logic, though she might just decide he was out of his mind, also.

"I called his office for an appointment to buy one of the boarding houses he built on my old block," Eddie said. "One evening he came out to show it to me, and I shot him down. People saw me do this. I ran and wound up in the Corridor. Cops came after me. And I came past here, to where the ash trees—"

"Wait, why did you kill Clifford What's-his-face?"

"He destroyed my family financially," Eddie said. "Guy's a fucking snake, I'm not sorry I killed him. He ruined our block. I'm not being prejudiced about it. He and his wife cheated Mrs. Denihan's family to put those two houses up on that property, and then he panicked the whole neighborhood, deliberately. Nobody knew he owned those boarding houses when they sold to him."

"When was that?"

Eddie frowned at the sound of it: "Seven years from now, or so."

Marypat had her hands folded on her lap, as though to keep warm.

"But I'm—I feel dangerous, now," he told her. "Things keep happening because of me. People are dying."

"Who?" She didn't sound frightened.

He almost told her about Marc Tcholowitz, but refrained. "This kid I went to school with, Timpone. He died before finals last June. Because of me. He walked into traffic and died."

"Is that the guy from McCanton who died in Whitestone?" she asked him. "It was in the paper and everything. Eddie, he died smoking angel dust."

"He wasn't smoking it, he took it thinking it was mesc. That doesn't matter," Eddie said. "He only got high because of me. He never would have. My friend Kelly is the same way. Now Kelly's never going to be a cop, because I turned him on. And…other stuff has happened."

"Have you murdered someone?" she asked softly.

"No," he lied.

"Then why did you say you were dangerous?"

"I might be," he said. "I'm kind of violent without warning. It's like I have a thirty-one-year-old's anger, but I have a teenager's temper. All my feelings are too intense, because of what I know about the future. Out of all my friends, only Desmond hasn't gotten fucked up somehow because of me."

"Desmond? That's the man of my dreams, right?" she quipped.

In the dark she could not see the sharp glance he gave her.

"Do you really believe this, Eddie?" she said. "I'll let you try to prove to me that it's real, and I'll believe you if you do prove it. But you do the same for me, if I can show you it's not true."

At that Eddie heaved a tremendous sigh. "You know something?" he said. "No bullshit, you are the most fabulous woman I ever met. No girl could fill your shoes once I lost you."

"Let's talk about the future," she said. "Tell me something I can see happen and know you're right."

"Let me think," he said, picking her up by the ribs and seating her once again on his lap.

She did not pull away. Three kisses later he had her cradled in his arms. As he unbuttoned her shirt again, she lay still, plainly aroused at the womanly feeling it gave her to submit to him.

Yet she was by most measures still a child, thirteen, fragile no matter how precocious. Her breasts when he had known them—in those days when he had imagined that he somehow owned them—had filled his palms. Tonight they appeared egg-sized, barely reason to wear a bra.

"How do you know all this stuff about me sexually?" she wanted to know. "Did I tell you?"

"No, we learned it together," he said. "When you become lovers with someone, you and that person find out these amazing things about each other all the time. Just what you find out about yourself is amazing. It's better than drugs."

"So far, *I* like it better," she said, making him laugh. Then she thought of something. "Do you take my cherry?"

He nodded.

"When?" she asked.

"December, your sophomore year." he said.

"No way!" *She's going along with it. It's fun. She doesn't believe it.* "Are you kidding me? I give it up when I'm still a sophomore?! I'm a slut!"

"No, think of it: I'm a senior then, right?" he said. "You can't just let me graduate without getting laid."

"Nice argument," she told him. "I always thought I was pretty horny for a girl."

"Definitely," he said. To illustrate his point he buried his face into her exposed cleavage.

"Do you think you'll fuck me sooner this time?"

He answered with a nonchalant nod. She liked it. They made out a few minutes, until she paused to speak.

"There would have to be things you'd know that would prove it to me," she said. "Just stuff you had to learn from knowing me, things you couldn't learn any other way."

"Well, I've been screwing your cousin Eileen," he said.

Marypat's eyes bulged. "Eileen Mangan?! No way!" she declared. "I hate her! I can't stand her!"

"I know," Eddie said. "That was the idea, I think."

"Oh, God, Eddie," she said, shaking her head.

"Isn't that childish?" Eddie said. "I won't call her again."

"That bitch told you she's my cousin?" Marypat asked.

"No," he said, "I just recognized her one day, where she works."

"We used to be close when we were little," she said.

"Yeah, I know," Eddie admitted.

"So, okay, you knew Eileen was my cousin," Marypat said. "Christ, I can't believe you would do it with her. She's *skanky*, Eddie."

"And your father's named Jim, your mother's Eunice," he began.

"Uh-uh," she said. "Stuff about my family you could have found out from church."

"I only go to church to see you," he said. "Hey, wasn't I right about your grandmother being Hungarian?"

"That's right!" she said. "Okay, that's another thing. I forgot about that. But if we were lovers, the way you say, then you should know deep secrets I never told anyone else. I mean, right? Wouldn't I tell you things, if I had intercourse with you?"

"Intercourse?" The word made him wince as he mulled over her suggestion. "All right, yeah, I can think of things."

"Like what?"

"Is it going to freak you out?" he said.

She shook her head.

"Okay, when you were young, like before kindergarten, your Uncle, uhm." He bit his upper lip, trying to recall the name. "One of your uncles, the balding one?"

"Uncle Alfred?"

"No. He's not actually related."

"Oh—Uncle Edwin."

"That's him," he said, not noticing how triumphantly flip he sounded. "He had you give him a hand job when he was baby-sitting you. Remember?"

There on the unlit bleachers, Eddie could not see her expression. Nevertheless, he knew right away that she'd predicted wrong: It *had* freaked her out, plenty.

He touched her face. Her mouth hung open, though no sound came out.

"Are you okay?" he said.

Her cheeks were wet. Soaked.

"Eddie," she whimpered.

"I'm sorry," he said. "I asked if you would freak out. I should have braced you."

"It's *true,* Eddie," she said.

The resignation in her tone stopped him cold. *She believes me.*

"Who did you make this deal with, Eddie?"

"I'm not saying," he told her. "It's not something you should know."

"What do you have to do?" she asked, her voice small and awed. "What's your part in the deal?"

"I don't know."

They listened to the crickets.

"You just made a deal without knowing what you owe?" she asked.

"When you're dying, you say whatever they want to hear," Eddie reflected. He held her close but stared at the tree silhouettes surrounding the meadow. "I was supposed to go see someone, and I haven't."

She mumbled something he didn't catch.

"What did you say?" he asked.

She shook her head.

"No, come on," he urged her.

"My Uncle Edwin," she said. She spoke as though retrieving this memory had aged her ten years. "I haven't thought about that in a long time. That used to bother me."

"There's a reason I just put it like that to you. I'm used to the future," he said. This tangent engrossed her quickly. "In the future everybody goes on television and talks about stuff like that. Every day, talk shows have Women Who Dance Naked At Church and Gay Fathers Who Boned Their Daughters' Boyfriends and everything else. I'm not exaggerating, it's all over the cable."

"Do we ever get cable TV in Queens?"

"Yeah." He cleared his throat. "After I leave."

"Eddie, don't be like that," she said. "You're mad at me for something I haven't even done. It's not going to happen the same way this time. You said so. It's all different."

Tell me about it. Eddie tapped his foot. "They make cop shows with real cops, too," he said. "There's a fourth network."

"My girlfriend Ginny? Her father works for ABC," Marypat began, and as she told him this story he noticed that she sounded her age. Whatever he loved about her, he saw it here in its infant stages.

Even touching her, just playing with her breasts, felt a tiny bit unnatural. A mature thirteen-year-old was still thirteen, even if Eddie lusted for her from inside a fifteen-year-old body. Yet the alternative would drive him mad: Push her away, watch from afar as she plays the field. *Watch her fuck around.*

The element about her that he loved was there—her character, her outlook. *Her pussy. Wait till I see how much character she shows sucking my best friend's cock while I'm at Purchase, staying faithful.*

Eddie put a hand to his forehead, interrupting Marypat's chatter.

"What's the matter?" she asked.

"I have a headache," he lied.

"I don't have any aspirin," she said, helpfully. "What disease did you say you have?"

"I don't have it *now*," he said, rather too crisply.

"Sorry," she said.

"I had a virus that makes your immune system collapse," he said. "You die from other diseases. Pneumonia, usually. Fucking government just let people die. No one did anything."

"Is it like science fiction? Is it a plague?"

He shook his head. "The science-fiction things in the future don't stand out once they happen. You just get used to them, and you don't remember how it was without them. Like banks. Ten years from now, every bank will have a computer room where you go to take out money, any hour of the day. Two in the morning, you can go get money or deposit a check. Everybody has a bank card, like a credit card. And you only notice these things when they break down."

She nodded so timidly that he wondered whether she had understood. He chastised himself for smoking pot with someone so young. Then she asked, "What about being gay?"

"I wasn't gay," he said.

"But you said something about gay people? Before."

"People think of this disease as being a gay thing," he said. "A lot of gay people had it first."

"Like disco."

All the hairs on his neck shot rigid in anger. "It's not a fucking joke, huh?" he said.

"I didn't—"

"You didn't *what?* You didn't think I might be sensitive about my own death? Which wouldn't have *happened* if it hadn't been for you?"

"Eddie," she said.

He seethed in quiet.

"Eddie," she said again, "did I give this to you? From Desmond?"

"No," he fumed.

"You became gay after we broke up," she said.

"*No,* I got it from shooting heroin," he said.

"But isn't it venereal disease?"

"*No,* it's in your *blood.*" His voice deliberately showed his distaste for this discussion. She did not catch the hint.

"You know for sure you don't have this now," she said.

He knew that tone, very well. "Yes, I am sure." He did not move his jaws as he spoke.

"Do you do heroin?"

No, I haven't yet had my heart ripped out by you and my "No, I haven't yet started doing heroin," he said, holding her by her shoulders.

His voice got louder. "Because I haven't been away at college, earning a degree in fucking computers so I can marry you, and I haven't been turning down more pussy than I ever knew existed—"

She pulled away. With one hand he seized her by the chin, brought her back to hear him up close.

"And I haven't come home for fucking Christmas," he said, "to find out that *you're pregnant from fucking Desmond!*"

Cunt!

In one movement his hand turned her head all the way around on her neck. Her spine did not snap, but popped inside, faintly.

❦ ❦ ❦

At some point Eddie deduced that the noise he heard all round him was a steady stream of gibberish issuing from his own mouth, so he shut up.

I killed her.

She lay limp in his arms, her head twisted backward.

"Oh...how..." He pressed his ear between her breasts. Heard nothing. Nothing at all. Not a murmur.

Inside him, something fractured, leaked away its vital fluid. The shock had subsided. Pain swelled to fill its wake.

Not now. Think.

Her warm but cooling flesh weighed heavy in his hands. *She's dead. Deal with it now, cry over it later. Bury her.* No matter what he did, he would have to go home for a shovel, which meant hiding her till he came back, which meant someone might find her. Plus his parents would want to know where he was all this time. Plus people smell bodies buried in the woods sometimes. *Too many pluses.*

Each second he remained there with her gave an eyewitness another chance to enter the soccer field from Roosevelt Avenue and see him rocking a dead thirteen-year-old in his arms on the bleachers.

Under the bleachers.

He carried her to the far end, to that small portal where drunk teenagers pissed and rats prowled. Again he held his ear to her. Nothing. *Dead.*

He placed her on the floor inside and struck his lighter. Nothing moved in this meager light. Any rat in here would have bolted already. The ceiling was the underside of the topmost bench, just low enough to prevent him from moving easily while crouched upright, but if he knelt, the floor's rubbish and scag cement would rip his knees to shit.

Eddie doubled over with his feet spread wide, and waddled apelike down the passage, dragging Marypat by her upper arms. She weighed less this way than he expected. He had to bring her in as far as possible.

At first the tunnel smelled the way he had anticipated, beery and urinous, but a few feet into the darkness the air hung stale, and a few feet past that Eddie met a stench that grew heavier as he inched toward the passage's sealed end. He knew the smell. Rodents must have died in here. *Things die in here, and no one can tell from outside. That's good.*

In the darkness his boot scraped the cinderblock wall to his left. He nearly lost his footing on a charred two-by-four.

Something small scampered across his right foot. He jolted upward and smacked his crown against the concrete.

"Shit!" he hissed. He dropped Marypat. Her head thumped onto the filthy concrete. He struck his lighter again. Nothing moved.

The sight of Marypat's body—her corpse, now, with its shirt unbuttoned, *not even fourteen*—the sight of it overcame him. He could not pick her up again, nor drag her an inch farther.

With a start he spied blood upon his hand. His own blood, from his forehead. He had scraped it on the cement.

Undress her.

He touched her shirt with one hand, kept the hand there. Slowly he felt his way along her hem to a button and tugged. The button would not give.

"I can't do this," he told no one at all, and in seconds had stumbled headlong out of the crawlspace.

The night air cleared his head. He didn't glance behind him as he left the soccer field via the horse trail that ran through the Corridor. At first he took the trail toward the Farm—toward the ash trees. Gradually, though, he lost momentum and came to a halt.

"No," he said out loud, and went home instead.

SEVEN

By the time he arrived home, Eddie had a plan.

As he reached the lawn he could hear his mother's squawk in the kitchen, so he entered the house unnoticed through the front door. Immediately his parents' voices came clear, reliving their first or second Christmas together, sometime in the 1950s.

"We didn't even have a goddamned tree, Joe," Mrs. O'Kane reminded her husband. "You got so drunk you didn't buy us a tree!"

Through a narrow strip of the kitchen doorway, Eddie watched the irises float heavenward in his father's pink-liquid eyes. The old man looked polluted.

"You know, you might find someday," Mr. O'Kane slurred, calmly, trying to sound witty, "there are people in the world suffering even worse than you, who don't stand around—"

"You don't care whether we had a tree—that's the point! I *know* you don't!" she barked. "Not that we couldn't afford it, Joe, but you just couldn't give a good goddamn once you've got a snootful."

While spying from the hall to judge whether his mother had consumed enough wine yet to fall asleep early tonight, Eddie saw a shadow in the corner of his eye and flinched: Kevin, slouched before the TV. He nodded just once as Eddie entered the living room.

"Why are you up already?" Eddie asked.

"Who can fucking sleep?" Kevin frowned without taking his eyes off the set. "They're like children, these two. I'm amazed the both of us aren't in fucking Creedmore."

"But you do have to work tonight?"

"Yeah, I'm doing overtime," Kevin said. He sounded strange, flat. *Has he started getting high?* "It's a pleasure going to work, leaving this shit behind. I should pay my boss."

Eddie looked at the TV and then back at Kevin. "So what time is it?"

"Like ten, almost."

"And you have to go to work when?"

Kevin stretched and yawned, without showing the vaguest symptom of enjoying it. "I should leave by eleven," he decided. "Hey, has Chrissy called for me, that you know of?"

Eddie shook his head.

"Oh," Kevin said, deliberately unimpressed, "because I thought maybe you got the phone. If the old man or Ma gets the call, you know, I don't get the message."

"Was she supposed to call?" Eddie asked, devoting his full energy to appearing interested.

Kevin shook his head. "Forget it," he said.

Eddie left him and went upstairs. In his room he lifted the chipboard casing off his clock radio to retrieve three red pills from his hidden cache of downs.

In the bathroom mirror he saw dry blood crusted on his face along his hairline. Kevin had not even noticed this wound.

After he washed his forehead Eddie bounded down the stairs into the kitchen, thus interrupting his mother's detailed recollection of a parish card party where the old man drank himself onto the church steps. Eddie had been three during this incident, supposedly, last time he heard the tale.

"Hey," Eddie said.

"Where have you been, huh?" his father said sternly, obviously hoping to direct his wife's artillery toward any other target.

"I was at church," Eddie said.

"Oh," Mr. O'Kane replied, as though teenagers routinely returned from Mass at ten PM with bloody scrapes on their foreheads.

Eddie's mother, on the other hand, fancied herself a wise and admirable parent when drunk. "Edward," she said, "have you done like I asked and called the ASPCA?"

"Don't worry about it," he said.

"Edward, it's the only way you're going to find that dog if she's sitting in the kennel there," she said.

"Ma, the dog's gone two months," he said. "Wherever she ended up, she's not coming back. No animal lives that long at the ASPCA."

She went into a mild tirade about how she only meant to help, "but sure, everybody shits on me, I'm the old ogre," and so forth. Eddie pretended to ignore her as usual and focus on making a sandwich, but he kept his eyes trained on her, on both his parents, the whole time, waiting for them to stop paying attention to their drinks.

Abruptly Mr. O'Kane rose from his seat to visit the bathroom, and for the last few steps his wife followed, harping on him about something he did a month before their wedding.

Eddie tugged apart one capsule over his father's scotch and water, and nearly opened the other two into his mother's wine glass, but feared she might taste it. Instead he opened the refrigerator. Her carafe of lousy white still contained perhaps two glasses. Half an hour, at most, when she was this charged.

Into the wine he dumped both capsules' worth. He lifted the carafe and swilled it to dissolve the powder.

A moment later his mother marched into the kitchen, almost on cue, and tossed down the rest of her glass. In a flash she had it refilled. If she tasted anything funny, it didn't worry her.

Mr. O'Kane returned from the bathroom and mumbled something polite. Eddie opened the back door and slipped out into the yard, glad to escape one of his parents' weird civil moments while they chose some new reason to fight.

Oddly enough, Eddie had never set foot in the yard next to his, nor the one beyond it. Both these neighbors had always been old couples who spoke with accents, though the Germans next door were nicer than the McGowans.

Eddie hopped the storm fence into the Germans' yard. Careful to avoid their vegetable garden, he padded to the McGowans' redwood fence. To scale it he had to climb where it nearly met the Germans' garage.

From the top of the fence he whistled faintly, to make sure the McGowans had brought their Irish setter inside for the night. Then he jumped down into their yard. His right foot connected with a stone or cement walkway he couldn't see, while his left sank to the ankle in soft earth.

Unfamiliar and unlit, this enclosure halted Eddie. He did not take a step until his pupils adjusted as much as they could to this more intense darkness. Barely could he even discern the McGowans' house; if he paraded through their dog's shit, he wouldn't know.

He crossed the yard slowly, probing ahead of himself with one foot. He found a cheap plastic seat that he thought might work as a stepstool so he could hop the fence on the other side. He set the chair with its back against the redwood, and stepped onto it.

Just as his fingers touched the top of the fence, the chair snapped out from under him. He landed on his ass.

Five seconds passed. No response within the McGowan household.

Clumsily he picked himself up and crept alongside the house to the front, careful not to let their dog hear him. Eddie unbolted the gate and shoved it open just a sliver, just wide enough to let him peek at the gold Duster outside on the street. The watchman sat still as a statue at the wheel.

Eddie knelt and opened the gate all the way, let it come to rest against the house. Doubled over, hidden by Mrs. McGowan's azaleas, he snuck down Mrs. Denihan's side alley into her backyard.

He had never stood inside this yard before, either, but knew the white metal benches for years. More than once he had wondered to himself whether anyone had ever sat in them.

A hedge separated Mrs. Denihan's yard from the lot. Behind her garage he passed around the hedge. He peered down the alley at the street. The watchman couldn't possibly see him back here.

Leaning against one of the houses Eddie spotted a cement boat—a square metal bowl, three foot by three, for mixing concrete. He laid it on the ground beside the skiffs of new bricks. These bricks were the main reason for the guard.

With the bricks stacked before him as a guide, Eddie had to estimate the size of the entrance under the bleachers. Finally he decided to take a hundred bricks; better safe than sorry. As quietly as possible, he loaded them into a wheelbarrow. Mrs. Denihan's house had remained dark every night since her departure, but other neighbors might hear him.

First he carried the cement boat back across Mrs. Denihan's yard and through the McGowans' gate. He brought it inside to the back, where he slid it over the redwood fence onto the Germans' property.

On his second trip a large sack of brick mortar proved much harder to get over that last hurdle. For all purposes a bag of stone, it weighed too much for him to hold by one end and fling.

On the other side of the fence he heard his parents' back door open.

"Eddie?" his mother called.

He nearly answered.

"Eddie!" she called again. "Eddie!"

Someone in the house said something to her, and she responded, "Oh, shut up," before closing the door.

Carefully Eddie set the sack on the ground.

The darkness of the McGowans' yard no longer slowed him. Either they were asleep or not home. He tiptoed alongside their house on the left side, and unbolted their other front gate.

Anyone in a car parked two houses away could not see Eddie here; the McGowans' stoop shielded him. From outside on the Germans' lawn he peered at the gold Duster. The watchman seemed asleep. In any case, Eddie could travel to his parent's yard from here all but invisibly.

The O'Kanes' front door opened and slammed. Kevin stormed out, not just talking to himself but frantic, nearly violent. He climbed into his Delta 88 and tore away.

Eddie slipped back through the McGowans' gate, rounded their house, crossed Mrs. Denihan's yard and got his wheelbarrow. It was heavy but he could move it. At first he wondered how to proceed without damaging her hedge. Then he realized it wasn't Mrs. Denihan's yard any longer. This was now Clifford Manchesi's hedge.

With an all but jovial flourish, Eddie rolled right over the shrubbery.

❧ ❧ ❧

When he entered the kitchen he found a note from his mother taped to the fridge. EILEEN CALLED, I DON'T APPRECIATE YOU WALKING OUT OF HERE AND LEAVING FOOD OUT, I'M NOT A MAID.

"Not a cook either, that's for sure," Eddie added.

She had put his sandwich in the refrigerator. Right now his appetite for food seemed as distant to him as his appetite for Eileen, but he knew he had to eat, if only to kill time until his parents passed out.

"Go to bed, Joe," he heard his mother say.

They were in the living room. His father lay on the couch, wearily raising his head from a stoned rest.

"Go upstairs, Joe," Mrs. O'Kane told him. "Don't sleep on the couch. Joe? Joe? Come on."

She herself had lost a good deal of balance. At most she had fifteen minutes left conscious and upright.

"Ma, let me give you a hand," Eddie said.

His mother glanced up, startled, then said, "And where the hell have you been? You just walked out of here and left that kitchen a wreck."

"Yeah, I'm sorry,'" he said, lifting his father onto the stairs.

"I'm not a maid, Eddie, I don't mind you making something to eat but you have to think about me, huh? Think about the poor slob who cleans up."

"Sure, I see that," Eddie grunted, forcibly guiding his father up along the banister.

"And I'm the big nag—I get nothing but abuse," she went on, struggling to keep her head upright. "I ask too much, that people should pick up after themselves."

Save it for your husband. Eddie marveled that he had put himself into this position out of fear that she might fall down the stairs.

Once they got past the staircase, Mr. O'Kane feebly propelled himself into the master bedroom, dragging his feet, and dropped onto his side of the double bed. With one fluid movement Eddie pocketed his father's keys off the nightstand. Then he bid his mother good night.

"Oh, I'm not going to bed yet," she said. "I just want to watch a few programs in peace. If your father sleeps down there on the couch, his back hurts him for a week. Then I have to hear it."

Eddie went downstairs as quickly as possible, leaving his mother's woozy chatter behind him.

Eating his sandwich a few minutes later in the kitchen, he listened as she took the stairs one step at a time. She had her slippers on, probably her bathrobe, too.

When he finished his sandwich he went up to his room and put on a black hooded sweatshirt. On his way back down he glimpsed his mother in the living room, asleep in the warm spot left by his father.

"Hey, ma," he called.

No answer.

Stealthily Eddie walked out the front door and closed it behind him. As he crossed the lawn he took his father's keys from his pocket.

As always, Mr. O'Kane had parked his van at the front of the driveway. Eddie climbed in, adjusted the seat and mirrors. His hands shook as he inserted the key in the ignition.

This is fucking insane. Marypat is dead. He had actually wished for Marypat to die, years ago, when she married Desmond. *I fucking killed her because of something that won't ever happen, now. She's lying dead inside those cement seats.*

His whole body gave in to a shudder. This tremor peaked and subsided. A calm tide of cunning filled its stead.

Eddie started the truck, backed it down the driveway to the yard and killed the engine. No one in the house heard a thing. Inside the yard where the driveway ended Eddie had left the wheelbarrow, full of bricks and that bag of mortar.

First he had to retrieve his cement boat, however. This time he traveled much more calmly, using the Germans' gate at the front of the house. He grabbed the boat and carried it swiftly to his father's truck, pausing only to close their gate again.

Eddie loaded the bricks into his father's van rapidly, efficiently. At one point, he noticed that he had placed too many toward the back door, and redistributed.

Lifting the wheelbarrow by himself proved too difficult. Eddie thought ahead carefully and decided he didn't need the wheelbarrow anyway. Yet he couldn't leave it beside his house, in case Manchesi's contractor came searching the neighborhood tomorrow.

Beside their garage a pile of lumber sat moldering. Eddie's father intended to build an awning or something with it, and it would remain there in the yard until they sold the house. Eddie snatched up two six-foot lengths of two-by-four and set a gangplank from the ground into the rear of the van. It bowed beneath the wheelbarrow's weight but held up. Eddie chucked the boards into the van and closed the back doors.

❦ ❦ ❦

Driving felt very natural to Eddie. Twice he passed cops and barely noticed. He drove to Roosevelt Avenue and approached the Corridor from its western border.

The first time he passed the entrance to the soccer field, three cars came in the other direction, and out of nervousness he didn't stop.

He looped the block and returned in the opposite direction. This time he pulled to the curb and watched other cars pass, waiting for a gap, when suddenly five guys a few years older than Eddie strolled out through the gate, swigging beers.

They don't know anything, just kids in there drinking. They didn't see her. They'd be freaking.

They paid Eddie no attention, so he decided to wait for them to leave and then drive in. When the group got half a block away he changed his mind and drove ahead, far ahead, past the Corridor altogether. He pulled over next to the first payphone he saw and left the motor running.

His idea was to call 911, but that wouldn't work. Instead he asked the operator to connect him to the nearest police precinct.

"Hello, One-oh-ninth," a woman answered.

"Hi," he said. "Does DNA testing exist yet?"

"Excuse me?"

"If you find a dead body, say, and there's blood on it—not just the victim's blood, but someone else's. Can you tell for sure whose it is?"

The woman pondered the question. "I don't think so. Son, have you found a body?"

"No, ma'am," he replied. "Have you ever heard of DNA testing?"

"D and A? No, I haven't."

"And you've been trained for evidence collection, at crime scenes and so forth?"

"Yes," she said. "I sure have."

"Have a good night," Eddie instructed her, and hung up.

The wind at his back now, he sped up Roosevelt toward the soccer field, passing those guys he had watched emerge from it. No one else cruised the road in front or behind him, not a soul.

Then he crossed the double yellow line, jumped the curb and drove right into the entrance. The gate on the right scraped the side of the van but gave. A second later he was inside.

First he flashed the high-beams at the bleachers, making certain all partiers had departed. A pair of empty six-packs holders stood along on the concrete.

Eddie put the van in PARK and hopped out with his father's all-weather extension cord. He swung both gates closed and tied them together with the cord, keeping the knot on the inside.

He drove carefully across the soccer field in the dark. Every few feet he flicked the headlights to check the terrain. Once he frightened a rabbit, who fled toward the horse trail.

Finally Eddie reached the bleachers and backed the truck to the structure's far end. He climbed out, opened the van's back doors, anxiously avoided staring at the portal behind him.

Water. He forgot he needed water.

But he knew where to find it.

His father kept oversized fittings inside white plastic four-gallon buckets. Eddie dumped two of these onto the floor of the truck and took the empty pails. Then he locked the truck.

While he jogged the horse trail to the Farm, he told himself again and again that he would have time to think everything through tomorrow, that he would have all the time in the world, that he would figure out how he had gotten himself into this nightmare and chart a course back out. He told himself whatever he needed to hear.

The Farm stood quiet, unguarded. He picked his way through the crops to the nearest water tap, past a pile of harvested potatoes. In this moonless starlight, the brass faucet glowed a peculiar mint color.

No. It can't fucking be.

The ash trees had advanced onto the Farm.

He blinked, hard, as though his vision might clear in the dark. The trees remained where they stood.

Cool air hit his face from somewhere nearby, and Eddie forced himself to ignore the ash grove. He filled first one bucket, then the other, and tried to carry them. He couldn't, until he spilled off between a third and half from each.

Traveling the horse trail in the dead of night, hauling so much water it hurt his arms, Eddie anticipated breaking at any second, just collapsing into mindless agony. Every fifteen or twenty feet he stopped to rest. At last he made it back to the soccer field. Nothing had changed.

Studiously ignoring the opening he had come to seal, Eddie unlocked his father's van and unloaded the bricks onto the ground around the bleachers. The thought occurred to him that he should have used the wheelbarrow to cart the water buckets, but he let that go.

He pulled out the sack of mortar and the cement boat, and stopped dead in his tracks when he realized he had not brought a trowel. Thankfully, his father had one, not a cement trowel— probably one his father used to spackle walls after replacing pneumatic lines—but it would serve.

Time to make the donuts.

Eddie faced the entrance to the tiny crawlspace. *Take her clothes off. They can take fingerprints off buttons. I might have bled on her, too, or left my hairs on her. I have to undress her.*

He didn't want to.

Have to.

He would pay any price to keep from crawling inside that foul tunnel again. Nearly.

Can't leave those clothes in there.

This time, at least, he would have his father's flashlight, a huge rectangular one with a high setting that his father swore mountaineers used at night in the Himalayas.

Kneeling, Eddie put one hand on the threshold, and felt something wet. He clicked on the light. The whole surface was sopping. *Of course.* Those guys with the beer had pissed here.

"Goddamn it," he cursed out loud, wiping his hand on the ground. His anger braced him.

Almost casually he aimed the beam of light down the tunnel toward where he had left Marypat. She lay sprawled, just as he had left her.

Beside her a rat stood erect on its haunches, clicked its teeth and then retreated farther back into the darkness.

Oh, fuck me, I am not crawling in there. I don't care if I hang.

Eddie extinguished the light, rose to his feet and set to work mixing concrete in the cement boat.

❦ ❦ ❦

As it turned out, Eddie had brought plenty of bricks, enough to lay a double wall. He could not tell how long the job took.

Once while he worked he took a break to smoke some hash, and soon after wished he hadn't. It made him jumpy as hell, and he kept thinking how easy his father's red-and-white truck would be to spot from a distance, how recognizable it was if someone passed on the horse trail. Anyone could see it here.

When he fitted the last brick and patched it with mortar, Eddie felt neither triumph nor relief.

I killed her.

The love of his life, last time at least. But dead now, and he could not change that, not by going to jail or anything else, unless... *No.*

Either way, he couldn't afford this debate now. He went to pull the wheelbarrow from his father's truck, until he considered what little he knew of homicide investigations. No, the wheelbarrow linked this job to the construction site down the block from Eddie's house. So did the cement boat. The few spare bricks, as well.

Eddie packed all of it, including the paper wrapper from the mortar, into the van and locked it. With the flashlight he checked that nothing remained, that tomorrow or the next night or sometime soon drunk teenagers would come here to piss and marvel that the Parks Department had walled up the tiny doorway.

He drove across the soccer field, and through the foliage saw a car pass outside on Roosevelt Avenue. Though he had not guessed it in advance, this was the riskiest part of his scheme: He could not possibly tell from in here whether cops were outside on the road, and if they saw him pull out of here, they would arrest him. They would note the stolen construction materials in the van.

So if the city ever tore down the bleachers, ten or twenty or forty years down the road, anyone with a library card could figure out who had walled the skeleton up inside them.

Not once as he crept back across the field did Eddie flick on his headlights. He shifted into PARK twenty-five feet from the gates, and went out to unfasten them. The extension cord untied much more easily than a rope would have.

With the gates free, he ducked his head out to peek. Outside on Roosevelt Avenue he saw one car approaching, so he watched it pass. Then he ran back to the truck.

He swung out over the sidewalk onto the blacktop and floored it homeward. Not until he left the Corridor behind him and reached a red light at Franklin Avenue did Eddie realize he had forgotten to switch on his headlights.

Roosevelt Avenue led to Northern Boulevard, which took him to the waterfront. Down the block from an empty factory building, on a street with broken curbs and no sidewalk, Eddie parked and opened the back doors once more.

He kicked the left-over bricks onto the pavement, then shoved the cement boat and the wheelbarrow and the paper sack after them. He used his father's whisk broom to clean out the red dust, and positioned the two plastic buckets to look as though they had spilled their contents by accident.

Before he drove home, Eddie examined the place on the van's right side where he had rubbed the gate entering the soccer field. A scrape about eighteen inches long revealed the steel under the garish white paint. He wished it had happened lower down, on the red part, but it made no difference. His father would never suspect Eddie, in any case. No one knew Eddie could drive, for starters.

Eddie brought the truck home and parked it in his father's standard spot. In the house he found his mother unconscious on the couch where he had left her, only now with religious broadcasting on the television. He took a shower, and smoked a joint with some hash in it, and listened to his radio in the dark.

The cops will ask Ruthanne if Marypat had any boyfriends. And Manny—he'll tell them about me in a second.

Neither Ruthanne nor Manny knew Eddie's last name, though. If she recalled seeing Marypat leave with Eddie, Ruthanne probably still could not send the police to him. And even if she could, so what?

So if the cops talk to me they'll see murder written all over my face, that's what.

His clock radio read 4:10 AM. The idea of attending folk mass at ten in the morning to feign shock at Marypat's absence danced fleetingly across his brain, but he shot it down.

It made sense not to go, anyway, since he hadn't gone last week and Marypat had commented upon it. In all likelihood she had mentioned it to Ruthanne. Steering clear of church altogether would make him just one more boy from the parish who'd had eyes for Marypat Cooper once upon a time.

I'm a guy who talked to her at church, made out with her a few times. How many of her friends could she have told about me? Nobody's going to know I did this, nobody.

An Ian Hunter song came on that reminded him of the night he first made love to Marypat, right before Christmas his senior year. The DJ said the song had just come out. This news made the memory more painful, though Eddie couldn't say how.

How the fuck are those trees moving across the Farm like that?

The sun came up before Eddie got any sleep, and he didn't get much.

EIGHT

Nobody who knew Eddie had seen him with Marypat Cooper, and within a week some juvenile delinquent had spraypainted SATAN'S REVENGE across the clean new bricks on the bleachers.

Eddie survived school that week, barely. Kelly got expelled for coming to school dusted Tuesday; he arrived forty minutes late for first period and then called Brother Edmund "Smegmund" to his face.

While recuperating during the summer O'Shea had gotten religious (though maybe he always had been and Eddie hadn't noticed, since they only saw each other at school) and had written several letters to help Matherson return to McCanton.

Weirdest of all: Matherson himself no longer scorned authority figures and in fact seemed destined to become one. He came by twice to visit O'Shea just before homeroom and called Eddie "Ed." These days Matherson and O'Shea ate lunch together, debating theological viewpoints.

During that first week Eddie made a point of avoiding newspapers. Since he had no contact with fellow parishioners or neighbors, he did not have to face constant reminders of what had taken place the previous weekend.

Wednesday he woke up to his clock radio playing the rock station, and on the hour the DJ introduced the more somber newscaster, a woman who very seriously concluded her opening tease: "And in Queens a thirteen-year-old girl has been missing since Saturday. More after this."

Commercials followed, three of them. Then, predictably, the newswoman read all the less lurid headline stories first. Eddie had plenty of time to change the station or shut off the radio. He did neither.

"The family of a thirteen-year-old girl in Queensborough Heights are praying today for her safe return. Police say Marypat Cooper is a freshman at the parochial Hill Academy in Jamaica Estates and a popular singer at Saint Mary of Bethlehem Catholic Church. The girl disappeared Saturday after an ecumenical concert at a nearby Jewish center, according to police. Sports, when we come back."

Other than that, Eddie heard nothing.

On Friday morning Powers, who sat behind him in Physics, came and said, "Fucking cops took Coogan out of Cream Puff's class."

This news surprised Eddie. Stunned him, in fact. It instantly made the most dreadful sense to him.

"His old man runs a TV shop, right?" Powers asked Eddie.

Eddie took a second to shake his daze before answering, "No, a gas station. Where I live."

"I bet his father got robbed and they shot him," Powers said. "Most dangerous thing in the world, running your own business someplace."

Eddie could not muster a shrug.

That night Eddie went to the Coogans' after dinner. He tried their back door, but no one answered. When he rang the side door Mrs. Coogan let him in solemnly, and he followed her into the kitchen, where Desmond sat at the table with his father. No one had eaten dinner, or could, evidently.

"Hi there, Eddie," Mr. Coogan said, his manner so deliberately tranquil it would panic any child.

"Hey, Mr. C," he said. "What's the word, Desmond?"

"You hear what happened?" Desmond said.

Eddie shook his head. "All I heard is, the cops came to school looking for you," he said.

"Yeah, and they should have come here, with me present, if they wanted to see him," Mr. Coogan said. "They were way out of line, picking him up at school. I'd like to put my foot in someone's rear end over it."

"Are you in trouble, Desmond?" Eddie asked.

Desmond glanced at his father.

"Not as long he's telling me the truth, he's not," Mr. Coogan said.

"You know this girl that's missing?" Desmond asked.

Eddie carefully said, "No."

"It's been in the *Daily News* all week, this girl from MaryBeth's disappeared last weekend," Desmond said. "The cops think I kidnapped her."

"They're *arresting* you?" Eddie asked, bewildered.

"No, not unless they find evidence," Mr. Coogan said. "They won't."

"They better not," Desmond said.

Eddie said, "But why would they accuse you?"

"I don't remember even meeting this girl," Desmond said. "The cops asked her friends if any weirdos ever bothered her, and her friends say yeah, this guy's got her pictures all over the wall in his house and prank-calls her and what."

"I know the girl's father," Mr. Coogan said. "Friend of mine."

"So they think you're her weirdo," Eddie said.

Desmond nodded. "I never met her, that I can remember," he said. "I never prank-called anyone, either, and I don't have her picture on my wall. I have no idea why they're saying this."

"Might be they have the wrong Desmond, or whatever," Mr. Coogan allowed.

"That happens," Eddie said.

"But they still went about it wrong," Mr. Coogan said. "That sneaky shit gets my back up."

"Probably what it means is, they don't have anything better," Eddie said. "When there's no trail leading anywhere, they play whatever bet's on the table. They'll back off of you, once they find a real clue or they close the case."

"That could be years." Desmond placed a hand over his mouth.

"But they can't stay on your back for years," Eddie said. "You didn't do anything, all they can do is try to make you confess. I mean, if you don't even know the girl."

"Damned sad thing, whatever's going on," Mr. Coogan said.

"Maybe she ran away," Eddie suggested.

Mr. Coogan shook his head. "Not a chance, if you knew her. This'll be bad news whatever they find out. What gets me is, they could've just had Jimmy Cooper call me and ask me to bring

Desmond over. Would have done that, no questions asked. I know Jimmy Cooper since Eisenhower was president. The man's my friend."

The older man's nervous anger made Eddie uncomfortable. Whatever point Mr. Coogan was arguing, he most of all needed to convince himself.

After they discussed it awhile, Mrs. Coogan asked Eddie if he would join them for frozen pizzas, and Eddie said yes. He and Desmond ate theirs in the TV room, watching *The Odd Couple*.

"Your pops looks peeved," Eddie said.

"Should have seen him when he got to the precinct," Desmond said. "Man, I was glad I had cops there to protect me. My father would have socked me clear into next month, easy."

"Is it freaking out your mother?" Eddie said. "She didn't say anything whatsoever."

Desmond shrugged. "Her stomach's bothering her," he said, and ate his pizza.

Eddie's appetite blanched. *It's happening to her now.* He put his plate on the coffee table, where it cooled until *The Odd Couple* ended and Eddie split.

❧ ❧ ❧

The next day Eddie took a long walk across most of the Corridor, stopping well before the Farm, and saw that new graffito on the bleachers. In a distant way he knew he should avoid the soccer field, should forget he knew it existed, yet this imagined threat seemed dull and unlikely. The soccer field lost whatever dread it held for him the minute he arrived there.

The masonry, if sloppy, would hold. Nothing else here seemed important.

Later he smoked a joint as he hiked the horse trail in the opposite direction. He reached the street and went home. The day hung gray and stagnant.

He felt better, though. Rotten though it might sound aloud, he had forgiven himself. This new temper of his had gotten the better of him, but he would control it. From here on out.

"Edward?" his mother called when he came in the house. She had barely reached the head-weaving stage. "Did you hear about the Coogans? Desmond's been arrested, right at school. Why didn't you hear about this?"

"I did," he said. "They didn't arrest him, they just questioned him. He didn't kill that girl."

"She's dead?" Mrs. O'Kane asked, horrified.

With the cuff of his left sleeve Eddie wiped his forehead, just once. "No," he said. "I just mean, that's what everyone's expecting, right? She's not kidnapped, or they'd have heard. Anyway, Desmond didn't even know her."

"Can he prove that?" she asked.

"What are you, a cop now?" he said. As he spoke she rolled her eyes and returned to the kitchen. "Ma, take it from me: Desmond didn't know the girl."

With a start he saw Kevin watching television—watching *golf* on television, for Christ's sake—in his bathrobe. He gave no sign of noticing Eddie's presence. Kevin's lower jaw moved very, very slowly in and out, grinding his teeth.

"Hey," Eddie said.

No answer.

"Hey," he said again. "Kevin?"

"What?" Kevin spoke with so little inflection that his voice seemed to come from the TV.

"Are you all right? Why are you up?"

"I'm *up*," Kevin shouted, "because my goddamned *mother* cannot understand that I work at goddamned *night!* That's why I'm *up!*"

"Oh, will you stop?!" Mrs. O'Kane pleaded from the kitchen.

"This is every fucking day, Eddie," Kevin said, lower. "Betsy McSo-and-so from the Rosary Society blows the janitor at church, and Ma wakes me at three in the afternoon to share it with me."

Eddie entered the kitchen as his mother recapped her carafe of white wine and replaced it in the refrigerator. "Where did you hear this? About Desmond," he asked her.

"Mary Flood," she said. "And your father drove past the fight."

"What fight?"

"Jimmy Cooper's cousin went to the gas station and punched Desmond's father, Eddie, I thought you knew all about it," she said.

"Jimmy Cooper's friends with Mr. Coogan, though," Eddie said. "They used to work together. They're friends."

"Not anymore."

Eddie left, claiming he was headed to Mass, and went to the Coogans' house. On his way he finished the rest of that joint and watched the sun set.

He arrived to find Desmond painting the front of his family's home. Mr. Coogan sat nearby on the steps, right eye bruised and swollen; beside him lay the pistol he carried when he drove each day's receipts to the bank.

"Hey, Eddie," Mr. Coogan said tautly.

Desmond turned around, and Eddie saw that Desmond was in fact spot-painting, applying a coat of white over red spraypaint letters three foot high: WHERE IS MAR

"Hi," Desmond said.

"You need some help?" Eddie asked.

"Nah," he said.

"Who did this?"

"Little piece of shit I gave a job to ten years ago, and didn't say nothing to his family when he stole from me," Mr. Coogan said. He spat on the lawn.

"You caught him? Painting this, I mean," Eddie said.

Desmond said, "That's why it only says MAR." With a wet rollerful of white he covered half the A.

"Ran like a sonofabitch when he seen me pull in the driveway," Mr. Coogan said. "Kid's got to be almost thirty years old, now. Running around pulling this crap."

"Do I know this guy?" Eddie inquired.

"Doubt it," Mr. Coogan said. "Grew up next door to Jimmy Cooper's mother in Garden City. Must live around here now. Only hired him as a favor to Jimmy. 'He's a good kid,' Jimmy says. Bullshit, he's a thief. Only I never told Jimmy, because we were friends."

The raw wound around Mr. Coogan's eye distracted Eddie, who could think of no comment to make.

"This isn't covering it," Desmond decided, studying the wall ahead of him. "I can still see it."

"It's not going to cover it, Desmond," Mr. Coogan said. "Just make it less noticeable. We have to paint the whole front of the house to cover it or else you see lines where the paint dried at different times. Probably have to prime the hell out of that red to cover it."

They three stayed still for a time. Then Mr. Coogan added, "Maybe we'll have to sand it off." Desmond got back to work. Eddie watched him, hands in pockets, not speaking much. Finally Desmond finished, and Mr. Coogan got to his feet.

"You'll have to excuse us, Eddie," Mr. Coogan said. "My wife isn't feeling well, or we'd invite you in."

"That's all right," Eddie said. *She's dying.*

"You're a good friend for coming over at a time like this," Mr. Coogan told Eddie. "Appreciate that."

"I didn't know this had happened," he said, with a nod at the wall.

"That's not what I meant," Mr. Coogan said, following Desmond inside. "Good night, Eddie."

"Take it easy, Eddie, I'll see you," Desmond said.

"Good night," Eddie replied. "Don't think people are all like this jackass, painting stuff on people's houses. People won't be so quick to judge. They'll see you're telling the truth."

❧ ❧ ❧

As it turned out, Eddie was very wrong. Not only did Mr. Coogan have to close the gas station early Sunday afternoon, but he had to bolt on his enormous storm shutters after someone chucked a pipe through one of the windows in his garage doors.

149

That night someone spread a flyer with Desmond's sophomore picture from the McCanton yearbook next to Marypat's graduation shot from MaryBeth's.

Photocopiers with enlargement would not arrive this far downmarket for several years yet, so Desmond's face was unrecognizable. Every house and car for three blocks in any direction from the Coogan's received at least one copy.

DO YOU KNOW DESMOND COOGAN OF 44-13 JASMINE AVENUE IS A SUSPECT IN THE DISAPPEARANCE OF MARYPAT COOPER LAST WEEKEND? the flyer asked, handwritten in block letters. *ANYONE HAVING SEEN THESE TWO TOGETHER OR KNOWING IF DESMOND HAS EVER MET OR MENTIONED OR TAKEN PHOTOGRAPHS OF HER OR OTHER GIRLS, OR GOING TO 10:00 MASS, PLEASE CONTACT POLICE.* It gave the detectives' names and the number for the 109th Precinct.

Everyone at McCanton acted weird when Desmond showed up for class on Monday. Cream Puff came right out and asked him what the police had wanted, according to Powers. Desmond claimed he wasn't allowed to tell. But everyone knew; at least twenty-five members of the junior class lived in Queensborough Heights, and each one no doubt had his own tale. By third period, Eddie had heard at least seven different versions.

More ominous still, Matherson made a point of inviting Desmond to eat lunch with him and O'Shea. "Come eat at our table, if you feel like it, dude," was how Matherson put it. The word *dude* sounded policelike in his mouth.

"Fuck that, Desmond, they're religious kooks," Eddie warned him. "Come on, let's eat out on the loading dock." And they did.

Once they finished eating, Eddie said, "My father told me you had to close down the station."

Desmond rolled his eyes, nodding. "I can't believe this shit," he said.

"Look, Desmond, do you need me to be your alibi?" Eddie said. "I could be your alibi, if you needed one, right? Or do you have one?"

Desmond shook his head. "I already told them where I was that night, and I said I was alone," he said. "The problem is, they don't know what happened or when, otherwise I could contact witnesses by using the credit-card record."

"Well, if you needed an alibi, I'd do it," Eddie said. "I know you didn't do anything to that girl. She's probably going to turn up somewhere, and you'll be in the clear. It'll just take time."

This view cheered Desmond, and when they returned into the building after lunch he fit in again. Nobody gave him a second glance.

That night, two guys with bats smashed the windshield and windows on the Coogans' Impala. Mr. Coogan came out on the lawn with his gun, and one vandal knocked him unconscious.

❦   ❦   ❦

Since shortly before Lenore died, Eddie had not visited Hawes. His business had beached, anyway, when summer school ended and he lost his easy daytime clientele.

Soon after school started he ran out of both dope and money. That meant he needed to collect more. Poobah's little black key still worked. Poobah probably assumed he'd misplaced the key. He must have had a spare. Wisely Eddie had stolen nothing reportable last year, so the school had not changed the locks. There were thousands, after all, three floors' worth.

Like Richie Webber's, number 1163. But the Cubs would win the World Series before Richie Webber would leave his dope unguarded in his locker again.

Webber's friend Timmy Bengler had learned no such lesson. In his denim jacket he left a dime of skunk, almost full. Eddie smelled it the second he opened 197.

After watching Matherson pontificate with O'Shea just before homeroom one morning, Eddie vowed to search the guy's locker. It *had* to be bullshit. Nobody could really get God that easily, so conveniently.

During gym that afternoon Eddie reentered the building, as though headed for the bathroom. Instead he trotted down the halls and located Matherson's locker within four tries.

No drugs at all, not even torn bits of roaches in the jacket pockets. Desperate, Eddie searched the pile of books. He opened the covers of notebooks and saw no Led Zep logos. Matherson had signed his textbooks neatly, noted the school year and written nothing else in the endleaves.

Near the top of the pile Eddie found a booklet from the Marist Brothers, the order who ran McCanton. GOD'S SERVICE AND YOU, the cover read.

I stand corrected. No matter. Other burnouts at McCanton would pick up the slack.

Starting at lunch, Eddie systematically catalogued all the sophomore potheads. When he had tracked down everyone's locker, he observed them as a group for a few days. Before homeroom each morning they congregated at the table nearest the candy machines.

One morning he saw them all slap each other five. One guy came in and started howling when he heard whatever news his buddies told him. Plain as day, and Eddie's hunch was right: Since none of them had suffered the disappearing-weed phenomenon last May, they all stashed their portions in their lockers.

Almost everyone hid it in the same spot, too, inside that obvious gap behind the metal lip, as though someone searching a McCanton locker might not check there.

By lunchtime, Eddie had gathered all of it, at least a quarter-pound of decent herb. He ate quickly and stepped outside for a few hits off a half-jay from one soph's pocket. Then he sat there pretending to study for an English test, and watched the would-be pot dealers turn on one another by the loading dock. It amused him.

That night he cut the sophomores' weed into nickels, and the next day he dealt it to the public-school kids down Roosevelt Avenue. With that money he visited Hawes, who didn't mention Lenore once and might not have remembered her. As simply as that, Eddie was back in business.

Autumn passed slowly, since Eddie shared neither the outlook nor enthusiasms of his peers. The public-school freshmen left the bus stop long before the first McCanton guys arrived, and Eddie ate breakfast in the Franklin Diner every morning. No one who knew him had any idea how much money he made or how he made it.

❡ ❡ ❡

One Saturday morning in October he awoke early. Outside his window a storm had stolen the sky so completely that all light in his room had turned rain-colored. Eddie pried his window open an inch and smoked a joint through it.

For the next hour or so, he lay still, listening to the storm abate. Then he put his radio on. The classical station put him in a good mood until the piece ended and it turned out to be a pledge drive. He tried the rock station, really low, but that woman newscaster came on and he didn't feel like hearing her.

Eddie tried the AM dial, where he flipped on the all-news channel for a while. He tuned in a talk station where some man interpreted the song "American Pie" line by line.

That entertained him, and the station played ads for a phone-in show later that day about UFOs, but when the poetry guy finished a religious show came on. Lazily Eddie spun the dial, and came back to the news station, during the quick movie reviews. He left it on.

None of the movies interested him. When the reviews ended and the commercials started, Eddie failed to notice, lost deciding what to do about food. He wanted a real breakfast, the sort he ate in the diner on school mornings, but cooking it might wake his parents. Even now that the rain had stopped, Eddie couldn't summon the energy to dress and leave for a diner.

The radio beeped. "Time is now one minute past nine. These top headlines this hour," and then static garbled the newscaster's voice. Eddie's antenna must have spun in the wind, for he could not fix his reception until the last news item:

"And vandals may have left a man dead at a cemetery in Queens early this morning. Police found watchman Pete Waters, 53, dead on the grounds of Mount Sinai Jewish Cemetery, apparently from heart failure. Said Mount Sinai spokesman Saul Derlitz:—"

For two sentences another voice spoke.

"Mr. Waters seems to have interrupted kids in one of the crypts, and taken a heart attack. I hope those kids can live knowing they took this wonderful man's life. I sure couldn't."

The newscaster told Eddie the temperature and went to a commercial. Eddie heard someone come in downstairs, and went down to find Kevin in the kitchen, eating corn flakes and staring at the stained white wallpaper beside the stove. He didn't have his holster on.

"Hi, Kevin," Eddie said.

"The hell are you doing up so early?"

Eddie shrugged.

Kevin ate some more, ignoring Eddie, who thought about watching cartoons.

"Listen," Eddie said abruptly, "do you know where Mount Sinai is?"

"Yeah, it's in the city," Kevin said.

"No, not the hospital," Eddie said. "The graveyard."

Kevin blinked into space a few times before answering. "Oh, sure," he said, "it's over by Edison. I got laid there when I was, like, fifteen."

"Would someone from Electchester get buried there?"

"Only somebody Jewish."

Kevin returned to his brooding and Eddie searched the living room for the phone book. He found it under the recliner. The number for Mount Sinai Jewish Cemetery was busy the first two times he called, and when he got through, a recorded message instructed him to call back Monday.

Up in his room he rolled a joint. He considered inviting his brother to smoke it with him in their yard, but no, Kevin wouldn't go for that. Eddie smoked it by himself, out the window.

The day outside retained that leeched noncolor from the storm. The air seemed clear, at least. From his window he could see into infinity, were it not for the treetops of the Corridor blocking his vision.

I remember Kevin going away to a rehab, Eddie told himself. *He got depressed, and he had a problem with pills.* Eddie's mother had of course insisted that no one ever discuss this issue. *If they're tranquilizers, he probably starts taking them on prescription.*

When he closed the window and padded back downstairs, his brother had moved into the living room to watch TV, so Eddie used the kitchen phone this time.

He had to guess which precinct he wanted. "Hello, One-on-seventh," a man said.

"Hi, are you guys handling the cemetery vandalism?"

"No, sir, I don't believe so," the man said. "What cemetery is that?"

"Jewish one in Electchester."

"Hold on a minute." The man asked someone else and relayed the answer to Eddie: "You want the One-oh-fourth."

Eddie thanked him and looked up the 104th Precinct in the directory.

"Hello, One-oh-fourth, can I help you?" A woman this time.

"Yes, I want to ask you about that, uh," Eddie said, suddenly wondering why he thought he could pull this off so easily. "There was, like—people breaking into the cemetery this morning?"

"Yes, sir, in Mount Sinai."

"Yeah, what was the name?" Eddie asked. "Of the crypt?"

"We haven't released that information, sir," the woman said.

"When will you?"

"I can't say that we plan to, ever," she said. "What you hear on the news is all I can tell you. Why do you need to know?"

"I want to make certain it's not a relative of mine."

"What's your name?"

Eddie tried to recall the name. Couldn't.

"Sir?"

"You know, I'm not sure which family name the plot is under, in Mount Sinai," he said. "Let me check the deed, and I'll get back to you?"

"Certainly, sir."

He hung up. *Damn it.*

From the television inside came the unmistakable voice of a nature-program narrator. "Fuck you, too," Kevin told the TV. "I'm sick of this shit."

Eddie sulked back upstairs to his room. From the bottom of his junk drawer he pulled a Sena ID card and read the name out loud to himself: "Marc Isaac Tcholowitz."

By force of will, Eddie made himself relax on his bed, listening to an FM rock station. The DJ made a big deal about new wave music's threatening rock'n'roll. In ten years, this same clod would probably claim to have discovered Devo.

The minutes dragged past.

The DJ played the Who. Eddie thought of Lenore. Outside his window, the day refused to brighten.

Finally twenty-five minutes elapsed, *Twenty-five minutes ago might as well be last year, to a police switchboard.* He practiced sounding older, rehearsed what he would say. Then he went down to the kitchen again.

"Hello, One-on-fourth." Same woman.

"Hi there, this is Rabbi Heineman," Eddie said. "Could I speak to the detective—I'm sorry, I don't remember his name, I spoke to him a few hours ago?"

"Why did you speak to him, Rabbi?"

"He called me about this thing, this disgusting thing that happened in Mount Sinai this morning." Eddie bit his lip, to calm himself. "I'm on the board for the cemetery, I live across the street."

"Just a minute, sir. Hold on."

The switchboard transferred him. It rang twice.

"Hello, Detective Hallahan," Detective Hallahan answered.

"Hi there, Detective, this is Rabbi Heineman," he said. "I think we met this morning at the cemetery."

"I'm not sure, sir, but can I help you?"

"Well, I'm counseling the Tcholowitz family," Eddie said, and let that hang.

After a moment the cop prompted him, "Yes, sir?"

It's the same name. "And this is embarrassing, but I lost their phone number, and I wanted to call them but I don't want to have to go to the temple and open my office."

"You need their number?"

"I wouldn't ask you except they were expecting me any minute, and this is such a hard time for them."

"No problem, Rabbi. I'm pleased you called me."

The detective recited the Tcholowitzes' number. Eddie pretended to copy it down, still numb from the knowledge that the name matched.

"I won't take up any more of your time, we appreciate your good work," Eddie told him. "Can you believe the lack of respect young people have today?"

"No, but I'll tell you," the cop said, "these were some cold-blooded kids we're talking about. They left that guy lying on the ground throwing a heart attack, and they still had the nerve to carry the body away. That's disgusting."

"It sure is," Eddie agreed, wondering what the cop meant. Hadn't they found the guard dead right there in the crypt?

"These kids, they get more ruthless every day. Breaks your heart."

"I know, I know," Eddie said. "Tell me, why are you certain it was kids that did this?"

"They get all full of this rock music and smoking dope and everything else, and they decide they worship the devil. That's the only reason someone steals a cadaver, that I ever heard."

He means Tcholowitz. The body's missing.

Eddie didn't pay attention to whatever the cop said next. When he heard silence on the line, he said, "It couldn't be adults that did this?"

"No adult could fit through the transom they used to enter the mausoleum," the detective said. "It was kids, or somebody real little."

Eddie thanked him and hung up.

NINE

On any horizon, the sky could darken in seconds to thunder. Yet nothing clean enough to call rain lay on the ground or hung in the air. As he walked down his street past the Germans' house and the McGowans', Eddie could not guess just where the sun might lie behind the cloud cover.

From inside the McGowans' redwood fence their Irish setter bayed, a throaty noise Eddie had never heard the dog make. This cry repeated, then stopped once Eddie had passed.

From the day they dug the foundations, and especially after... *what happened at the soccer field,* passing the construction on Mrs. Denihan's lot had never been easy for Eddie. Today for no tangible reason the place made him want to run. He very nearly did.

The aversion ebbed within him as he left the site, the way magnetic repulsion subsides as the magnets move apart. It did not disappear entirely, though. As he walked it followed him, a constant hum slightly too low to hear.

For a time Eddie let this curious feeling guide him. At each corner he decided which direction repelled him, and took the opposite. In quite a short while, he found himself choosing north exclusively.

He passed the staircases that descended to the Main Street subway terminal. He crossed Northern Boulevard near the RKO Keith's, a landmark theater that gangsters would level within five years. It had posters in the lobby windows for *Close Encounters*.

Further north he went. The streets sat lifeless. In the gutters lay crumpled newspapers and candy wrappers, limp without wind to scatter them. At a small house several middle-aged men squeezed a refrigerator in through an undersized door. No one noticed Eddie.

At last Eddie came to the borough's northern border: the shoreline of Long Island Sound. He veered away from the waterfront, into a tiny park beside the base of the Whitestone Bridge. He sat on a bench facing the water and the huge suspension bridge and the Bronx, which he saw clearly despite the overcast sky.

Get on the bridge. Cross it.

Eddie didn't really want to, of course. He didn't think the Whitestone had a pedestrian walkway, for starters. If it did, he didn't know where to find it. And noon had passed already, hours ago, so it would be night before he got back, so no way.

But he felt that push. *Don't stay here.*

No matter how gray the day was, it would not turn dark for some time yet. Eddie had no special reason to take comfort in this fact, but he reminded himself all the same.

Two gulls prowled over the Sound in front of him. He watched one catch several fish in a row. Snappers.

Leave. Go.

Surprised that he hadn't done so already, Eddie pulled his hash pipe from his pocket and loaded it with pot. A joint would have eliminated the risk of someone's seeing him, but he could spot only two other people in this whole park, a woman and her—daughter? Probably. The mother stood pushing the kid on a swing, in a small playground hundreds of feet away from him.

And to reach the park by car, cops would have to come down off the service road of whatever expressway fed the Whitestone Bridge. The road made a perpendicular turn at the very mouth of the park. Just by twisting in his seat to peer behind him, Eddie could see for blocks and blocks south, back past the exit ramp. No cop could get the drop on him.

So he turned around and fired his pipe up. When he lit it, the smell of the herb hung around him a long while. He marveled that even here, beside the open water, no wind blew today.

Then, gently at first, one did.

The sweet smell of marijuana smoke left the air. Another odor took its place, something foul, but just a wisp. *The Parks Department must have fertilized the grass.* Eddie ignored it and smoked another two pulls on his pipe.

This time the smoke he exhaled cleared more quickly. The aroma that replaced it wasn't manure. Something smelled not just fecal but rank. Putrid.

Not far from him stood a wire wastebasket, filled past capacity, and from where he sat Eddie studied its contents. He saw just one fly drop onto a cardboard box near the top, then career away.

He held off lighting the pot again. The smell grew, or perhaps he caught a better whiff, and it struck him that he found it familiar. The scent sparked a memory of the last place he had smelled it: beneath the bleachers at the soccer field.

Where I left Marypat. Try though he might, Eddie still could offer himself no excuse for her death. He had murdered a sinless child, no matter how badly he wished his anger mitigated the crime. She had done no wrong. *I broke her neck.*

Since no one connected her to him, and since no one had found her body (though by now, all the adults Eddie knew had quietly resigned hope that she was alive), he had suffered through his guilt by himself with his mouth shut tight.

One fact alone sustained him throughout: *Turning myself in will not bring anyone back.*

Eddie no longer had any friends with whom he could even broach this topic, in any case. Anyone he spoke to carried on about juvenile shit he could not fathom. Any time he sat by himself this way, straining to gather whatever did mean something to him, all he could think about was the love of his life, entombed behind bricks laid by his own hand.

An empty pretzel bag left the wastebasket and somersaulted across the rocks and flotsam into Long Island Sound.

The stench intensified.

There's a breeze. It made so little noise that Eddie hadn't sensed it. He rose from his seat. Whatever stunk, it wasn't in the trash or the water. He looked behind him, over the bench and out of the park, up the roadway.

Pacing toward him, stumbling, was a figure in a white sheet. A man. Something had happened to the man's head.

The woman at the swings did not glance away from her child, so Eddie could not tell whether she saw the man, too.

Christ, she has to smell that, though.

Through a herculean summons of will Eddie resisted his urge to flee, soaked though he was to the very marrow in dread. The man came closer, slowly closer. *Is there a hospital near here,* Eddie wondered, *an emergency room this guy wandered out of?* The gap between them now would equal two blocks, at most, and closed with each plodding step the intruder took.

Eddie focused on that young mother, pleading that she might turn around to face the roadway and make this sight vanish.

The wind picked up, and she knelt to zip her child's jacket. Then the two of them left the playground, hand in hand. The mother carried a folding stroller that Eddie at first mistook for an umbrella. The pair walked placidly down the asphalt path, dry leaves skittering around them.

They reached the exit. Without acknowledging any wounded man clad in a sheet limping toward them, now only a block away, the mother strapped her little one into the passenger seat of a compact car. She merrily climbed behind the wheel and pulled out.

At this distance, Eddie could make out great hatred seething in the man's contorted face. The head wound made him hard to recognize, especially since Eddie had only seen—

That's not a sheet, that's a shroud.

Jews bury their dead in shrouds.

The pipe dropped from Eddie's hand. Without picking it up he took off swiftly to his left, toward the park's far corner. There was no exit there but he would make one. He booked across the grass.

The wind slowed him, though not much. Nor did he let himself inhale enough of that stench to make him retch. Just as Eddie reached the black iron fence, the man in the shroud turned the corner from the service road. His skin appeared gray, slightly purplish.

Eddie hopped the fence and landed on the sidewalk running.

❦ ❦ ❦

Tcholowitz could not keep pace. Eddie rounded the first corner he came to and ran three blocks down Burling Street before his pursuer even reached that first corner behind him.

Block after block Eddie jogged south. He saw almost nobody on the street. At last a green El Torino passed him headed north, so he spun and watched it speed down Burling under the limbs full of dead yet somehow colorless leaves.

Four blocks away, the car slowed to a halt beside Tcholowitz, who paid it no heed.

They've stopped. They see him.

No. The car had only paused before turning.

Eddie continued forward, powered by the same unseen force that had guided him to the edge of Long Island Sound. That power propelled him a hundred times harder, now that he had the repellent directly behind him.

As he neared Northern, Eddie made a left turn at random. It took him down another anonymous tree-lined street full of mismatched houses. Then he took the next right, checking behind him that Tcholowitz had not arrived to see which way he went.

Eddie trotted a little past the halfway point, to a huge oak. He hid behind it and waited.

And waited.

Come on, fuckhead.

"Hey, what's going on?" a voice asked.

When he hid, Eddie had barely noticed the house beside him. A middle-aged guy raking leaves in the yard had watched him the whole time, apparently.

"Nothing's going on, sir," Eddie answered.

"No, I mean, what's up?" the man said. He wore typical '70s sideburns. "Everything cool?"

Eddie panted, checked the corner. "Yeah. I guess."

The guy came closer. "Who are you hiding from?"

Nervously Eddie explored the gnarled roots of the tree with the toe of his boot as he spoke. "It's a real long story. I didn't do anything illegal, or anything," he said. "I'm just checking to— *there!* Do you *see* that?"

Eddie's frantic tone took the stranger aback, for a second. Then the man stepped forward and bent over his fence to look where Eddie pointed. "What?"

Tcholowitz had rounded the corner without a moment's pause. He knew exactly which way his prey had run.

The wind flooded Eddie with its wretched stink. The sky had begun to dim overhead, but at this range he could discern Tcholowitz's features better than ever. The corpse's dead eyes shone black with venom. Its mouth gnawed the air spastically. *He knows where I am. He just knows.*

"What am I looking for?" the man asked.

"Nothing, sir," Eddie called behind him as he ran. He heard the man say something else, either "What the hell is it?" or "What the hell is that?", but Eddie refused to glance backward as he ran, fearing he might charge headlong into a car.

He turned down 67th Avenue. His immediate terror subsided, and in its place came a mad urge to assess his situation realistically. *That's the guy I killed, case closed. He wants my ass.*

As Eddie approached Northern Boulevard, he passed more pedestrians—people raking, kids throwing footballs to each other. No one noticed him bounding past them.

Two blocks from Northern, terror hit him anew, starting in his mid-spine. Tcholowitz had once again fallen in behind him on a straightaway. Eddie didn't even have to look back.

He zig-zagged, throwing a right turn and then the next left, then another right and another left, until he reached Northern near the Corridor.

A city bus drove past him, headed back into the Heights.

He charged after it, and boarded at the next stop. The driver gave him a bemused once-over as Eddie dropped his fare into the coin machine. "Can I have a transfer?" Eddie asked, between gasps.

"To what bus?"

"What have you got?"

"Well, where are you trying to go?" the driver asked.

"Far away." Eddie scratched his scalp, suddenly aware of the sweat pouring down his forehead and neck. "Where does this bus go?"

"I go to Fort Totten."

"Then what?" Eddie said. "You come back?"

The driver nodded.

"And I have to pay you another fifty cents to stay on?" Again the driver nodded, this time with a smile.

"Sounds cool." Five other passengers watched him, all puzzled by his entrance. Eddie staggered down the aisle to a seat at the very back.

"Are you all right?" an older woman inquired.

Eddie nodded. "Thanks," he mumbled. He saw his reflection in the window beside him very clearly now that evening had settled outside. He looked as though he'd gone swimming fully dressed.

"I had to run to catch the bus, is all," he told the older woman loudly, so that all the passengers could hear him.

"Usually people decide where to go *before* they take a bus," she observed, as though this insight might prove helpful.

She shut up and let Eddie alone. As he rode he watched the boulevard roll past his window. It occupied him, helped him calm down to the point of despair rather than frenzy.

What the fuck am I going to do?

By the time they reached the Heights' eastern border, all but one of Eddie's fellow passengers had disembarked. The bus crossed the woods into Little Neck, then followed the Clearview Parkway up toward the Throggs Neck Bridge.

There the bus turned right and traveled an unlit road to Fort Totten, where it made a U-turn in a cul-de-sac outside the guard booth. Eddie's last remaining fellow passenger, a guy in his twenties with a crewcut, rose and departed, waving at the driver as though they knew one another by sight.

After the soldier left, the driver let the bus idle awhile. Eddie walked up the aisle, digging coins from his pocket.

"You got change for a dollar?" he asked the driver.

"Don't worry about it," the driver said.

"All right." Eddie nodded. "Thanks."

"Feeling better?"

"As good as can be expected," Eddie decided.

He returned to his seat. Outside night had fallen. Like that park beside the Whitestone, the fort sat right on Long Island Sound. Eddie stared out his window at an odd green light across the dirty water.

The driver pulled out. They traveled the dark road until a red light stopped them at the foot of the Throggs Neck Bridge. Far above them several elevated roadways passed over and under one another, and out above the Sound.

Directly underneath the main lanes of this bridge, the clay never saw sunlight. Eddie knew it for a fact. The summer after his senior year—a few weeks before he left for Purchase—he and Marypat had dropped acid there. Aside from a few times when they shared hits off someone else's pot at parties, this was the only time they ever did drugs together.

They roamed the shore all night, combing the rocks, skimming shells across the water. After hours of talking and laughing together, they humped like weasels in Eddie's—actually, Kevin's—Plymouth, parked behind an enormous pylon.

Their lovemaking lasted forever. Finally Marypat asked, "Doesn't it seem like morning should have happened already?" and dug Eddie's brand-new watch out of his jacket pocket. It said 9:00 AM. Sunlight never came there.

The best time Eddie ever had shooting heroin, he was twenty-three. On the nod he dreamed he was back under this bridge with Marypat.

None of that has ever happened, now. None of it.

The light turned green, and the bus turned left, back toward Little Neck and Queensborough Heights, toward someone sixteen and dead and very, very angry.

❧   ❧   ❧

With three new passengers on board, the bus crossed the woods back into the Heights. Close to the far side it passed Tcholowitz.

His rotting lips formed a snarl that Eddie could not hear. From beside the blacktop Tcholowitz slapped the side of the bus. Only Eddie noticed. He watched out the rear window as Tcholowitz's shroud receded into a white dot chasing the bus down Northern Boulevard. By Booth, Eddie could see the white dot no more.

Eddie got off at Main Street and walked briskly. Though Tcholowitz had definitely covered an inexplicably great distance in the time it took the bus to reach Fort Totten and turn around, he hadn't just materialized out there by the fort. So Eddie could travel safely, this far away from him.

For all that, Eddie picked the route with the most streetlights. Main Street led him to Union. Three blocks later he reached a wide white one-story building, with metal lettering over the door: 109TH PRECINCT.

From the corner, Eddie could watch both directions from which Tcholowitz might approach. Either way Eddie would see him from far off, and lead him into the police station. This hallucination could not persist in there.

A youngish cop leaving the precinct house saw Eddie and asked him, "What are you standing here for?"

"I'm waiting for someone," Eddie said.

"Someone inside?"

"No, sir."

"Who?"

Fuck you, Kojak. "This girl from school," Eddie answered. "She didn't want to have to wait for me on Main Street by the subway, so she wanted to meet me here where it's safe."

The cop couldn't think of anything bossy to say. A squadcar pulled around from the parking lot behind the precinct, and the cop took the shotgun seat. Eddie watched them drive away.

At the next corner, something white emerged. *Just a car.*

One quarter of an hour passed. Tcholowitz did not arrive.

"Wait," Eddie said out loud, to no one but himself. *Wait, now, what in hell am I doing at a police station?* If he flipped out in front of cops, at the very least they would call his parents and accuse him of taking drugs.

Worse, explaining his pursuer to them could very easily lead to implicating himself. *Besides, no one else sees him but me, like it's a TV show where I go crazy and confess.*

Confess: Though he had not performed a sacrament in decades, this word still bore a very precise definition for him. As soon as he heard himself use it, he saw where he had to go: Mary of Bethlehem.

So he left, trusting much less his leeway with the time. The quickest route to MaryBeth's took him across the Back Parish, that odd quarter between the church and the western Corridor, where the streets curved and cut the blocks into pentagons and triangles.

As he followed a misshapen path toward the church, it dawned on him that the last time he had gone there had been to hear Marypat sing. He braced himself for any mention of her; judging from the girl's involvement in the parish, he could expect posted expressions of outrage, at the very least.

Rounding the sharp corner where Phlox Place met Cherry Avenue, he tried to picture the folk group playing Sunday Mass without her. *They must have canceled Folk Mass, I can't imagine how they could deal with—*

The fetid breath of the grave punched Eddie back a few steps. Otherwise Tcholowitz would have had him.

"What do you *want*?" Eddie shrieked, dodging the corpse's grasp.

Tcholowitz snatched at him. Up close, Eddie could see where the blighted flesh turned brown with lividity on the back of his attacker's naked legs.

"*What* do you fucking *want*?"

He didn't wait for an answer. Around him leaves leapt from the gutters as he ran.

Tcholowitz made a sound as he lumbered after Eddie, a labored heaving, and it stayed in Eddie's ears no matter how far into the lead he pulled. Once the church came in sight, Eddie glanced back to see his onetime victim still a quarter-mile down Cherry: The noise had sounded so close that Eddie had felt the dead man's breath down his neck the whole way.

Eddie crept up the path to the north side entrance of the church, slowly, noting the lighted windows. *It's Saturday night, they're having Mass.* That kept him outside. He waited as though guarding the door.

Tcholowitz marched steadily toward him. Every cell, every nerve in Eddie's hide screamed for him to flee.

The dead man flailed as he walked, yet he advanced so slowly.

When Tcholowitz started down the last block, the wind came with him. A rush of ice crystallized along Eddie's spine.

What if I'm at the wrong kind of church?

The dead man came rabidly forward, raving, chewing the night air, and at last came across the street to the church lawn. He showed no reluctance whatsoever.

Eddie swore, and darted inside the vestibule, where he held the heavy door closed with both hands on the handle.

Tcholowitz immediately began tugging from the other side. Death had not robbed him of physical strength.

"You stole from me!" Eddie hissed at the closed door. The stone walls made the empty space amplify him.

Desperately, Eddie looked over his shoulder, up at the small wooden doors that led into the church itself. Through the doors' tiny windows he saw ushers watching the liturgy.

Where is there a synagogue? Not the one up Roosevelt, that's miles.

BOOM! Eddie's grip slipped, just momentarily, and let Tcholowitz open the steel door half an inch before slamming it—ideal for attracting attention.

Behind Eddie, the wooden door opened to fill the vestibule with a priest's sermon for two seconds, until it swung shut. "What's the problem, son?" asked a man Eddie did not turn to see.

Why did I come here? What did I think would happen? "Son? Why are you holding that door shut?"

There is one place only. I have to go.

"Son, this isn't a playground."

Eddie set the door free. It flew open. Outside Tcholowitz tumbled onto his decayed ass.

Up the stairs Eddie charged, directly into the church. The priest, lost in his written homily, did not look up as Eddie barreled across the front aisle to the doors on the opposite side. An affronted murmur rippled through the surprised congregation.

Two shocked ushers greeted him. "What are you doing?" one of them stage-whispered.

"*Don't* stop me!" Eddie begged. "Please!" He pushed through the wooden doors into the south vestibule before the idea of grabbing him dawned on either usher. From the head of the stairs Eddie turned to look back.

Tcholowitz dragged himself through the church after Eddie with the fervor of a badger. The light from the altar showed Eddie the dead man's face in rotting detail for the first time.

Tcholowitz had no eyes, yet his sockets narrowed in fury. Three granite steps at a time, Eddie bolted down to the steel doors. *More stairs on this side,* he told himself. *Should slow the fucker down some.*

Outside the church, Eddie headed west. He maintained a steady trot, building his lead block by block. Never once did he look behind him, though he could feel when Tcholowitz had him in sight, could feel it all over his flesh.

Eddie reached Colden Street, which ran alongside the Corridor. He jogged two blocks to a rusted opening in the ancient storm fence and entered the Farm.

The ash trees had taken over. The Farm itself seemed cramped by their presence, by their number, swelling to fill the Corridor.

He felt that need to leave, the revulsion that had kept him out of there for the past six months. It meant nothing compared to his desire to escape Tcholowitz.

In huge careless strides Eddie crossed the planted lots, his boots sinking into the soft soil and mulch. He moved eagerly ahead toward the heart of the grove, and as he advanced the woods seemed to expand around him, seemed to grow longer and wider than the space he knew it occupied.

Tcholowitz's panting filled Eddie's ears again. He quelled the urge to check behind him.

Where are they?

"Hey?" Eddie called, without slowing.

Ahead of him the forest grew denser, until he came into a dark clearing. He knew this place, though he could see nothing.

"Hello?" he called, more softly, embarrassed to hear himself.

The clearing held still. He listened until suddenly the darkness around him writhed.

At the glade's dead center a fire shot to life, thrusting a thick blue smoke upward at the ceiling of tree boughs. This cyanic cloud slipped inside Eddie's sinuses and tickled the backs of his eyes. In that instant he knew the wretched odor, remembered perfectly the one other time he had smelled it.

From the growth around him emerged small people who loitered about the fire—dozens of them, three feet tall.

Their faces grinned at him, not humorously but wickedly, with cruelty, some male and some female, though their ugliness precluded much thought of their gender. They wore tightly fitted robes of some fabric akin to burlap. Constantly their jaws moved up and down, as though chewing.

Eddie's eyes adapted quickly, enough to let him recognize certain of these creatures whom he had met before.

One man smoking a clay pipe stepped forward, his expression neutral. He had a beard but no mustache, and spoke in a dry brogue.

"Well, good evening t'ye, Eddie O'Kane," this tiny man greeted him. "And are ye happy being fifteen again?"

Then Tcholowitz burst into the clearing, rushing headlong at Eddie.

"Brung a friend to meet us, I see," the tiny man quipped.

TEN

Eddie ran. The glade's inhabitants darted out of his way. No matter how fast he moved, however, he could not leave the clearing.

I must be dreaming. Eddie began to lose his will to run. He came to a halt.

So did Tcholowitz.

One of the little people—*the Good People, who used to call them that? Nana ?*—held in his hand a kind of horseshoe, using it like a giant magnet to steer Tcholowitz.

Such a horrid smell meant Eddie couldn't be dreaming, though. The wind had mysteriously stopped, yet the stench endured. And still the phlegmy rasp of the corpse's rotted lungs filled Eddie's ears.

"Been some time, Eddie," the little man smoking the pipe said. "Do ye recall m'name, even?"

"Brayson," Eddie said.

"And ye remember what's Gareth got in that box, there?"

Brayson asked, pointing with one withered finger at another little fellow perched on a log, staring into the firelight. In his fingerless right hand—which ended abruptly before the knuckles, in a bitemark shape—he clutched a minute copper box, eager for an excuse to open it.

"His fingers," Eddie said.

"Remarkable," Brayson said, his manner that of a hungover lawyer. "And with such a fine memory, still ye forgot to come see us? Now, how was that?"

"I didn't feel right coming here," he said.

"'Didn't feel right,' how? Keeping your end of a deal we made?"

"The woods," Eddie said.

No one answered.

"Every time I saw the ash trees, they kept me out. I couldn't come here. I can't explain it."

"I see," Brayson said, as though this answer satisfied him. From some unseen pocket he brought out a knife, and began paring his fingernails.

Eddie's vision improved slightly in the firelight. He could detect dozens of them, all watching him from around the clearing. Brayson and Gareth were both near enough for him to see the fine pattern of lines that covered their skin. Their hide resembled a snake's, or a smooth lizard's; countless creases in their faces and hands formed scales. Once Eddie noticed it, they all appeared vaguely reptilian.

"So," Eddie said, quivering at how insane he sounded holding a conversation with these creatures. They sensed it, too, and smirked. "What do I do?"

Brayson gave his response an excessive degree of deliberation. "Well, I suppose," he said at last, "that, being fifteen and what, ye do whatever ye want."

"About him," Eddie said, gritting his teeth and pointing at Tcholowitz, whose constant gurgling reminded Eddie of a Tourette's patient he once saw in San Francisco.

"Oh, *him*," Brayson said. "Don't know what to do there. Any idea why he's so fond of ye?"

A few snickers jeered Eddie from the dark.

"Hey, man, fuck this," Eddie spat. "You didn't warn me about this."

"Ye didn't tell us ye had it in mind to kill people," Brayson spat back. "Seems to me ye had some story about saving yer dog. How is the pup, by the way?"

A brisk chortle cut short in the dark to Eddie's left.

"Look, you guys are controlling him," Eddie said, pointing at Tcholowitz, and then at the one with the horseshoe. "I see you steering him with that thing."

"Observant man," Gareth said, not glancing up.

"Get him off me," Eddie demanded. "You want me here, I'm here. Yeah, I should've been here already, but I'm here now. Tell me what you've got to say."

"No, seems to us ye go over that first part a bit too easily," said a woman whose name Eddie had not heard. "Should have been here already, months ago."

"All right, so I didn't come," Eddie said, sweating, and not from the fire's heat. "So what?"

"So what?" Brayson repeated.

"Yeah," Eddie said. "So what?"

Brayson nodded at the one with the horseshoe.

In one breath Tcholowitz bounded six feet forward. Eddie fell whimpering upon the ground.

Brayson exhaled flowery pipe smoke before speaking. "Don't tell us 'So what' again, Eddie," he explained flatly. "Ain't really befitting a man in yer shoes. We decide what matters and what don't."

Tcholowitz moved back, as though drawn by an invisible leash.

"You've been following me all day, leading him toward me?" Eddie asked them.

Several shook their heads.

"No, sir," Gareth said, still entranced by the flames. "We just helped him get out and about. He knew right where to find ye. Good at it, ain't he?"

"Eddie, I want to bring ye somewheres," Brayson said. "Up to taking a walk with us?"

With a sullen nod Eddie rose to his feet. Gareth pried himself from the hearth to join Brayson, and the others followed. Eddie had dirt on his hands and clothes, which made him resemble the little figures surrounding him, leading him through the thicket.

Tcholowitz came too.

"Leave him here," Eddie pleaded. "I got your point, leave him here."

For just a second they brought Tcholowitz close enough to make Eddie cower behind a tree.

"Should ye be giving out orders and such, do ye think?" Brayson said patiently. "Rather rude, forgive my saying so, and it ain't going to help ye one way or another."

Eddie closed his eyes.

"And besides that," Gareth said, "ye can't expect we're to let ye tell us what guests to invite? After all, ain't there those who'd tell us to avoid the likes of Eddie O'Kane?"

They resumed foraging. After a little way, Eddie assumed they were leaving the weird place, going out to where he had come from. Soon patches of normal moonlight lit the ground. The Good People had brought him back to the Corridor, near the horse trail.

Except for Tcholowitz they all moved silently. Eddie towered over his other companions, yet they covered the unlit terrain much more deftly than he. At the end they all had to wait on the trail while their taller prisoners navigated a thicket of ragweed. Tcholowitz mowed directly across like a tank, and Eddie followed in his wake.

From the dark he emerged, and saw where they had brought him: the soccer field.

"What, uh," he began.

Brayson waved for Eddie to follow them through the fence onto the field. They led him straight to the bleachers.

In the moonlight he could see his companions much more clearly, their crude garments and their mannerisms, and the tools they carried. They had writing on their clothes, characters that Eddie mistook for Hebrew.

And as he reached the great stone bench, he saw a small crew of them scampering about the far end. The end he had bricked up.

"Eddie, want ye to meet Eammon," Brayson said.

"Quite a pleasure," Eammon told Eddie with a smile. Despite his height, Eammon projected a sense of great physical might.

He held a sledgehammer.

Somebody else had a chisel—no, it was a drill, a hammer drill. One of the Good People stood holding it steady against the bricks Eddie had laid.

"Don't do this," Eddie said.

Eammon wound up and pounded the drill. Brick fragments whistled past Eddie's head on either side. Quick as a flash Eammon had struck it a second time, a third.

"Don't." Eddie just gave up.

Two bricks flew to pebbles. Eammon's fifth shot knocked a hole clear through Eddie's wall. The woman who had spoken to Eddie back among the ash trees ignited a fuel lamp to illuminate the rectangular hole.

Immediately something black pushed out from inside the enclosure. It fell to the ground and dashed away as another followed it. This time Eddie could see the rat's face, its polished black eyes.

"Awful sloppy masonry," Eammon judged, ignoring the rodents that scampered over his feet, "though no one asked my opinion."

Tcholowitz's breathing grew louder.

Something appeared in the hole. Something a purplish gray Eddie knew very well by now.

"Eddie," Marypat croaked.

And then she wailed, so shrilly that the Good People themselves winced. Eddie pressed his hands over his ears. She continued, never pausing to breathe, her scream piercing with rage, wrenched through her crushed larynx.

The second syllable of Eddie's name was what she howled the entire time.

"The lady sounds upset, Eddie," Brayson observed in a diplomatic tone.

"Put it back!" Eddie shouted. "Put the brick back!"

"Ah, women." Gareth dismissed the din around them with a wave of his undigitated hand. "Always find something to go on about."

"Cover the hole! Cover it!" Eddie hollered. Hot sweat stung the lower rims of his eyes. "Whatever you want, I'll do it! Make her stop!"

"Yea, certain they will," Brayson said to Gareth, as though Eddie had not spoken. "Yet this girl's got a point, has she not?"

Eddie dropped to his knees, and in desperation tried to crush his own skull with his hands.

"Stop it," he begged, feebly.

"Edward, don't ye want a moment alone with your sweetheart?" Brayson asked. "Who knows how long it'll be till ye see her again?"

Eddie shook his head.

"Sure, ye do." Brayson pointed at the hole.

From five feet away, the rotted face in the hole was a blur.

"Get over there, Eddie, we want ye to see her right up close," Brayson said. "Or will ye want to hear me tell ye twice?"

Eddie brought his face up to the missing brick. Behind him, that woman angled the lantern to shed light directly inside.

Small wriggling things were eating Marypat's face. Well-fed flies escaped through the hole, along with a stink that would gag a dung beetle.

"A dead virgin always smells the worst," Gareth said.

"Don't be superstitious," Brayson told him.

"More of a tragedy, ye have to agree, though?"

"She's got no eyes," Eddie groaned.

"Right, well, the ants got those, most likely," Brayson said. "First thing they home in on, unless ye got blood on ye."

"Make her stop," Eddie begged.

"No, we can't, Eddie. We can't make her stop," Brayson said. "What we *can* do, mind, is make it so ye don't have to listen. But since ye didn't listen to me when I said to come see us, ye can listen to her awhile."

Since he had no choice, Eddie did just that.

"Ye left her for the rats," Brayson reminded him.

"Hell hath no fury," said Gareth, "like a woman gnawed."

Eddie wondered in a detached way why he could hear Brayson and Gareth so clearly even as the torment of the dead pommeled his ears from front and behind.

"Tell ye what, Eddie," Gareth said, fiddling casually with his precious metal box, "ye want to know why we're showing ye this?"

Eddie nodded.

"Cause ye thought ye could do as ye please and forget the whole affair," Gareth said. "We want ye to know it ain't that way at all. Ye didn't come to us until ye were made to come. Next time we tell ye to do something, will ye wait for us to make ye do it?"

Eddie shook his head.

"Now, that's a fine thing," Brayson said as he gently tapped ash from his pipe. "Cause next time ye have to beg us for help, ye kiss a dead girl."

❦ ❦ ❦

Brayson refilled his pipe as he led the party back to the horse trail. Behind them Eammon and two others set to work repairing the rent in the bleachers.

From the soccer field the Good People herded Eddie up the trail to the Farm. There Brayson hailed two of their number carting a metal spray pump. *I saw that can in the drying shack once.*

They set the can upright. One aimed the hose and the other plunged down the handle, spraying jet after jet of liquid onto Tcholowitz. They soaked him fairly quickly.

Then Brayson lit his pipe and chucked the match on the corpse.

Tcholowitz fell to the ground, writhing in flames. His wheeze rose in pitch to the hiss of flesh on a white-hot skillet. An unnatural wind arose, but dissipated rapidly.

"Don't smell too good, either," Gareth said to Brayson. Eddie could tell Gareth wanted to return to the fire.

"What do your friends have in that can?" Eddie asked them.

The one with the hose shot Eddie full in the face.

"We're none of us friends, Eddie," Brayson advised him solemnly. "That's not a word to toss about."

It was water. The fluid dripping from Eddie's nose and chin was purely water. He kept his mouth shut and watched Tcholowitz smolder.

The fire lasted twenty minutes, and as it burned Tcholowitz's noise became fainter and fainter in Eddie's head, until just the barest hum remained, the shadow of an echo.

Tcholowitz collapsed to embers. The last wisp of breath flared his coals pink, then blew them out.

"Feel better about that, Eddie?" Brayson said.

"Yes."

"I expect so." A chunk of whatever Brayson smoked had shot down his pipe into his mouth, and he turned his head to spit onto the dirt beside him. "Now, then, we need ye to do something," he went on.

"What is it?"

"Ye have to kill someone for us," Brayson said.

Numb, Eddie accepted this information without talking until it became obvious they wanted him to, and then he asked, "Who?"

"Not a nice sort of fellow, take our word," Gareth said. "A man named Clifford Manchesi."

The name brought a grunt from Eddie's throat.

"Know him?" Brayson asked.

Eddie snorted. "That was who I killed the night I met you," he said.

"Was it, really?" Brayson replied, in a way that told Eddie, *Little fucker already knew.*

"Done him once, ye ought to be good at it by now," Gareth reasoned.

"How do I do it?" Eddie asked Brayson.

Brayson shrugged, drew from his pipe. "That choice is yer own," he told Eddie. "Whatever kills him."

"You've got to give me some time, I can't just do it tomorrow," Eddie said. "I don't even know where to find him. He himself won't come anywhere near the neighborhood until after he's bought everyone out on Poplar. That's years from now."

"Take a couple of full moons," Brayson told him. "Can't take ye longer than that, Eddie. They can't trace ye, ye never laid eyes on the man before."

Eddie nodded. Then a thought occurred to him. "Is he going to come back after I kill him? Like, uh…?" Eddie asked, pointing at the withered pile of ash where Tcholowitz had fallen.

"Not until long after he's in the ground," Gareth said.

"Will you dig him up and send him after me?"

"Will ye give us a reason to?" Brayson rejoined.

They knew he wouldn't. Eddie bid them good night and dragged himself away.

As he stumbled through the Farm he glanced back once, expecting to find the Good People vanished. It frightened him to see them all standing exactly as they had before he left, all still, all watching him.

He didn't look back again after that.

The people who lived on Colden Street all owned dogs, and every dog barked or snarled as Eddie passed. Now that his terror had subsided, Eddie's limbs felt limp. He wouldn't reach home and couldn't stand the place right now, anyway. Almost by instinct Eddie traveled to the Coogans' house.

❧ ❧ ❧

When he reached their house and saw Desmond's patch job over the spraypainted letters, he remembered the Coogans had trouble. Too late, though, for he could travel not one step further.

He walked into the yard and tapped lightly on the window to the TV room. Desmond opened the door.

Behind Desmond, sipping soda on the couch, sat Eileen Mangan.

Without meaning to, Eddie gulped.

"How you doing, Eddie?" Desmond greeted him.

Eddie mopped his forehead with his sleeve. "Got company, have you?"

Desmond snickered. "Why do you sound Irish all of a sudden?" he asked. Eddie had not seen Desmond smile since the vandalism had started.

"Come on in," Desmond said, then louder, to Eileen, "This is the guy I mentioned to you. This is Eddie O'Kane. Eddie, this is Eileen Mangan. You can trust this guy, Eileen."

Eddie nodded, mute.

Eileen returned the gesture. "We've met," she told Desmond.

Don't act like I know she knows Marypat. "Yeah, how have you been?" Eddie asked her.

"You know the whole story about what's been happening? With my father?" Desmond asked Eddie.

"I think so," Eddie said.

"Someone hit him with a bottle by the A&P on Sena today," Desmond said. "He's got a bad concussion. And Eileen's cousin is missing. That's what everything's about."

"My cousin Marypat disappeared," Eileen said somberly. Eddie had never seen her this serious about anything. Dark circles puffed around her eyes. "This business of them attacking Mister Coogan doesn't help anything."

Desmond nodded, relief evident in every breath he drew.

"My uncle *knows* Mister Coogan," she said. "So does my father. The only reason they didn't call here is the detectives told us not to. They said not to have anything to do with the Coogans until evidence ruled Desmond out. My asshole cousins hear this and tell the world."

"It's all been a misunderstanding," Desmond said. "I can see why people get upset over a thing like this."

"Yes, all right, but that doesn't help find Marypat," she said. "And those cops didn't find any reason to suspect you at all, just some gossip she told two of her friends." To Eddie, she explained, "These girls said he had photos all over his room and he was beating women up and all this. It wasn't true."

With some discomfort Eddie swallowed and said, "So what do you think happened?"

She gazed at her feet. "I don't want to think it," she said. No one said anything for a moment before she added, "But I have to know."

"Sure, anyone would," Eddie said.

"It drove me crazy, I have to tell you," she said to Desmond. "I wanted to march over here. I kept dreaming you had her locked in your basement."

She looked directly at Eddie and said, "I know Desmond never met her. I could tell as soon as I laid eyes on him." She touched her temple with her finger. "I'd know if he were hiding something from me. I'd *know*."

Eddie acted unfazed.

"When someone's obsessed it puts a haze around them, around the place where they live. I can see it right off," Eileen said. She nodded at Desmond. "He even showed me his room."

"Yeah, this is weird," Desmond said. "They said I had her picture on my wall. We *do* have Marypat's picture on the wall, in my father's office. Eileen's, too."

"Where? Inside, or at the station?"

"Right inside," Desmond said. "Eileen found it just before. And this is what's weird: You pointed Marypat out one night. Remember? You asked who the girl in the picture was?"

Eddie rubbed his head, donned a thoughtful expression. "Wait, yeah, I remember," he said. "I thought she was my cousin. She looks just like my cousin. In that picture she does, anyway."

"When was that?" Eileen asked.

Don't panic. "When was what?" Eddie asked.

"That you pointed out her picture?"

"Oh..." Eddie dug deep. *Behave like I don't know what she's thinking. No nerves. No.* "Had to be last summer. July, I guess. We were watching *Twilight Zone* that night. Wow, how appropriate."

Desmond and Eileen both glared at him.

"I mean, for a weird coincidence like that," Eddie said.

She doesn't know. She doesn't.

❦ ❦ ❦

The next day Eddie awoke to an unnaturally quiet house. A tiny ringing whined in his ears, as though he'd gone to a loud concert. He listened for his mother's voice downstairs. When he didn't hear it, he guessed she was at church.

But his clock radio said 12:16. Neither of his parents ever attended Mass this late.

He put on his robe and went down to the kitchen. "Hello?" he called. "Hello?"

Kevin would be long asleep at this point, so Eddie vowed to enjoy having the house to himself while it lasted. He made himself cereal and tea, and scoured the house for the paper.

He found it outside on the lawn. No one had brought it in yet.

Eddie reclined on the couch, sipping his tea and reading. He gave no thought to the time. When he returned to the kitchen to make toast, the clock read five after one.

Where the hell are they? Eddie wondered, though at the same time he could hardly say he missed them.

After finishing his toast he picked up the phone. His memory failed him, and he had to ask information for the number he needed. He thanked the operator and dialed.

"Hello?" a woman answered.

"May I speak to Kelly? I mean, to Dennis?"

"Just a second." Shuffling sounds followed. Then:

"Hello?"

"Hey, Kelly?" he said. "It's Eddie."

"Oh, hi," he said. "How are you?"

"Great, how have you been? Sorry I ain't been in touch."

"I haven't been doing anything. Nothing at all," he said. "Just working. I got a new job, did you know that?"

"What are you doing?"

"I work in the office at the zoo," he said. "It's pretty cool. But it's, like, nine to five."

"Well, that's cool, if you like it," Eddie said. "What are you up to today? You want to hang out?"

"Actually," he said, and Eddie could almost hear Kelly concoct the rest of this sentence before delivering it, "I'm not sure we should hang out right now."

Eddie said, "Oh."

"I mean, not like we used to hang out," he said. "I, well—some things are different now. I'm not with Jan, for one thing."

"So," Eddie said, pulling teeth, "you're involved with someone new."

"Not exactly," he said. "I've had some changes in my life."

"What are you, gay?"

Kelly didn't react. "No," he told Eddie. "I just have a newer, more personal relationship with Jesus. Things are really turning around for me, these days. I have to thank Matthew, I never thought he had it in him to reach out like that."

"The Book of Matthew, you mean."

"Matt Matherson," Kelly said. "From McCanton."

I won't have this on my conscience, at least, Eddie told himself, with a scratchy chuckle. While Kelly pontificated, Eddie searched his denim jacket for his hash pipe.

Left it in that park beside the Whitestone Bridge. The feeble laugh still left in Eddie's throat nearly choked him.

"...you know, church once a week, take Jesus out for an hour and put Him back," Kelly was saying. "But just the fact that Matthew would come see me after I got bounced from McCanton, that opened my eyes to the power of faith as a lifestyle. I should—"

"Kelly, can I call you back?" Eddie interrupted him. "Someone's at my door. I'll call you in ten minutes."

"Sure, Eddie," he said.

He dropped the phone into its cradle, then held his head in his hands. His legs ached from running so much yesterday. *That dead shithook would have ripped me to pieces if he caught me.*

"But he didn't," Eddie reminded himself.

His mother kept the phone book under the couch. Eddie looked up "Manchesi" and found no one with a C.

Without showering he dressed and walked out the front door, down the block. Mrs. McGowan waved at him from her stoop as he passed. "How are you, Edward?" she asked.

"All right, and yourself?" he replied.

"As good as an old woman can be," she said.

The construction site next to Mrs. Denihan's made Eddie want to move away from it. He stayed only long enough to memorize the company name and phone number on the plywood placard.

"Isn't that an awful mess?" Mrs. McGowan asked him as he returned to his parents' house.

Eddie nodded.

"Real sneaky, too, didn't say nothing to us," she said. "Not very neighborly of them."

"I suppose not," Eddie said as he returned to his house. "Have a good one."

For some time Eddie sat in the living room, mulling over his options. Manchesi's company had no listing in the Yellow Pages. The exchange for the number meant it must be in Corona, or Maspeth. That made sense.

He drank more tea. At half past two he decided his parents had run away to join the circus. *Might as well not be here when they come home.* He put on a jacket and went out.

Halfway down the block he felt that pressure again, that repulsion from the construction site. The sensation reminded him of, of...

Of yesterday.

Eddie's eyes widened. He stared past the incomplete buildings, at the untouched earth behind them, where he had buried Jabberwocky.

It can't be.

Yet sure, when he moved away to where he couldn't see the spot that he alone knew as her grave, the feeling waned.

That ringing in his ears from when he woke up had not gone away, though, nor lessened. It stayed at one steady volume, minuscule, insistent. The longer it stayed, the fuller it grew. It could make reason difficult.

There's only one way to know, he told himself.

He had surprisingly little trouble bringing himself to the Corridor. Whether recent events had forged his nerves into steel or the place no longer seemed scary on its own after last night, he crossed Colden Street onto the Farm with neither a tremble nor a sigh.

The ash trees had lost their power to intimidate him. Today they seemed merely unpleasant, a taunt he could easily endure. He did not enter the grove, but he would, some night soon, he knew. That fact neither cheered him nor caused him grief.

They won't let me get in trouble. Whatever I'm up against, I don't have to sweat the cops. Too much.

For the first time ever, he found an actual soccer game taking place on the soccer field. Spectators sat on the bleachers, spilling soda and yelling at the teenagers on the grass.

Eddie stayed on the horse trail until the game ended. While he waited he marveled at how colorful the world seemed to him today; it made it easy to disregard the drab day before, the nightmare.

The game took an hour, if that long. The two teams shook hands and posed for pictures. Eddie crossed the field unnoticed by the throng departing.

He felt no push. The bleachers did not repel him.

Did I dream all that? Did it happen?

The spraypaint still said SATAN'S REVENGE over the bricks Eddie had laid. But the two he had watched the Good People smash to fragments last night were indeed no longer there.

Those two had been replaced with *old* bricks, weathered ones that matched the original masonry. No one but Eddie would notice this change, except that the N and G in the graffito were newly incomplete.

This whole thing, the whole time I've been back—have I really been here? Am I dreaming it? I could be crazy.

Eddie knelt beside the wall, pressed his ear against cold brick. No sound. Then—

Something rustled, inside.

ELEVEN

Eddie wandered around for a few hours before he returned home. When he came in the house he found his father angry, silent, nursing a scotch and water in front of the television.

"Edward, where have you *been*?" his mother sobbed from the kitchen.

"I went for a walk," he said. "What's the matter? I woke up and there was nobody here."

"We were at the hospital," Mrs. O'Kane said. "I have awful news, Eddie, something terrible has happened."

She's drinking scotch, too. What's going on?

"Kevin," she said, and took a sip to steady herself. "Kevin has taken his own life."

Eddie either sat upon the stairs or fell there on his ass.

"We were at the hospital all night," she said.

"What happened?" Eddie asked.

"I found him in his room," she said, tears running down her cheeks. "He's laying in the bed and I can smell the vomit, so I says, 'Kevin? Kevin?' He won't wake up. And then I called the ambulance, and when they come they found a note. He put it under his pillow."

197

"How did he do it?"

"*I* don't know," she replied, as though annoyed by Eddie's question. "What did I ever do, Edward? Why should this happen to me? They said he would just have woke up a vegetable."

"But how did he kill himself?" Eddie asked again.

"I don't *know*, we weren't here," she said, her breath rank with liquor. "Edward, did he say anything to you? Was it that girl he was seeing? Carol Anne, what was her name? Caroline?"

Inside himself Eddie could already detect numbness and anger blooming to soothe the wound.

"I did everything I could for him, Edward, I'm only human," she went on. "Maybe if I weren't the only real parent he had, if your—"

"Shut up," Mr. O'Kane warned her, loud enough to hear from the next room yet with little energy.

Mrs. O'Kane finished her drink. As she mixed another she laid her head against the refrigerator door, crying. Then she pulled herself together, and poured herself more scotch.

Eddie went inside. "What did he do, though?" he asked his father. Mr. O'Kane moved his upper body in a way that might have been a shrug but more resembled a stunned yawn.

"Ma?" Eddie asked.

"What?"

"How did Kevin kill himself?" he asked once more, patiently. "Did he cut his wrists open, or what?"

"Poisoning," she said.

"He poisoned himself?" Eddie said. "What kind of poison?"

She closed her eyes, trying to recall. "Setacrol?" she said. "Secatol? Something like that."

"Seconal?" Eddie asked.

She nodded.

Where did Kevin get...?

Eddie dashed upstairs to his room. Without even closing the door behind him he tugged the top off his clock radio. His stash sat untouched.

"Edward?" his mother called from downstairs. "What's the matter?"

"Nothing," Eddie said. He picked up one of the red pills and slid it into his pocket, then replaced the top on his clock radio.

"Edward, come back down here," she demanded.

Eddie returned downstairs.

"Now, I'm going to tell you something," she said, in the besotted manner she adopted when speaking as matriarch, "This is a tragedy for our family. This is nobody else's business."

"Fair enough," Eddie said.

"We will not discuss this with anyone," she continued. "When someone asks the cause of Kevin's death, we will prefer not to discuss it."

"All right," Eddie said, "I get the idea."

"It's not anything against your friends, Eddie. Please don't think that I'm telling you your friends aren't as—"

"Ma, huh?" Eddie snapped.

"Okay," she said, and went inside to sit beside her husband.

For many minutes Eddie stood in the archway to the living room, watching his parents watch a PBS show about Charlie Chaplin.

"Ma," he asked, "did you ever notice him using drugs?"

"No," she said. "Neither of you boys ever got into that nonsense, thank God. I raised you with some brains."

Which reminds me. Eddie walked into the kitchen, where he chased the seconal with a belt of his father's scotch. He went up to his room to lie down with some music.

The pill relaxed him, but allowed him to think.

In the middle of a Cars song he rose from his bed and marched down to the living room.

"You two lied to me," he said.

His father appeared not to hear.

"When?" his mother asked.

"You led me to think Kevin went to a rehab or had a nervous breakdown," he said. "You never told me he tried to kill himself. If you had told me the truth, I could have stopped it from happening. This one isn't my fault."

"You're talking through your hat, Edward," Mrs. O'Kane said.

So enraged he trembled, Eddie held himself in place. *I'm not killing anyone else. No one. Not Clifford Manchesi or anybody else.*

His mother's head bobbed drunkenly as she sat regarding him.

"You brought it on yourself," he said. "If you weren't so secretive, your son would be alive now. You're just jealous when somebody's actually got something to complain about."

"Thanks," she scowled. "I give, give, give, and all I get is abuse."

Eddie left them and went upstairs.

The priest whose homily Eddie had interrupted Saturday evening said a brief service for Kevin at the hospital chapel late Monday morning. Eddie had never met this priest, which was odd because he had gone to Mass every weekend until he left for college.

Maybe I even changed the rectory. Maybe Reagan won't be president. During the priest's mealy-mouthed platitudes about not judging "our" fallen brother, Eddie examined the ceiling. *I've done all of this.*

That night Eddie went to the Corridor and entered the ash grove. It seemed smaller, though he refused to study it closely. It took longer for him to lose himself among the trees than it had Saturday, but eventually he found himself crossing the weird territory toward the hidden glade.

The fire puffed with a percussive flash that punched Eddie in the chest.

"What have ye to tell us, Ed?" Brayson greeted him.

"My brother died," he said.

Brayson said nothing.

"I want you to fix it."

"Fix what?" Gareth asked, eyes fixed on the fire. "Bring him back?"

"No," Eddie said. "I want to start over."

"Can't help ye."

"Just make me thirty-one again," Eddie said. "I'll give all of this up, if everybody can live again. Marypat and my brother and Frank Timpone. Even Marc Tcholowitz."

"Ye'd die yeself."

"I don't care," Eddie said. "I want to go back."

"Noble of ye," Gareth said. "Can't be done, though."

"Why not?"

"It's not like ye could understand," Brayson said. "Ye are who ye are, when ye are."

"Send me back a second time, and make me even younger," he said. "I'll start from there, and I'll know to watch my temper."

"Wouldn't help ye, if we did," Gareth said. The flames held him hypnotized. "Only reason a child behaves itself is fear of retribution. Save for that, a child is the best murderer what can be found. And grown up as ye are, ye ain't got that particular fear no more."

Brayson spat a chunk of whatever he smoked. "Not to mention, ye'd killed before we met, or we never would've."

For a time Eddie watched Gareth unthinkingly toy with his metal box of fingers. That chewing motion they all made—they actually *were* eating something. Gareth chucked a dark piece of plant matter into his mouth.

"Found Clifford Manchesi yet, have you?" Brayson inquired.

"I'm not killing anybody," Eddie said.

"How's that?" Brayson said.

The clearing went silent. Gareth even took his gaze off the fire to stare at Eddie.

"I'm not killing anyone, for any reason," he announced. "It's immoral. I'm not a murderer. You can't make me."

"Dead wrong there," Gareth said.

"Send a whole cemetery after me," Eddie said, feeling strong. "Send all of hell, send the devil. I don't give a shit, I'm not killing anyone. You want to make my life a torment, go ahead."

"Right now I'll give ye a chance to forget what ye just said," Brayson replied. "Ye don't want us mad at ye."

"Our deal is off," Eddie said, and turned to leave.

"Sorry to hear that," someone said.

It took him a long time to get out of the ash grove.

v v v

When he left the Corridor Eddie went to Desmond's house. Mrs. Coogan let him in. "How are you, Eddie?" she asked.

"All right, I suppose," he said. "Yourself?"

"Oh, you do that brogue so well, Eddie," she said with a laugh. "Did you learn that from your grandmother?"

Eddie stared at her.

"She was Irish, wasn't she?" Mrs. Coogan asked.

Eddie nodded. "Yes."

"My grandmother was, too. She couldn't read or write," Mrs. Coogan told him. "She came off a farm. She was so hysterical, all the things she went on about. Elevators scared her to death."

"Superstitious."

"Yeah." Mrs. Coogan winced and rubbed her side. "Desmond's on the phone, Eddie. Just go on in and tell him you're here."

"Thanks," he said. "Mrs. Coogan, did your grandmother believe in the Good People?"

"The what?"

"The Good People," Eddie said. "Like, leprechauns?"

"Oh, the Wee People," Mrs. Coogan said. "That's what she called them. She wouldn't let my father walk the dog in the park at night for fear of his meeting the Wee People."

"What did she tell you about the Wee People, do you remember?" he asked.

"Nothing I can think of. Wait, don't they appear in mirrors if you walk in a room with the lights out?" Mrs. Coogan stared at the wall, straining her memory. "No, I think that was the Devil. My mother wouldn't let my grandmother talk to us about things she believed in." She winced again, pressed one hand onto her rib cage.

"Your side still hurts," Eddie said.

She nodded. "Don't know, I've pulled something," she said.

"Please see a doctor," Eddie said.

This remark caught Mrs. Coogan off guard, and she muttered something and left him. She feared doctors, Eddie knew. *I just made her feel stupid.*

Eddie went inside toward the TV room. Right as he reached the open doorway to Mr. Coogan's office, the sound of Desmond talking inside stopped him. Desmond could not see him.

"Think about it, though, what you're telling me about my friend," Desmond said. "I don't know anything about this stuff. You've shown me a few things—okay, I agree you have some kind of gift. But you want me to believe Eddie could do this because you had a dream?"

The buzz escaping Desmond's ear from the receiver, even at this distance, sounded unmistakably feminine.

"That's a really fucked up thing to say. The guy's my friend," Desmond said. "Maybe your dream meant something else. I mean, all your dreams can't be predictions, right? You could

have just replayed him in your dream because you saw him here...
How do you mean? No, you said it, what did you mean? Just from
meeting him, you know him better than I do?"

*Has to be Eileen. Has to be. She doesn't want to tell him she's
fucked me.*

"All right, tell me exactly how you dreamed it," he said, and
listened to her response. "Like a football stadium?... Smaller?"
She went on. "*What* did it say?"

The blood froze in Eddie's veins.

"And she had no eyes," Desmond said. "Did this scare you?"

Eddie's leg twitched.

"That's why you're so worked up about it, because it just
happened," Desmond said. "A dream is like a chemical in your
head, and when you wake up, it seems more real than it does a few
hours later. The chemical drains out of your head in six minutes,
then you forget the dream, usually."

Eddie crept back toward the kitchen and called, "Mondo?"

"Hold on," Desmond said to Eileen, then yelled back, louder,
"'Sup, Eddie? I'll be right with you."

"Take your time, Desi-Lu."

"Listen, I have company, I have to go," Desmond said. He
lowered his voice. "I'm glad you called. I'll call you... Can I call
you later tonight? Just let me think a little... Of course I'm taking
you serious. But you have to, you know, meet me halfway... Yeah,
okay. Bye-bye."

*She's got a vagina and will talk to you—of course you're taking
her serious.* Eddie entered the office wearing a neutral face. *Can't
keep you out of my sloppy seconds, can I, huh?*

"How you doing, man?" Desmond greeted him.

"Evening," Eddie said.

Desmond sighed. "Just talking to that girl, Eileen, from the other night," he said. "Where do you know her from?"

"She works down Main Street," Eddie said, as though that answered the question.

"Yeah, she lives in College Point," Desmond said.

"Whitestone, actually."

"I guess. I gave her a ride home the other night, after you left," Desmond said. "She was going to take the bus home, middle of the night. I drove her home."

"Anything happen?"

"Kinda, yeah." Desmond grinned.

Eddie slapped him five. "My man!" he said.

"You know, we made out," Desmond said. "I'm taking her to the movies on Saturday."

"Go for tit. Practice on the ironing board," Eddie advised him. "Seriously, you should smoke a joint with her, loosen her up."

"She's not into that shit," Desmond said.

Oh yes, she is.

"She's real worked up, about her cousin and all," Desmond said. "She says some real strange things." He shook his head, recalling them privately. "Strange."

Fine piece of ass. Just get past the used part, dumbass. "Like what?"

Desmond shrugged, unconvincingly, and changed the subject. "Say, Eddie, you ever see when gangs write their names on buildings? Like the Crew does down by Sena, on walls and places?"

"Sure," Eddie replied.

"You ever see one anywhere called 'Satan's Revenge'?"

By its own accord Eddie's jaw lowered and raised several times. "Whuhm," he said.

"'Satan's Revenge'?" Desmond repeated. "It sounds like I've heard of it. I wonder if we did work on a car they smashed up and spraypainted. I know we did two by the Crew."

Liam came in, wearing pajamas and carrying a plastic cup. "Hi, Eddie, how are you?" he said. "Guess what? I'm going to school tomorrow, but I'm not going to be at school. You know how come? You know how come, Eddie? We're going to an aquarium."

"That sounds great," Eddie said.

"Why are you here, Eddie?" Liam asked him.

Why did I come here?

"My brother died," he said.

"What?!" Desmond said.

"Kevin killed himself," Eddie said.

"I'm sorry about that," Liam said, sincerely.

"Shit, I'm sitting here bragging about getting some leg, and this happened to you?" Desmond said. "Oh, man. What happened?"

Eddie examined his fingernails. "I don't know, he took a bunch of pills," he recounted. "We're not having a wake."

"How's your family taking it?"

"They're drunk."

"I'm very sorry about that," Liam said. "My grandma died, two years ago, Eddie."

"Liam," Desmond said, "would you let me and Eddie talk alone for a while? You're supposed to be in bed, anyway."

"Listen, Liam?" Eddie said. "Do me a favor, okay? Don't tell anyone about my brother, all right? My parents don't want anyone to know."

Liam thought it over. "What about my mother?" he asked.

"Nobody," Eddie said. "Please? Not right now."

"But I'm not supposed to lie to my mother," Liam said. "Lying is always wrong."

"You don't have to lie," Desmond said. "This is respecting Eddie's family's wishes."

"But I'm not allowed to lie, ever," Liam protested.

"I'll come explain it to you later, all right?" Desmond said. "For now, just go to bed and don't say anything."

Liam did as his brother instructed him.

"Christ, I'm ready to shoot his religion teacher," Desmond said after Liam departed. "Can't run a stop sign in front of him these days."

Desmond consoled Eddie until Eddie decided he had stayed long enough. Visiting the Coogan household certainly had displaced Kevin's death as Eddie's main concern.

"Man, I should be home with my family now," Eddie said.

"Sure, yeah," Desmond said. "You want a ride?"

"No, thanks," Eddie said.

"If there's anything we can do, you know to just ask, man," Desmond said. "You just ask. You were here for us, when we had trouble. Remember that."

"That's all done with?"

Desmond nodded. "Jim Cooper called my father and they talked for an hour. My dad says Mister Cooper wants to call me and apologize. But I hope he doesn't, man, I wouldn't know what to say. Anyway, though, it was just a misunderstanding. It's over now."

"That's good to know," Eddie assured him, and went home.

❦ ❦ ❦

Death lay heavy upon the O'Kane home. The streetlight in front of the Germans' house had burned out, leaving their whole stretch of the block dark. Occasionally it would flicker a dim blue for a few seconds, then blink out again.

Eddie came in the front door. His parents sat where he had last seen them, the positions they had assumed when they came home from the hospital. His father's head hung sideways on his neck. It took his mother nearly two minutes to begin harassing Eddie.

"Edward?" she said.

"Yeah?"

"Would you please," she slurred, "carry your father up to bed?"

"Let me see what I can do," he said. The old man would offer him no help whatsoever this time. Eddie grabbed him by the shoulders. The man's head lolled.

"Too dangerous, carrying someone this drunk upstairs," he told his mother. "Let's just lay him out on the couch."

"No, then he gets a bad back and it lasts for weeks," she said.

"Maybe that'll teach him not to get shit-faced," said Eddie.

"Nice mouth," Mrs. O'Kane grumbled. "You could show your father some respect, Edward."

"If he showed himself some, sure, I could." Eddie pulled his father sideways, pushed a pillow beneath his head, and swung his limp feet onto the couch. He tugged his father's shoes off.

"Probably ought to be helping *you* on the stairs," Eddie muttered, watching his mother sway up the first few steps.

Mrs. O'Kane went to bed. While giving her time to fall asleep, Eddie checked the crawlspace under the basement stairs. His father kept paint there.

Eddie selected a half-can of outdoor maroon, a color closer to brick red than he had expected to find. Along with an old brush whose bristles had grown coarse enough that he wouldn't feel bad chucking it, Eddie carried the paint up to the front door.

He tiptoed up the stairs to peek in his mother's room. She had passed out. "Ma?" he said, from out in the hall. She did not respond.

He found the truck keys in his father's jacket, on the kitchen table, and carried the paint and brush outside. From the back of the truck Eddie snagged his father's flashlight.

The construction site kept unnerving him whenever he passed it, so he pulled out in the other direction. The truck felt even bigger to him than last time. Yet he handled it without a catch, and drove calmly up Roosevelt to the soccer field. He parked outside, and carted his supplies in through the entrance.

Some kids were hanging out on the bleachers, drinking.

"Hey, man," one of them greeted him.

"What's up?" Eddie replied.

"Do I know you, man?" the guy said.

"No," Eddie said, walking past them to the far end.

With a sycamore stick he pried the lid and stirred. Though the moon cast enough light for him to read the graffiti, he switched the flashlight on and set it on the ground behind him to shine where he had to paint.

First he covered the actual words, then he laid a thick coat to make the job look professional, or at least systematic.

"Hey, man, what are you doing?" another of the kids asked.

"Working," Eddie said.

They ventured closer.

"I work for the Parks Department," he said. "I was supposed to have this done this afternoon. I figure I'll just do this little bit and say I ran out of paint, I can do the rest tomorrow."

"Oh," somebody said. "Cool."

They ignored him after that. He ran out of paint after completely obscuring SATAN'S REVENGE and leaving only a third of the bricks exposed. He carried the empty can and the brush with him back to the truck. The teen alcoholics said nothing to him.

He began to feel vulnerable as he came out onto Roosevelt Avenue. He drove slowly, careful not to give any cop a reason to pull him over.

Again he took the longer route, deliberately avoiding the Corridor as much as possible. When Eddie paused for a stop sign before turning onto Poplar, several blocks from home, he thought he spied movement on the sidewalk, something small darting through the shadows.

He drove on, and parked in his father's spot minutes later. After checking that the truck's position matched exactly the way he had found it, Eddie climbed out, and noticed the empty paint can and brush on the passenger seat.

Goddamn it, Eddie cursed his paranoid stupidity. *I forgot to chuck the can and the brush. Where the fuck am I going to throw them here?* His parents' garbage cans wouldn't do, for Mr. O'Kane would notice and want to know where the paint had gone. *Me wasting six cents' worth of anything makes the old man shit green twinkies.*

The Germans' cans stood on the far side of their stoop. With the streetlight out, no one saw Eddie haul the can and brush over there, holding the handle out, careful not to stain his jacket.

The Germans' garbage cans had metal-spring cords that kept the lids shut tight. Only old people ever owned these, in Eddie's experience. It made opening them a hassle, and he had to press the can down hard into the Germans' trash.

When he closed the lid he glimpsed red paint on his hands. *Fuck.* To see how much he had gotten on himself, he held his hands up, letting the light from the McGowans' porch illuminate them.

The streetlight in front of Mrs. Denihans lot worked, so he walked over there. Nowhere on his jacket did he find any red, though his wrist had somehow caught the wet arc of the can's mouth.

All at once Eddie realized how close he now stood to the construction site. He felt no urge to flee. It no longer affected him. Had that repulsion been psychosomatic? On reflex he had avoided passing this place in the truck tonight.

Scratching his arm, Eddie set off for his house. As he walked he sensed that tingling anxiety the lot had provoked in him; it spread tangibly from his heart outward.

He stopped walking, and squinted.

Limping toward him down Poplar, from the direction he had just driven, Eddie saw a dog.

It sensed him and quickened its injured gait.

That's her.

The Germans' streetlight emitted a few weak blue sparks. In the brief flashes Eddie saw that this dog had no snout.

He barreled across his parents' lawn to the front door, tugging his keys from his pocket. As he reached the steps the keys pulled free of his jeans, and flew from his hand.

They landed on the lawn. Or in the garden. Somewhere.

Jabberwocky reached the edge of the O'Kane property. Eddie glimpsed part of her skull protruding from her bashed face.

The truck keys had a house key on the ring. Eddie jammed it into the lock upside-down, then had to yank it hard to pull it out and reinsert it.

A noise traveled with the dog: a snarl trapped in her crushed septum.

Eddie pushed through the front door into the foyer, and slammed the door shut. He fell back against it.

Outside, the dog's throttled cry rose in volume.

Deal with this. They mean fucking business.

Eddie entered the kitchen and grabbed a section of the Sunday paper. He twisted it into a knot on one end.

When he returned to the front door, he opened it just a crack, to peek at the dog. With her nose feeding maggots and dirt caked to her moldered hide, she was no longer Jabberwocky, at least.

Eddie closed the front door and lit his newspaper torch. Then he ran through the kitchen to the backyard. As soon as he stepped outside he sensed the dog's approach around the side of the house.

Eddie moved directly to the garden hose. It hung on a metal rung beside the tap, close to the garage.

Long before Jabberwocky came into view, Eddie had the hose raised and aimed. *I wish I'd put the light on back here before I came out.* At first sight of her he pressed the valve open.

The hard jet of water slowed the dog's hobbled advance even more, but nothing would dissuade her. Clumps of hard clay dissolved from her matted coat as Eddie blasted her. Very quickly she was soaked head to tail.

Eddie dropped the hose and charged at her with the torch.

She did not ignite.

The torch went out. Eddie swerved around the dog and raced back into the kitchen. Again he slammed the door behind him.

It didn't work. Which made sense; would they show him any magic he could imitate himself? Eddie flicked on the outside lamp. Now he could clearly see his former pet out there, accusing him blindly, gurgling as though trying to expel through her nose.

What happened to her back leg? Eddie killed the kitchen light so he could study the situation. *When I buried her, nothing had happened to her leg. Tcholowitz limped too, but having his brains hang out of his head could cause that. Something happened to that dog's leg.*

Tiny worms writhed in the water that trickled through her fur. *Could one leg decompose faster than another?* he wondered. *Maybe some kind of grub in the dirt near that leg ate through the muscle.*

Mr. O'Kane kept gasoline in the garage, in a clearly marked safety can, but to open the garage, put on the light and close the door again would take too long. Jabberwocky would get in there with him.

The dog's frustrated bray grated on Eddie, so he went inside to the living room. Mr. O'Kane had not budged upon the couch.

Eddie peeked out the rear window, to see the misshapen dog follow him to this section of the house. *She just knows.* At least he couldn't hear her too well. He could ignore her here, and think.

His father had turpentine in the crawlspace down the basement. That should light. *Or is there lighter fluid around anywhere, for the hibachi? Is it with the yard furniture?*

While Eddie wracked his mind for better suggestions, he glanced about the room. By chance he looked out the back window again.

Next to his dog stood a dead woman, arms flailing in slow motion.

The moonlight turned her leeched skin white and cast shadows into the melted hollows of her former eyes.

Lenore looked horrible. And furious.

TWELVE

"I didn't kill you!" Eddie told Lenore, in quite a loud voice, as he backed rapidly away from the window.

His father did not stir.

"I didn't kill you!" Eddie said again, lower. "A doctor killed you! Go see him, *I* didn't kill you! I went with you, your *friends* wouldn't!"

She either could not hear or did not care.

Why doesn't she break the window? She won't touch the house.

Eddie moved into the kitchen again. He reached the door and peered out. The dog rounded the corner of the house faster than Lenore did.

Her leg's fucked up, too.

The outside bulb made the sight harsher—the grave's ruin of Lenore's face, obscene stains on her cerement. Eddie wanted to turn the switch off, but the image of upright corpses circling his house in utter darkness terrified him. Once he had seen it, he couldn't ignore it.

As she stumbled, Lenore made a grinding sound. Eddie listened closely and realized it came from her throat, a scream with no mouth. Someone had sealed her lips, somehow.

She came right up to the door.

They sewed her mouth shut when they buried her.

For some reason that thought turned Eddie's stomach. He staggered away from the door, keeping his eyes on Lenore— on *Lenore's dead body; that's not Lenore, remember that's not Lenore*—until he reached the door to the basement stairs.

He turned on the lights and went down. Immediately he heard Jabberwocky scratching the screens outside the windows over his stereo. Even without seeing them, he could not stand knowing his two visitors were right outside the window.

His father's workshop had no windows. Eddie closed the door behind him and sat on the paint-spattered stool.

On the workbench his father kept an old radio that had once belonged in the kitchen. Eddie switched it on. All he could tune in besides white noise was a religious program, so he turned it off.

Sitting still, frantic, Eddie became aware of the chill sweat dammed at his hairline. Follicles on his arms relaxed and lay flat. His heartbeat gradually retarded to normal.

Not his hearing, though. That tiny whistle had continued all day, since he woke up, same as yesterday. Music or conversation or even just traffic or the wind would drown it out. But here in the silent shop, Eddie could hear it fine.

As he paid attention to the whistle, it grew louder, too loud to call a mere ringing. A whine, that was the word for it. This whine had lurked in his head for days now.

Since they burned Tcholowitz.

It had never left Eddie's ears, that phlegmy heaving that had hounded him around northern Queens Saturday.

"I'll lose my mind." He spoke just to hear himself.

Fuck this dungeon. Eddie opened the door agam and walked briskly to the stairs. As he passed the window where his pursuers waited, gooseflesh rose on his arms.

Eddie climbed the stairs all the way up to his bedroom. He put a classical station on his clock radio, with the sleep lever depressed.

Wisely, he chose not to peek down even once at the specters below in the yard. Instead he tugged the shades over both windows and lay on his bed, in the dark, trying to recall the last time he had smoked pot. He did not feel the desire, either.

A symphony kept him from listening to anything else. Fatigue set in. He slept in his clothes.

❦ ❦ ❦

Just before noon Eddie woke. For several minutes he stayed in bed, eyes closed, mercifully unaware of the previous night, the previous day, the night before that and so on.

He turned the radio on. Organ music.

Sometime later Eddie's parents arrived home with such an eerie calm that at first Eddie mistook them for burglars. He had to strain his ears to hear them. They barely chided one another. A stranger would doubt they had ever argued.

So subdued were they that Eddie clearly heard the tinkle of ice cubes landing in glasses, and commented to himself, *There, that'll fix everything.*

His mother padded up the stairs, her stride steady, sober.

"Edward?" she called softly.

"Yeah?"

She pushed the door open and said, "I tried to wake you this morning, do you remember? You've been sleeping in your clothes."

He shook his head.

"We buried Kevin," she said.

Stretching, Eddie rubbed his eyes.

"I'm not putting an obituary in the *Daily News,* and they won't announce it at church," Mrs. O'Kane told him. "So no one should be asking you about it. But if they do, let's keep this a family matter."

Ears still ringing.

"By that I mean, prefer not to talk about it," she went on. "If someone asks you about your brother, say that: You prefer not to discuss it. They should respect that."

"We talked about this already, Ma," Eddie reminded her.

She nodded as if mildly insulted, and after a moment concluded, "Well, we buried Kevin today. I thought you would want to know."

She left. Eddie did not object.

Buried with no wake.

Suddenly he recalled why he had drawn the shades, what he had wanted to ignore out there. Already today his parents had opened and closed the front door, at least twice. Could Lenore or the dog slip past them and come inside?

He sat upright, filled with panic. By the time he had risen to his feet, however, the urgency had subsided. Of course Lenore wasn't in the house.

More than that, he found the very idea of these ghosts silly. Autohypnosis played a great role in all magic, after all. The

Good People—*God, are* they *even real?*—the Good People had to understand psychology pretty well, and should know what demons would torment him most.

Eddie jerked the bottom of the shade so that it raised, letting the sunless day fill his room. First he stared at the Corridor to the west. Then he looked down into his own yard.

Lenore was no mirage. Neither was the dog.

They stood patiently watching him, the way he knew they had all night. The daylight showed Lenore's features plainly, especially the fetid dough that filled her sockets.

He pulled the shade down again, and walked downstairs.

It proved impossible to eat breakfast anywhere on the ground floor without their watching him through a window. After moving three times Eddie brought his bowl of soggy Lucky Charms upstairs to his room.

Once again, as he sat down shielded from his pursuers, Eddie felt his pulse slow and his flaring nerves relax. Exposed to Lenore or Jabberwocky, his body recoiled on the cellular level, not just with nausea.

After he ate, Eddie listened to a Beethoven piano sonata and decided he would not leave the house until he killed the two creatures outside. By the time the piece concluded and the disc jockey spoke, Eddie still had no further plan.

He trotted down one flight of stairs and then the other, down to the basement. A crappy couch with large pink cushions had dominated one wall of the cellar for as long as Eddie could recall. He seized two seat cushions right away and pressed them into the window well above his stereo.

It worked. By blocking every window in the basement he could ignore them. He converted the place into a bunker, then swept the floor while blasting dinosaur rock albums.

His mother came down here to do laundry once a week, if that often. His father mostly used the workshop to store parts from work, rather than waste valuable booze time building birdhouses and the like.

So Eddie had his fort to himself. Here he could figure out how to rid himself of his problems, or else wait them out. The sudden security made him giddy. He turned the stereo up, sang along.

That made the ringing rise in his ears.

Tcholowitz's voice, the last cry of his soul as he perished in flame, hummed in Eddie's skull loud enough to detect over Deep Purple. It made thinking difficult.

And Eddie badly needed to think. To start with, why was Lenore here? Sure, he had killed the dog, fair enough. But Lenore's death had *hurt* him. He hadn't killed her by any stretch of the word, except...

Except that she hadn't died the first time.

This reason ultimately made sense to Eddie, though not enough to explain why her decrepit remains would trail his every step until he dispatched them. Honestly, he had meant Lenore no harm. Perhaps he had used her, but he had not killed her, even through negligence.

Not that I'm not a murderer, anyway. He dropped his face behind his cupped hands. The record ended, and the arm carried the needle back to the beginning.

"Do you want dinner, Edward?" his mother offered from the top of the stairs. "I'm cooking hot dogs."

"Sure," he said. "Please." He climbed the stairs to the kitchen.

It had still been daylight when Eddie sealed off the basement, and it surprised him to see the darkness out the back door.

His mother had set the kitchen table. "How many hot dogs you want?" she asked.

Lenore appeared at the door, wailing at him around her bound lips.

"I don't know," Eddie said, instantly unable to imagine eating. "What do I usually eat? Two?"

"Two or three, usually." She looked at him. "What's the matter?"

Outside Lenore clawed the air angrily. *She wants to rip me up.*

"What's the matter with you?" Mrs. O'Kane asked again.

"Nothing," he said.

Lenore moved closer to the door. Very clumsily she began to strip off her burial clothes.

"What are you staring at?" Mrs. O'Kane wanted to know.

"I've got a headache," Eddie said. It was no lie, either. "Cut me some slack, all right? My brother's dead." *I didn't even get to see him buried.* He didn't say that, though.

"What, are *you* cracking up, now?" his mother asked him.

"You don't think my brother dying is something to make me depressed, a little?"

"Oh, 'depressed,'" she sighed. "You people today with this 'depressed' nonsense, you don't even know what it's like to have something to be depressed about."

"I don't feel good," he said simply.

"You still want to eat?"

He nodded. "Let me take it downstairs with me."

"Oh, no, I'm not running a cafeteria here. I'm not a cook in a bunkhouse," she said.

No bunkhouse would have you. "I know that," he said. "I just don't feel too good." It amazed him he could lie so calmly with Lenore glaring at him, with his every hair a nail sticking straight out from his skin.

"And did you lose your house keys, sport?" she asked.

"No," he said.

"You must have," she said. "I found a set out on the front lawn."

"Wait, yeah, those are mine."

"You left them there on purpose?"

Eddie paused. "No," he said. "Of course not."

"Then how did you know where they were?"

"I just guessed," Eddie said.

"Have you been smoking pot, Eddie?" she asked.

"No," Eddie said. *Not today.*

In the living room his father sat on the sofa, eyes locked on one part of the wall, swilling his drink. Eddie said, "Dad?" once, to no response. Then his dinner was ready.

She gave him three hot dogs. He poured mustard on them, carefully ignoring the back door, and brought them down to his command post. As soon as he calmed himself his appetite returned. The three hot dogs disappeared.

The couch had sacrificed all its cushions to fortify the windows, so Eddie couldn't lie down. He leaned back in the broken recliner, with Yes on the turntable. By annoying him, his mother had distracted him from the ringing in his ears, which had thereafter dropped in volume.

I can pour flammable liquid on them from the upstairs windows, and try igniting them that way.

I could trap them in the garage.

I could let them chase me into the back of the old man's truck, then lock them in there and drive the truck somewhere. Leave it under a lake or something. A reservoir.

It came to him as he sat brooding exactly why he found the logic behind Lenore's return so disturbing: It implied that something held him responsible for anyone who died earlier than they would have since his deal.

Not just people who died by Eddie's hand—anyone who walked in front of a truck but hadn't done it last time, anyone who ODed or caught a stray bullet, anyone who—

Eddie sat bolt upright, palpitating.

They'll send Kevin.

♉ ♉ ♉

Later that night, after Eddie slipped up to his room and smoked a joint out his window, when his father had gone to bed and his mother passed out in front of the television, the real contest began.

Back down the basement, he put his Traffic 8-track on. During the sax solo on "Low Spark" there emerged a feedback he'd never noticed on the song. It had a different reverb than the rest of the instruments, and climbed in volume gradually.

It went off-pitch. Eddie turned the volume down. The sound was not coming from the recording.

Eddie turned his stereo off altogether. It could not mask this noise, anyway, which reminded him of a siren.

The cellar felt too empty without music. Eddie turned off the lights and went up to his room.

As soon as he reached ground level he heard that siren much more clearly. It filled the sky outside. The pillows in the windows downstairs had muffled it.

He got up to his room and flipped on his clock-radio. No use.

Eddie miraculously managed to read a magazine for a short while, by letting the noise lull him. The hum seemed to him more and more similar to a human voice.

But relaxing to the monotony triggered the other sound: Tcholowitz's breathing.

Which suggested one possible source of this newer hum.

"Jesus Christ," Eddie swore, rising from his bed. At the windowsill he inched one storm window high enough that he could thrust his whole upper body outside. Below, Lenore and Jabberwocky flocked dutifully to his latest appearance.

The cry hung in a cloud of sound over Queens, over the world as far as he could see, yet he could tell at once the point from which it issued.

They had opened the bleachers again. What he heard was Marypat cursing his name at the pitch of her lungs.

All day Eddie had braved awful straits, and he had accepted the challenge to best the corpses roaming his parents' yard even if that meant hiding in this house until they decomposed. And he had further braced himself to endure even the advent of his brother's appearance among them.

For all that, he had not anticipated Marypat's scream.

So he fought it. He blasted the radio, took cotton from the bathroom to plug his ears. Neither ploy helped. Marypat's voice rose above even Foghat, while earplugs only succeeded in amplifying Tcholowitz's constant rasp inside Eddie' s head.

Compared to these two, Lenore's guttural grind and his dog's bray sounded soft, musical. Marypat's howl, especially, took on the properties of noxious gas seeping through the windows and doors to inflate Eddie's room. Second upon second the air pressure increased. Marypat's scream smothered him.

The roof will shoot off the fucking house. The windows will burst.

Eddie squeezed a pillow around his head again. Tcholowitz's tone had become a hiss. Perhaps it would weaken, given time. Months.

Why am I still here? Eddie asked himself. *Give the fuck in.*

Very deliberately he slowed his respiration, hoping to force his body out of panic. Instead, he began gasping. His lungs felt crushed.

Keep thinking loud, keep the sound out, he told himself. *Keep the sound out keep the sound out keep the sound out keep it out keep it out not really here, I am dying somewhere, medical ward on Rikers they have a hospital floor in Central Booking Queens or I'm lying in the woods somewhere, in the Corridor I'm lying there imagining fucking leprechauns and dead people and all this shit, thirtyone years I live and now I die with dirt in my face dreaming about shit I heard when I was four fits I should die in the Corridor I live in California how many years and I go like the elephants, I die like the elephants, I go back to the place where no one will find me, keep it out a body in the Corridor might lay there for years no the kids therell be kids all over me, kids find a body they freak out and nowadays kids are warped, wait is it nowadays no its yeah it is, its not the seventies really its not really, REO Speedwagon is not the next big thing and I have not killed Marypat Cooper, nothing in me ever in my whole life could make me kill her no matter how bad she hurt me, nothing even if I didnt see her for, what? keep it out keep it out thirteen fourteen years Im dying I know I could never hurt her twist her head around I dont care she fucked Desmond, keep it out theres an answer Im just going to find it, keep it out keep it out keep its just too much theyre playing inside my head there cant really be dead people outside they make me see things and hear things smell things they can do this thats how magic works is people believe in it, keep it out keep it OUT how LONG can they KEEP this shit UP IM SWEATING I CAN SMELL HER FUCKING VOICE IN HERE FUCK IT GO IM DRIVING THERE IM GOING*

❦ ❦ ❦

Eddie still had his father's truck keys in his jacket pocket. The old man hadn't needed them yet, or hadn't said so. After his guests arrived last night Eddie had left his jacket on a chair in the kitchen. It had not moved.

Eddie stormed into the kitchen and put his jacket on with barely a nod at Lenore in the yard. He took out his father's truck keys and selected the key that would unlock the driver's door.

Then he charged across the kitchen and out the front door toward the truck.

The air rushed into his ears as he ran. He hadn't noticed this wind while he hung out the window upstairs. It hurled a garbage can lid at him as he reached the blacktop. And the very air smelled foul, but everything reeked to Eddie now, everything.

He opened the door to the truck just as he heard Jabberwocky's claws behind him clicking steadily on the walkway from the yard. He leaped into the truck and pulled the door shut. He probably didn't need to lock it, but he pushed the button down automatically.

A light went on in his parents' bedroom window.

Oh fuck. He leaned across the seat onto the passenger side, glad that the Germans' streetlamp had burned out.

Up in the window, the shade raised at one corner. Or did it? Eddie held still, and heard the voices build in his head once more. *Keep it out keep it out keep*

Lenore appeared outside the truck.

She's naked.

Lenore had tugged off her cerement. Eddie had not noticed her exposed breasts in the corner of his eye as he left the kitchen, because her torso no longer resembled human flesh so much as mulberry clay.

We used to make love. In his mind Eddie saw her riding him on the bleachers the first time they met.

When he looked upward again, the bedroom window had dimmed. His father must have switched on a reading lamp.

Eddie turned the key in the ignition, not looking at the house. It didn't matter if they knew. Either way, he had to take this truck.

When he pulled away, he thought about driving slowly, leading his pursuers into a quarry or a vault. *Fuck it, no, the soccer field.* He drove directly to Colden Street and parked in front of one of the Korean houses where the dogs never shut up.

Over the Farm itself, Marypat's wail hung dense with tremolo. The sound floated over the treetops, cascaded onto the crops.

He crossed the Farm to the horse trail swiftly, and reached his destination soon. The storm fence, the foliage—it all vibrated to the cadence of the slain virgin's rage.

It grew worse when he entered through the fence. Here, out on the mown grass of the playing field, Marypat's wrath made the earth itself rumble. As he approached the bleachers, Eddie lurched with nausea at the smell, yet kept his eyes on the far wall, watching for the little culprits.

No one awaited him.

His sleeves rippled from the power as he arrived at the source of the scream: a hole the size of one missing brick. That brick lay at his feet. Eddie picked it up and slid it into its slot.

She stopped. The vibrations ceased with her, and the stench.

Crickets sounded abnormally loud. Eddie stood holding the brick in place, glancing about for company. None showed. He took his hand away from the wall, and the brick did not wriggle out. She could not push from in there.

What have I done?

It was no time for such a question. As they had Saturday night, the masons had drilled a small trench out around the brick. No one was here to mend the wall properly.

Eddie crossed the field again, and took the horse trail until he reached ash trees. As though he did so every day, he entered the grove casually, confident. With Marypat shut up, not much could ruffle him. The clearing would appear before him presently, he knew.

To either side of his path the woods quickly became weird, limbs bent and malformed. Unimpressed, he continued at his own pace.

The fire flashed its blue smoke. Eddie's throat felt the familiar tickle.

"Smart man, Eddie O'Kane," Brayson greeted him. "Very smart."

"Got a smart mouth, too," added Gareth, gaze trained upon the fire.

"Okay, I'm back," Eddie said. "I changed my mind. I'll kill Manchesi."

Brayson accepted this news without reaction, and lit his pipe. Gareth rubbed his nose with his good hand. The others milling about seemed indifferent to Eddie. The fire, that's what they watched.

"How do I make the sound in my ears stop?" he asked Brayson.

"Which sound ye mean?"

Eddie swallowed. "Tcholowitz's voice. I can hear him. It was louder until..." Eddie changed his mind and said, "It was loud until a few minutes ago."

"Very faint, is it?" Brayson nodded.

"Yes," Eddie said.

"Get used to it."

For several seconds Eddie stared at his smaller companions, then at the flames, which danced with too much symmetry to be natural. Tiny pictures flickered between them.

"All done throwing fits, are ye?" Brayson asked him, exhaling smoke from one side of his mouth.

"Yes," Eddie said.

"That's good."

"Someone knows about us," he said.

Every eye in the dark glade blinked up at him.

"This girl saw me kill Marypat in her dream," he said. "She's psychic. I think she knows my whole situation."

"What makes ye think that?" Gareth asked.

"Just a feeling I get."

"Don't try and evade the point," Brayson scolded him. "Ye have to understand: We tell ye what to do and when to do it. Won't have any more horseshit about that."

"Okay, agreed," Eddie said.

"No, not 'agreed,' Eddie," Brayson said. "If ye agree it means ye have a say in the matter, and ye do not. That's what we're to make ye understand. Mind how ye talk to me."

Eddie answered with a nod this time.

"He's telling ye the truth," Gareth said to Brayson. Eddie detected a wisp of alarm in the tiny man's tone.

And then, in the fire, Eddie clearly saw Eileen talking to Desmond. They were both naked, in her bedroom. If Eddie moved closer to the hearthside he could make out what she said.

"Woman's got the Sight," Gareth fretted, scratching one tooth with his thumb.

That's why he's always staring in the fire. They see things there.

The Good People paid careful attention to what Eileen told Desmond. For the first time in this place Eddie could study his surroundings. His eyes adapted to the peculiar light, and the ceiling began to appear woven of tree branches.

Behind him, the path he had traveled to reach here resembled a hallway through deep forest. A white mist floated there, aglow with a glimmer from the outside world.

"Don't give the Devil ideas," Brayson told Gareth calmly. "If it turns into a problem we deal with it. Not likely they'll believe anything she says about us."

"After all," someone else agreed.

"I have to know," Eddie interrupted, "is someone going to patch up that wall where you knocked the bricks out?"

"If we get around to it," Gareth said.

"I'm just asking, should I patch the bleachers myself?"

For an answer Brayson spat, and replaced the pipe in his mouth. He regarded Eddie with a placid but adversarial air.

Nervousness began to spread throughout Eddie's body, physically, making his spine twitch. Steadily the feeling grew worse, until he recognized it: his physical fear of the dead.

Lenore and Jabberwocky were coming down the path behind him, through the snowy fog.

Brayson exhaled a large lungful of flowery smoke, and asked, "Eddie, ye have such a fine memory, haven't ye?"

Eddie shrugged, barely.

"Let me ask ye," Brayson went on, "what did I say would happen the next time ye came to us in this position?"

Next time ye have to beg us for help, ye kiss a "You never said anything about it," Eddie replied.

"Ho!" Brayson chortled, as did several around the fire. "Fine riposte, that, Eddie," he said, with less mirth.

Jabberwocky arrived first. Eddie told himself not to flinch, that they couldn't let the things touch him. But then the dog lunged toward him and he dodged it.

They took amusement, the Good People did, in the spectacle of Eddie O'Kane hopping away from his dead pet. When at last they reined the dog in with one of those magic horseshoes, Eddie looked up and discovered Lenore had reached the glade.

Someone held her fettered, as well, though he could not tell who that was. But she stayed in place, brimming with hatred for him. He stepped closer, and she moved not one muscle toward him.

"What d'ye know?" someone said behind Eddie. "Eddie's been kind enough to bathe his dog, here. Sprayed her with a hose, ye did."

The makeup on Lenore's face no longer matched her complexion. It stood out, as though someone had sprayed rank meat with peach-colored powder.

Brayson cleared his throat and spoke: "Now, Eddie, I'm going to ask ye again—"

With no prompting, Eddie seized Lenore by her hair and kissed her full on the cheek. The contact with his lips made his guts reel.

The Good People stood before him, aghast.

"That's what I had to do, right?" Eddie said, and gagged a little, feeling that rancid powder on his lips.

Slowly, almost respectfully, Brayson nodded.

"That was revolting," Gareth commented flatly. "Put me off m'food, if I ate food."

"I've done far more revolting things," Eddie said.

THIRTEEN

Eddie backed the truck into the driveway at a little past one, and turned the radio off. He had put it on solely to drown out that whine in his ears, that minute incessant burr, now three voices strong since the Good People torched Lenore and Jabberwocky.

Not a single light shone from any window of the O'Kane house. Eddie climbed out of the truck, apprehensive for no sane reason; anything he should behold in terror lay behind him for the night.

The air had become brisk, or perhaps he had fled the house in such terror that he hadn't noticed the temperature. The chill preyed easily upon his exhausted bones. His shivering made it difficult to unlock the door.

His mother had left the living room. Eddie took his jacket off and dropped it on the couch, unable to recall the last time he had seen his family's television off.

Then he smelled something foul. The fresh air had revived his olfactory nerve, so his nose awoke to a sickly yet familiar whiff of necrotic perfume. What he smelled was Lenore's grave.

Eddie spun on his heels, checking for her. She was not present.

He entered the bathroom and flipped on the light. In the mirror he saw a smear of undertaker's pancake makeup painting his cheek.

His hands stunk, too. Soap alone would not clean his face or fingers; the powder had taken on an oily character, thick with debased matter from Lenore's skin. Eddie scrubbed for half an hour, and threw two washcloths in the kitchen trash when he finished.

When he returned to the living room, his jacket too reeked of Lenore's casket, on the sleeve that had rubbed against her back while he kissed her. The couch smelled where his jacket had lain.

She was real, Eddie told himself solemnly. *Only I can see them, but they're real.*

He spot-washed the couch with Lysol. The odor prevailed. He removed everything from his pockets, and brought his jacket downstairs to the washing machine before going to bed.

❦ ❦ ❦

His mother woke him at ten the next morning.

"Your school called. They want to know why you haven't been there," she said.

Eddie rubbed his eyes. "So what did you tell them?"

"That you would be in later this afternoon."

"No, I won't," he said.

"Oh, yes, Edward. You're not taking advantage of our grief and playing hooky," she warned him.

"Call a truant officer," he said, and rolled over, back to sleep.

Later he woke up on his own. His father had gone to work. Eddie couldn't blame the man. His mother sat in the living room, half-paying scant attention to an old movie on TV.

"You're going to school tomorrow," she informed him.

"Can't wait," he said.

After breakfast Eddie searched the kitchen for his jacket. On his way to check the living room, he remembered putting it downstairs on top of the washing machine. He remembered why.

Instead of going down the basement, he returned to his bedroom and put on a heavy gray sweater.

Downstairs as he opened the front door, his mother asked, "Why does the couch smell like disinfectant?"

"I don't know," Eddie said, and left.

Outside he watched workers unload a van full of ceiling fixtures for the Manchesi buildings. Again he memorized the phone number from the contractor's placard, since he had no pen on him.

Eddie meandered toward nowhere in particular, over the less-traveled streets of the neighborhood. While passing a hardware store he saw two clerks, one clutching his own bleeding hand, dash out to a car and speed away. Outside a laundromat a woman dropped her clean clothes on the sidewalk and berated her two infant sons for causing her to do so.

The candy store on Negundo had in its front windows a huge blowup of Marypat's graduation picture. HAVE YOU SEEN MARYPAT COOPER?, the poster asked.

Almost by their own choice, Eddie's eyes dropped to the ground, to the gutter. As he walked away he studied the mulch that lined the curb, all leaves and pollynoses, and seed pods.

Seed pods. *The Good People eat seed pods. Those things stank worse than garlic. Where did I recognize those pods from?*

For some minutes Eddie loitered on a corner down the block from the candy store, straining to recall. Eventually it came to him.

He got to the Farm in fifteen minutes. He expected to find the place packed with Koreans tending their plots, but only a handful were present. No one paid any mind as Eddie steered a path toward the curing shack. He crossed one row behind that woman with the red coat, who knelt with a trowel in her hand. She did not see him.

From twenty feet away, Eddie knew the shack lay full of those pods. At the doorway the aroma nearly overpowered him. It did not remind him of any other plant.

Eddie snatched one pod off a bowed card table. Whoever owned this shack had placed this table inside here to increase the surface area for laying produce. By itself the pod didn't smell at all; the Good People had to crack them open before the scent arose. Quite a few pods must have broken in storage, though, for the shack reeked.

He walked over to the woman in the red coat. "Hi," he said.

"Oh, hi," she answered, smiling, turning.

"What's this?" he asked, holding up the pod.

"Not mine," she said.

"I know, but what is it?"

She looked at it. "I don't know in English, sorry," she said.

"Who grows it?" Eddie asked.

Now she got to her feet, and examined the pod more closely. "I don't know," she said. "Sorry."

"Whose shack is that?" he asked, pointing. "Who built that?"

The woman wore the expression of one struggling to sound diplomatic. "Not here," she said, and smiled.

"Thank you," Eddie said.

She nodded, and knelt again. Eddie returned to the shack, and checked all the adjacent plots. Somebody had to grow the things.

"Sir?" the woman called.

Eddie turned.

"There!" she said, pointing outside the Farm, over the fence, at a Korean man with white hair carting groceries down Colden Street. "That him."

Eddie thanked her and took off, the pod still clutched in one hand. The old man stepped out onto the street and turned to the right before Eddie arrived on the asphalt behind him.

"Sir?" Eddie asked.

The man turned.

"Hi," Eddie said. "Did you grow this?"

The man looked at Eddie's pod and nodded, smiled.

"What is it?" Eddie asked.

This question the man did not comprehend. A small boy passed them, whom Eddie asked, "Do you speak English?"

"Yeah," the boy said, without an accent.

Gesturing politely toward the old man, Eddie said, "Ask him for me what this thing is."

"That's a yimcha," the boy answered.

"What do you call it in English?"

The boy thought hard, then grinned and shook his head.

"How do you eat it?" Eddie asked.

"You don't eat them. You break them and rub them on your chairs in your house, and your dog won't go on the chair, then," the boy said. "I think cats, too."

The old man said something to the boy.

"He says you can use them in soup, but you don't eat them," the boy explained to Eddie. "They use them across the street to keep the rabbits off the farm, he says."

Eddie said, "Ask him why he grows so much of it."

The boy and the old man conversed for half a minute. The boy laughed a little.

"He leaves them for the, uhm," the boy interrupted himself, trying to translate. "I don't know what you call it, they're like little people?"

Slowly Eddie suggested, "The Good People?"

The boy frowned. "I don't know, they're little and they live in the woods, and if you grow the yimcha for them they won't wreck your farm. They say it was their farm first. It's like Halloween. In Korea kids go out and steal stuff from people's gardens, and make believe that the little people did it."

"These little people, though, they're Irish?"

"No, they're not even people, they're really small."

"But they talk like they're Irish, though."

"No. They talk Korean. But old Korean," the boy said. "They speak..." He paused again. "What do you call your family when they're dead?"

Eddie considered it. "Ancestors."

"Yeah! They speak the same way our ancestors did," he said. "And if you're bad they do stuff to you."

"Ask him if he knows anything about them," Eddie said.

The boy blinked twice. "It's just a story," he said.

"Ask him," Eddie insisted.

The boy did, and the old man smiled at Eddie.

"He says if you want to hear about them, you can talk to him with his daughter there," the boy told Eddie. "At his house. She speaks English."

Eddie nodded and smiled at the old man. They walked onward. The boy walked with them. Dogs barked.

"Why do you care about Korean stuff?" the boy asked Eddie.

"Oh, I don't know," Eddie said. "Just find it interesting. You like these things?" He held up the pod.

"I think I ate the soup. But you hardly taste them."

"They smell so strong, though," Eddie said.

"No, they don't," the boy said. "They don't smell at all." To prove his point he picked the pod from Eddie's grip and held it under his own nose. "See? It doesn't smell."

They had reached the old man's house, which had a storm fence around it. In the yard a German shepherd rose to its feet and began barking.

"Here," Eddie said, snapping the pod into two splintered pieces. Instantly that fragrance attacked his nose. "Now smell it."

The boy sniffed, loudly, and shrugged. "Doesn't smell."

To bring the pod directly beneath his own nose would make Eddie's eyes water. "You don't smell that," he said, incredulous.

The boy shook his head.

Suddenly the old man spoke sharply to the child, who replied in Korean and then looked from the old man to Eddie and back again without speaking.

"What did he say?" Eddie asked.

The child would not answer, and left, hastily.

The old man unlocked his fence, entered his yard, and relocked the gate. From the man's expression alone, Eddie knew he was no longer welcome to follow.

Behind the fence the dog advanced, snapping, baring its teeth. The old man continued into his house without looking at Eddie once.

Eddie dropped the pod on the sidewalk and marched back down Colden Street, accompanied by a chorus of howls. Every house down here had a dog, and every dog screamed for Eddie's blood.

In the few minutes since Eddie had left it, the Farm had acquired half a dozen new farmers. One played Korean music on a tape player. Three men stood chatting near the toppled refrigerator, holding cups of coffee. Atop the fridge sat a thermos.

The trio stopped talking when they noticed Eddie. He pretended he hadn't been watching them and headed away from them, down a narrow aisle between rows of plots.

Nervous energy sent him right to the very limit of the property, to the hump-shaped land wall. On the other side lay the horse trail. He did not climb the mound, but studied the pods growing upon it. *They plant them here to keep the rabbits away. The old man must just pick them and dry them in his shack.*

As a cloud dimmed the sun, Eddie surveyed the ash trees along the Farm's western border. To judge by the distance from the water tap, the grove appeared wider still than before.

In the brightest light of day, these trees stayed dark. No sun whatever leaked down onto their soil. Eddie had never seen another forest where the trees angled themselves this way, concealing the copse's heart.

Do they all know about this? Eddie peeked sidelong at several people tending their ground. *Do all the Koreans in Queensborough Heights know the Good People live in the ash trees? Did the Good People always live here, until the city cleared this strip for the Farm?*

Before he left, Eddie wanted another pod so he could identify it. He took the path past the woman in the red coat. She waved at him as he returned to the shack.

The shack sat empty. Not a single pod remained.

Eddie leaned back from the doorway, checked in all directions. Nobody could have unloaded the old man's shack into a wheelbarrow and left. The other farmers would have stopped them.

Ducking his head, he stepped all the way inside the shack. The spraycan in the corner was the one they had used on Marc Tcholowitz, Eddie was sure of it. He crouched to look at the drain on the floor, which was just a metal grate over a hole.

With both hands he lifted that small grate, and could see far down into the dry earth, could see that this was not a drain at all but an underground passage.

❦ ❦ ❦

Clifford Manchesi's office in Maspeth faced out onto Grand Avenue. None of the four people inside—Manchesi himself and three women—noticed Eddie peeking furtively in the front windows as he passed by several times.

Finally Eddie walked around the block. In the parking lot behind Manchesi's building stood an Olds 88 and a Dodge Dart. Eddie did not know which car belonged to Manchesi.

At the end of the block this street fed diagonally into the service road for the Expressway. The parking lot connected with the street via a ramp driveway. To the left this ramp bordered the bus stop where Eddie had arrived not twenty minutes ago. The bus stop would provide his excuse to wait there for Manchesi to drive out.

The sun would not set for some time yet. Eddie had at least an hour to wait before anyone left the office, and it made no sense to risk having someone see him loiter at the scene of the crime.

He returned to Grand Avenue, and took a right. He traveled at least ten blocks before he came to Krista's Polish Diner. Food sounded good to him, but as he entered the diner he remembered that he had only four dollars and some change.

"Table for one?" the waitress asked.

"Can I have a table if I just drink coffee?"

"Sure," she said.

She sat him next to a window, through which he watched the sky darken. The diner wasn't crowded. Eddie spotted a clock over the counter. It said four-thirty-eight.

He began to relax in an oddly sinister way. Kevin's pistol, tucked safely inside his inner jacket pocket, made him powerful. Only because it might make him stick out in her mind, Eddie squelched the urge to flirt with the waitress when she brought him coffee.

"Need anything else?" she asked.

"No, thank you," he replied. She smiled at him.

Eddie drank two refills, and at twenty after five rose from his table to pay his check at the front. As he opened the door, the waitress said, "Thanks!"

"Thank you," he said. *She'll remember me now.* "Listen, how do I get to the Knights of Columbus hall?"

She gave him careful directions. He made her repeat them twice, so she would definitely recall sending him there if anyone asked about him. Then he thanked her again and left.

If night had not completely fallen on Maspeth when Eddie stepped from the diner, it had long done so by the time he reached Manchesi's office again. The lights inside were lower now, yet they shone brighter in the darkness. Only two people remained working: Clifford Manchesi and a woman entering figures from a ledger into an adding machine.

Eddie rounded the block. Whoever owned the Dart had left.

What if he gives his accountant a ride home?

He leaned against the bus-stop sign, spat on the ground, stared at the lights on the Expressway. *Fuck it. I'll come back tomorrow, or the next day. Those little fucks can wait until I get him alone.* He put on his gloves.

Behind him Manchesi's back door opened. Eddie glanced over his shoulder too late to see who had climbed into the Olds, but the driver was alone. For a minute the car idled, warming up, before it pulled from its spot and headed for the driveway.

Thirty feet away he saw the ledger woman at the wheel. When she passed he turned his head, as if scanning the horizon for the bus, so she could not see his face. She drove away. He checked again: Manchesi was not in the car with her.

Two people came from the next block, carrying books, speaking softly to each other. Eddie avoided meeting their gaze until they came so close that he realized both men were retarded. They passed quietly.

How the fuck does Manchesi get home? Eddie wondered. *I'm not leaving here by public transit.*

After making sure no one saw him, Eddie made his way down the driveway and across the lot, to the back door. From outside he saw no one in the office. He pulled the door open and slipped inside.

Clifford Manchesi sat at his desk, sorting a sheaf of papers. His teased haircut reminded Eddie of the father on *The Brady Bunch*.

"Yes?" Mrs. Manchesi said. "Can I help you?"

Her voice jolted Eddie. He had not seen her enter.

Now she and her husband both stared at Eddie, waiting to hear him explain his presence.

"Can I use the phone?" he said. "I mean, or—can you call me an ambulance?"

"What's the matter?" Mrs. Manchesi asked.

"Somebody got hit by a car outside," Eddie said, slipping into his lie effortlessly. "I'm sorry to bother you, but you're the nearest building with lights on. I found the guy out there. He looks pretty bad."

Mrs. Manchesi rushed to the back door. "Where is he?" she asked as she stepped out.

"Turn right at the sidewalk," Eddie called after her.

"He's not on my property, is he? The parking lot?" Clifford Manchesi asked, picking up the phone.

Don't worry, scumbag. Eddie shook his head.

Manchesi turned toward the phone and dialed 911. Eddie came up behind him and from his pocket pulled out Kevin's gun.

"Hello? I've got an emergency," Manchesi said. "We need an ambulance on Grand Avenue and—I'm sorry, not Grand Avenue, it's—"

From six inches away Eddie fired directly into the back of Clifford Manchesi's skull. The bullet exited through Manchesi's forehead and sank into the wall. All at once the cheap beige paneling wore a scarlet supernova.

Manchesi landed face-first on his desktop with a loud thud. The black-and-white calendar on the desk blotter instantly became black-and-red.

From the receiver in Manchesi's hand the operator's voice buzzed, insectile yet audible: "Sir?... Sir?... Hello? Sir?"

Meticulously avoiding any contact with his victim, Eddie reached forward to press down the cradle and break the connection. The handset broadcast a click and then a dial tone. Eddie nearly grabbed the phone to hang it up, but stopped himself.

A set of keys lay on the desk beside Manchesi. His wife's blue sedan, which Eddie had seen parked in Mrs. Denihan's driveway every day for years, was parked out front. *She's picking him up on her way home. Do they have only one car?* Eddie picked up the key ring, a plastic bull's head with TAURUS embossed across it.

The back door opened.

"You know what?" Mrs. Manchesi said, without breaking stride. "I should bring my bag, I have PhisoDerm."

As she picked up her pocketbook she glanced at Eddie and her husband's corpse. She paused.

"Cliff?"

Eddie raised the gun and fired at her face.

The bullet hit the wall behind her. She took off. A scream bounced from her lungs, rising in pitch as she ran out the back door into the parking lot.

Eddie's first impulse told him to stay right on her heel, as if he should tackle her. Outside he sprinted to catch up. Then, as he closed in on her near the driveway, he stopped and raised the pistol.

This time he did not repeat his mistake of aiming for her head. He nailed her in the back, and then fired a second round, which dropped her to the asphalt.

Calmly Eddie approached her.

"Don't kill me!" she gasped.

He trained the gun on the back of her head.

"Don't! Don't!" Her voice sounded wet. She choked as blood filled her throat.

"Wh—wh—" She could not speak.

"Are you asking why?" Eddie said. "Is that what you're trying to say, why?"

She moved her head up and down, still gagging.

"Because you and your husband take over old widows' estates, and destroy people's families." It sounded hollow, even to Eddie. *The truth is she's dying just because she's here.*

"Nm," she gurgled.

"I know just what you and Cliff are doing in Queensborough Heights," Eddie told her. "He's going to fill those buildings up with people out of the projects, and scare everyone into selling cheap. I know all about it. It's not going to happen. You shouldn't have gotten greedy with somebody else's neighborhood."

She could no longer hear him.

"That's why," he said, and shot her through the head. She lay flat.

The shot echoed. Suddenly Eddie realized he had just fired

this thing three times on a fairly quiet street. He stared around, checking for witnesses.

At the bus stop stood not one or two but a crowd of onlookers, all staring wide-eyed at Eddie.

They had just watched him kill this screaming woman, had heard him declare his motive. Some held a hand over their mouth. Other than shifting from foot to foot, no one moved. No one spoke.

Why aren't they running or yelling? Eddie moved closer, looking at their faces, which resembled the two men Eddie had seen before leaving the bus stop before. *A retarded school must be down the next block. They're all here waiting for the bus.*

"Eddie?"

The sound of his own name sank a spear into Eddie's stomach.

Liam Coogan stepped off the line. "Eddie?" he said again.

Oh, fuck me.

"You killed that lady, Eddie," Liam said, frightened.

❦ ❦ ❦

Rather than cross Manchesi's office agam, Eddie led Liam around the block to Mrs. Manchesi's car. Her husband's keys worked fine. Liam sat in the passenger seat, and Eddie walked around to the driver's side.

A siren screamed, far away down Grand Avenue.

"Why did you kill that lady, Eddie?" Liam asked.

"I said I'll explain it to you," Eddie said through clenched jaws, pulling the sedan out into traffic.

He drove straight down Grand Avenue. Soon they passed a

squadcar and then another racing back toward Manchesi's office.

"Look, Liam," Eddie said, paying full attention to the road ahead of him, "your friends from school are going to tell the police that you left the bus stop with me. You have to tell them that it isn't true."

"But it is true."

"I know," Eddie said. "You'll have to lie."

"I'm not allowed to lie," Liam said.

"This is different," Eddie said.

"You killed that lady, Eddie," Liam reminded him. "When someone gets killed you have to tell the police. If you don't it's not right."

"Sure, I understand that," Eddie said. "But we're like family, Liam. Your family always comes first, isn't that right?"

Liam considered this point, and nodded.

"You have to protect your family, Liam. Those people back at that office have screwed up the block where I live, and that's— that had to stop. I had to stop them."

After several seconds Liam shook his head. "You can't ever kill anyone, even if they kill your family. My teacher said so."

"Your religion teacher."

Liam nodded.

"Liam, sometimes teachers are wrong, or they explain things in a way that you misunderstand," Eddie said. "Teachers aren't perfect. You have to think for yourself."

Liam shook his head. "It's wrong. It says it in the Ten Commandments," he said.

Eddie turned down a side street alongside a cemetery.

"Where are we going?" Liam asked. "I have to go home for dinner."

"I want to show you something," Eddie said, softly. On a block with two warehouses and no residences, he pulled over next to the fence.

"It's a cemetery," Liam said.

"Yeah, but it's full of rabbits," Eddie said. "Get out and look through the fence, Liam."

"I have to go home, Eddie," Liam said. "My mother gets mad if I don't get home fast enough and she has to hold up dinner. I have to go home now."

"Liam, you'll still get home earlier than you would have on the bus, because I'll drive you. Then we can ask your mother whether I'm telling the truth," Eddie explained patiently. "First, I want you to see something out there, so you understand what I did before."

Liam studied Eddie's face for a few seconds, eyes wide behind his thick glasses. "What do you want me to see?" he asked.

"Get out and look," Eddie told him, opening his own door.

Liam climbed out and glanced at the grass beneath his feet. There was no sidewalk here. A weak glow from the only streetlamp on the block reflected off the windshield.

"I don't see any rabbits, Eddie."

"Out there. You see that thing?"

Liam closed his hands around the cold iron poles of the cemetery fence. "What thing, Eddie?" he asked. "That angel?"

"Uh-huh." Eddie swallowed several times, but his throat still felt knotted. Then he told Liam, "Look real hard at the angel for a minute," and took from his inner pocket Kevin's pistol.

FOURTEEN

Eddie didn't know where to abandon Mrs. Manchesi's car. He thought about burning it, but that would just alert the authorities.

Naturally he could not ditch the car anywhere within walking distance of his house. He would drive over the Whitestone and leave it in the Bronx, if he only had the means to get home from there.

For a time he toyed with driving directly home and parking the car in Mrs. Denihan's driveway. The cops might assume Mrs. Manchesi had left it there. But the chance that the McGowans or the Germans might see him exit the car was too great.

He reached Roosevelt Avenue. On autopilot he had returned to Queensborough Heights. *I shouldn't drive around here, someone might recognize me in the car.* Eddie took the first left, toward Corona.

This direction made the most sense, in fact. No one in Corona knew him, for starters, and large areas there closed down at night. Most of the chop shops in northern Queens operated in Corona.

That gave him the solution. *Let someone steal the car!* Eddie followed the elevated subway all the way into Corona. When he began to pass bodegas and storefront churches, he turned down a dark sidestreet at random.

He killed the engine several blocks from the subway, and left the keys in the ignition. Mrs. Manchesi had a change dispenser mounted on her drive shaft, and Eddie emptied it, for train fare. Then he took Kevin's gun from his pocket, and shoved it under the passenger seat.

Outside the sedan, people watched him from stoops and doorways. Eddie departed nonchalantly and took the subway back toward Queensborough Heights. When he first boarded the train, he had the sensation that inside him his skin had torn loose from his muscles.

Minutes later, as his train descended to the Main Street terminal, Eddie wondered whether he should ditch these gloves. *Police labs can trace fibers.* He yanked them from his hands—it was too hot for gloves, anyway; he had only left them on out of nervousness. As soon as the doors opened he dashed to the garbage bin on the platform and chucked them in. Passing commuters regarded him as though he were crazy.

I should visit Desmond.

Maybe he *had* lost his mind, at that. Dropping by the Coogan house suddenly seemed to him the shrewdest move possible. *That way in case someone identifies me, Desmond himself will be my alibi. Even if I act weird, Desmond will think it's because Kevin died.*

Eddie climbed the steps to street level and set out briskly for the Coogans' home. A cool sweat dribbled down from his scalp as he walked, though he never flinched and it soon dried onto his skin.

The sight of the house made him pause very briefly, but he marched onward. *No one's going to think anything of it. If I'm there at roughly the time Liam died, no one will ever suspect me.* It made perfect sense.

He had no wish to pass the photos on the wall in Mr. Coogan's office, however. The very thought of seeing Liam's face, smiling, made Eddie's head perspire anew. So he entered the yard instead, and proceeded to the TV room. The lights were on back there.

When he reached the window, Eddie peered inside before tapping.

Eileen was here.

Eddie cursed softly, and lowered his hand without touching the glass.

She sat on the sofa, talking, a desultory frown pursing her lips. Desmond paced, waving his hands, agitated. Aside from occasional glances at Desmond when he turned his back to her, Eileen kept her eyes trained dead ahead.

She's telling him she used to fuck me.

Desmond raised his voice, loud enough to hear outside, though not clearly. *Feels great, doesn't it, pal? She laid your best friend. Tough shit, and it's your turn to chew.*

Quietly Eddie worked his fingers under the window. With careful, controlled movements he inched it upward, gradually letting Desmond and Eileen's voices escape the television room.

"That's a really fucked up thing to tell me, okay?" Desmond said. "I've gone along with a lot of this stuff, so you can't say I'm not being fair. This is a fucked up thing for you to say to me."

"I'm telling the truth," Eileen said. Eddie could hear her, but she did not speak as loudly. "I see hi—"

"Whoa, whoa," Desmond interrupted her, his voice low but urgent, "I don't need my mother overhearing this, all right? She's a little superstitious."

Eileen's voice stayed at the same volume. "I can't see the name of the cemetery," she said. "He's lying dead beside the fence. Eddie O'Kane shot him in the back of the head, twice, and then Liam fell forward on the grass. There aren't any houses."

Eddie's empty stomach contracted.

Desmond exhaled through his nose, his frustration audible. "Come on, he's late coming home," he said. "That's just a totally wrong thing to say, I don't care what kind of visions you think you're having. Besides which, you're talking about my friend."

"I know Eddie better than you think," Eileen said.

"Just lay off the shit about my brother, all right?" Desmond asked her. "I just can't deal with hearing you talk like that."

"It's what I see, Desmond."

The phone rang, Desmond snatched it to his ear and said, "Hello... You got it, Ma?" Then he hung up.

"You ought to take this serious," Eileen advised him.

"I'm not saying you're not serious," Desmond said. "It's that you keep saying something—"

A scream interrupted him. Mrs. Coogan was screaming. Desmond dashed in to the kitchen. Eileen sat on the couch, staring dead ahead at nothing, studying what no one else could see.

Eddie left. *I should stay to see what else she tells him.* Yet he couldn't. He couldn't.

❦ ❦ ❦

Lolling buzzed before the television, Mr. O'Kane acknowledged Eddie's arrival home with an indifferent shrug. In the kitchen Mrs. O'Kane seemed not to notice Eddie at all.

After draping his jacket across a kitchen chair Eddie bolted upstairs, closed his door and sat on his bed. *They won't arrest me just because Eileen says I did it. A cop comes to question me, he's going to take one look at my parents and nothing nervous I do will stand out. We had a suicide in the family days ago. They won't think I killed Liam.*

He still had some downs left, and could certainly stand to calm himself, but balked at the thought of speaking to police while under the influence. Maybe he would take one at bedtime. No cop would visit him in the middle of the night.

I have to make it known that I'm home. Eddie stood up, wondering whom he could call other than Desmond. He went downstairs again and used the phone in the kitchen.

"Hello?" O'Shea's mother answered.

"Hi, is Brian there?" Eddie asked.

"I'm afraid not," she said.

"Can you take a message?"

"Surely. Let me get a pen... Yes?"

Eddie licked his lips. His scalp felt wet again. "My name is Eddie O'Kane. I sit in front of Brian at school. In home room."

"With a C or a K?" she asked.

"Pardon? Oh, with a K."

"Does he have your number?"

"I don't know, let me give it to you," Eddie said, and he did. When he finished, he added, "That's my home number. I'm home now. You're talking to me at home."

Mrs. O'Shea didn't find his banter odd. "I'll make sure he gets this."

"Bye, now," Eddie said.

"Bye-bye," Mrs. O'Shea said.

As he hung up, he saw his alibi shaping up: *If I call a bunch of people, someone's bound to think it's earlier than it really is when the cops ask them later. I can say I wanted my homework from school.* He called Kelly's house, too, and left a message with Kelly's surly younger brother.

After the younger Kelly's rudeness, a resentful urge poured through Eddie. He put the phone back into its cradle, and told himself, *The fuck with this. I'm working for them—if there's a problem, they should take care of it.* With that he put his jacket back on and left.

Outside Eddie slipped his hands into his pockets. The fingers of his left hand closed around the keys to his father's truck. He had not planned to drive to the Farm, and in fact did not realize he still had these keys in his pocket. His father must have assumed these keys had disappeared, must have begun using a second set.

Eddie paused and glanced back at the house, gauging whether his father seemed lucid enough to notice the truck starting up and disappearing.

First Eddie felt something stab his forearm. Half an instant later the roar of a pistol filled his ears.

"Desmond!" Eileen screamed from down the block.

Desmond stood fifteen feet from the O'Kanes' front door. Eddie dropped to one knee. Desmond's expression changed at this sight, as though he hadn't expected to hurt Eddie by shooting him.

"Desmond!" Eileen screamed again, closer, running. Desmond turned to face her, and held the gun away from his side as though he no longer trusted his hand.

"What are you doing?!" she hollered as she arrived on the O'Kanes' lawn. "You shot him!"

Desmond stammered something to her. Eddie glanced at the doorway behind him. The shot that drilled him had then chipped a piece off his parents' arch. *He only hit me in the arm, and the bullet pierced me. He thinks he nailed me in the side.*

Without a sound Eddie rose and dashed to his father's truck. He already had the key in the door before Eileen or Desmond realized he had gotten up. They began to cross the lawn toward him just as he pressed the button down to lock the door behind him.

"You killed Liam!" Desmond said, raising the gun again.

"*No!*" Eileen cried, and pulled Desmond's hand down.

Eddie's left arm bled profusely, no question, but he could still use it. The bone wasn't even broken.

He started the truck. When he checked before pulling out, Desmond had started runmng down the block, in the direction from which Eileen had arrived. *He left her at the car—that's where he's headed.*

Eddie pulled left and accelerated until he came upon the crappy green Skylark Mr. Coogan occasionally let Desmond drive. Obviously Desmond had intended to hide by parking this far away from Eddie's house. Eddie rammed directly into the middle of the car—slowly, like a bulldozer—and pressed the pedal to the floor until the Skylark crumpled into a horseshoe.

When he stopped he heard Desmond yelling. Eddie shifted into reverse. For a few feet Desmond's car stayed wrapped around the front of the truck. Then they disengaged, and Eddie drove off.

"Fuck, this is for real now," Eddie told himself, examining the dark blood that poured from his sleeve onto his leg and the seat. Three blocks later he put the truck in neutral and pulled his sleeve down. The wounds did not resemble holes so much as slits. His hand felt numb.

He drove on. His old man's red-and-white van would stand out anywhere Eddie parked it, so it made no sense to try stashing it on a sidestreet. He pulled up directly across from the Farm on Colden Street. As he climbed out the ground weaved beneath him, just slightly, and he wondered how much blood he had lost.

Beneath his boots the soil of the Corridor felt soft, strangely moist. Eddie crossed the Farm sloppily, tramping over pristine plots and plants, until he reached the ash grove.

The repulsion these trees held for him had not dimmed, yet no longer deterred him. Finding the passage to the Good People's glade had become second nature to Eddie by now. Presently the woods around him transformed, as dependably as if he had walked through a door into a hall. He knew this path well.

Then the flames flashed, and his nose tingled, and he squinted so the blue smoke would not burn his eyes.

"Hi there, Eddie," Brayson greeted him.

"I been shot," Eddie slurred. He felt drunk.

"So I see," Brayson concurred.

Gareth sat on a log, staring into the fire. He spoke over his shoulder to Brayson, as though Eddie did not exist or did not matter. "This one's a problem, mind," he said. "She's got the Sight something fierce."

"No problem of ours," Brayson declared. "So, Eddie, set ye down and get comfortable."

"You have to change this," Eddie said.

"What's that?"

"You have to fix this," Eddie said again. "I was working for you when this went wrong. You have to fix it."

"How do ye propose we do that?" Brayson asked.

"Put me back in time again. Make me thirteen or fourteen," Eddie said. "I won't kill anybody this time. I can control it now."

"Quit being a fool, Eddie," Brayson said. "Ye're a murderer, that's why ye kill. Never would've met us otherwise."

Eddie glared at the Good People gathered around the hearth. It jarred him to realize none but Brayson was paying him any attention. Everybody, even Gareth, held a tiny swath of fabric in their hands, and they all stared either at this cloth or into the fire. In among the flames Eddie glimpsed Eileen.

"What did ye expect? Ye take up the body of a young boy, but ye got the mind of a grown man—a killer, at that." Brayson took his pipe from his mouth and spat a piece of that flowery blend he smoked. "Stands to reason ye should kill, what in a body full of youthful urges and no adult restraint, don't it?"

"I want to go back further," Eddie insisted calmly. "What do I have to do?"

"Find someone who can send ye there," Brayson suggested. "Nobody here can help ye. Meantime, ye can set down." Brayson took a pouch from his pocket and filled his pipe from the pouch.

"I have to do something about my arm," Eddie said. "If you won't send me back, I have to go to the hospital."

"Have a fine time in gaol, then, Eddie," Brayson said. "Think of us."

"You can't let them lock me up."

"How can we stop them?" Gareth piped in.

Eddie stamped his foot. "*You* got me into this—"

"And we're telling ye, set down," Brayson said. "Ye leave us and go out there, it's as good as driving to the police. Here, not a soul can touch ye."

"I left my father's truck outside on the street," Eddie said.

"What of it?"

"They might trace it to here."

"No one's coming in here," Gareth explained without looking up from the flames. "No living man can reach this place unless he's committed murder and has reached the brink of death."

Eddie ran his fingers through his hair. "All right, but my arm's fucked up," he complained, peeled off his denim jacket to show them his wounded arm.

"Here, set down," Brayson said.

At last Eddie did. A grotesque little woman stepped from the dark and touched both the entry and exit wounds on Eddie's left forearm with a dirty-looking poultice made of leaves. Eddie had never been so close to one of the Good People, and as she worked he studied the countless fine wrinkles crosshatching her skin. His wounds stopped hurting.

Eddie squatted there in the dirt, not talking to anyone, staring into the fire, for a long time. Days, it may have been.

❦ ❦ ❦

Eddie's arm did not hurt but frightened him whenever he examined it, so he didn't, especially once the faint discoloration around both wounds blossomed into larger black circles.

Hunger wracked him, but in large part due to psychology more than to malnutrition. Mostly he craved the physical act of eating. This craving pushed him to try eating a yimcha.

"Have a bite," Gareth said, tossing several pods in Eddie's lap. "Go ahead, ye might like it."

Even as he shook his head no, Eddie picked a pod up and smelled it. He broke off the tip and chewed it tentatively, then snapped off a bigger piece and chewed that too. And another. The pieces broke up into chunks of wood not quite soft enough to swallow. The aroma when he broke the pod no longer threatened to overpower him.

Then the taste suddenly revolted him. Eddie gagged, but because his mouth was full of gnawed pod pulp no one noticed. He continued chewing more slowly, so he could avoid the taste.

By this time, Eddie had lost all track of how long he had sat in the clearing, yet still he had not seen most of his companions clearly.

But now, as he nursed a mouthful of yimcha splinters, the darkness opened up to Eddie's eyes. At first he assumed the eternal night of the glade had lifted; all at once he saw each tiny person on the ground, and others marching through the woods around them. After a minute Eddie realized the Good People were in fact not just carrying but weaving the cloth patches in their hands.

Eddie gazed into the fire beside him. He had spent some time staring into it, watching the tiny flashes of pictures in there. But now the image came as clear to him as a photograph. The Good People watching the fire, chin hunched in one hand while the other absently wove the fabric, reminded Eddie of kids watching TV.

On the screen Eileen sat in the Coogans' back room, talking to Desmond and—was that Kelly? And Matherson? By allowing the image to absorb him, Eddie discovered he could hear their voices.

"Forgiveness is the greatest kick you'll ever find, Desmond," Matherson was saying. "I should know. I've tried 'em all."

"Fuck forgiveness," Kelly said. "The only reason not to kill him is because you'll get locked up. You should get the cops on his ass, and he should go away for life."

With his dirty fingers Eddie carefully removed the plant matter from his mouth, and asked Gareth, "Is it the yimcha that's doing this?"

"Where did ye learn that word?" Gareth asked, surprised.

"From a Korean. Is the yimcha what's giving me night vision?"

"Sure." Gareth watched the fire devoutly.

Eddie slipped the crap back into his mouth and watched in stunned silence for some time. The yimcha in his mouth cleaved into smaller shards. Eventually he attempted to swallow one, and gagged again, more noticeably.

This time Eddie just spat the stuff out. "To hell with it," he announced. "These things taste horrible."

"Indeed they do," Gareth agreed, cracking himself a small piece.

Eddie sat there with the pods in his lap. Very soon the darkness clouded his sight again, and the flames reclaimed the movie.

"Shit wears off quick," Eddie observed. He got no answer.

Later, much later, Eddie chewed up his last pod, and his vision diminished to normal. "Can I have some more?" he asked Gareth.

"Sure," Gareth answered. "Get me some, too, while ye're there."

"While I'm where?"

"Out there in that garden where they grow," Gareth said. "Have ye seen them, all along that little hill, there?"

"You mean out on the Farm?"

Gareth nodded.

"I'm not going out there!" Eddie declared. "Someone'll see me!"

Gareth shrugged. "I doubt that, it's after dark out there," he said. "But suit yerself, if ye don't want any bad enough."

Eddie lasted a short while before he got up and said, "Just take them off the vines along that big mound at the edge of the Farm?"

Gareth nodded. "Fill up ye jacket with them," he advised. "Bring back at least a couple pounds."

Eddie started down the path toward the outside. Halfway there he turned back and asked, "What about the tunnel?"

"How's that?" Brayson asked, suddenly interested.

"Can I just take the tunnel?" Eddie asked. "The one that goes up into the drain in the little shack."

Obviously deciding not to give Eddie the satisfaction of asking how he knew about the tunnel, Brayson shook his head. "Ye won't fit. Go on out, no one's going to notice ye. Not at night."

Eddie retraced his path down the trail to the outside. When he reached the strange passage where the trees formed unnatural silhouettes, he paused and stood very still. He could not say how long it had been since he had been alone. It alarmed him to find himself apprehensive about returning to the real world, the way old people fear leaving home.

He pushed himself the rest of the way and emerged on the edge of the Farm. For several minutes he stayed there, breathing. The absence of smoke made the air exhilarating.

But a smell rose to his nostrils, an unwashed odor threatening to become fetid. Eddie checked about him for its source, until it dawned on him: He hadn't bathed since coming here.

How long have I been beside that fire? He stumbled to the fence that bordered Colden Street. The spot where he had left his father's van lay unoccupied.

In the glow of the streetlamp Eddie studied his hands. He had lost weight, no question, yet that alone could not explain the state of his skin. It appeared as though his hide hung loose on his bones, waiting to rot off. This effect could not have come from mere filth, or even from some disease Eddie had picked up rolling in the dirt. His body had changed.

Eddie pulled down his left sleeve, to check his forearm.

"Oh, my fucking God," Eddie whispered.

The two wounds had each split his skin so wide that they now formed one rupture, a dark red chasm eaten out of his arm.

He touched one finger from his right hand down inside the fissure, and stroked the smooth flesh at the bottom. Contact with the cool air made this pink surface wither visibly before him.

"This will kill me," Eddie said, not caring if anyone heard. "I'll lose my fucking arm."

Eddie stared up and down Colden Street. His arm didn't hurt him, so he pulled the jacket sleeve back over it. He missed the world, but he felt cold and tired, and he wanted most of all to return to the fire. So he made his way down the edge of the ash grove to the mound that ran the inside perimeter of the Farm.

Here in the dark it was easier to ignore the state of his left forearm, so he took off his jacket and laid it open, to load. As he plucked pods from the vines Eddie marveled that he had not slept in ages, not since entering the glade however many nights ago.

But he would sleep as soon as he got back. He would chew a few pods and nod out watching the fire.

❡ ❡ ❡

As soon as Eddie returned, two things turned solid in his mind. First, he had in fact slept, more than once, on the ground here by the fire. He had spent the entire time miserable, grinding his teeth and wishing for a pillow.

Second, he did not want to sleep just yet. The Good People had filled the clearing, each eager to snag a handful of Eddie's pods.

"Now, look, I went out and collected these," Eddie said.

"And ye'll go collect more, soon as we tell ye," Brayson informed him, with a curt laugh. "Had ye not bothered our Korean friend, we'd be getting them delivered still."

They took as much as they wanted, and most disappeared back into the woods. Eddie managed to keep two fistfuls for himself. He sat down beside the fire, and carefully broke one pod into little pieces, and enthusiastically crammed his mouth with these plant fragments whose taste would soon make him retch.

Now that he had grown used to yimcha, now that he knew enough to break the pod into extra-small particles, Eddie could talk while eating them and gaping at the fire. Most of the people he saw there—almost all of them, actually—were strangers to Eddie, but he could not take his eyes off them. Eileen came up every so often.

"How do you control who we see in the fire?" Eddie asked Gareth.

"I don't," Gareth answered without removing his gaze from the flames.

"Who does?"

Gareth shrugged.

They watched in silence a while longer. Eileen and Kelly talked Desmond into abandoning hope of revenge. "Eddie O'Kane's probably lying dead in a sewer somewhere," Kelly said. Eddie found himself grinning involuntarily, wondering if Kelly might be right. He did not see Matherson among them this time.

Out of the blue, Eddie asked, "Why do you all talk like leprechauns?"

"Like what?" Brayson asked. Eddie kept forgetting Brayson was there, since Brayson sat far away from the fire, and Eddie never saw him look at it.

"Leprechauns," Eddie said. "Irish things, I don't know, little people."

"We ain't leprechauns," Brayson said.

"What are you?".

"You mean what are *we*, Eddie," Brayson corrected him. "And ye know very well what we are."

FIFTEEN

Sometimes Eddie would awaken on the ground, uncertain how long he had lain there, unable to recall falling asleep. More often they would rouse him to fetch more yimcha. None of the Good People ventured out the trail to the Farm; instead they sent Eddie to collect the pods for everyone. He made several trips each night, by his own estimate.

The Good People always knew without checking whether it was day or night outside the ash grove, in Queensborough Heights. Usually Gareth would send him out with a plastic sack and advise him, "Make a couple of trips, it's getting on daylight."

Eddie didn't mind the job. He liked getting out of the glade and away from the fire, though he always enjoyed the outside less than he expected. These were the only minutes he could spend alone.

The chance to examine himself in the light from the streetlamp always disturbed him, because he could not resist the urge to pull down his sleeve and see how much more of his arm had peeled away since the last time he'd checked. The wound turned green in places. And it made him smell bad. Eddie had met corpses who smelled only a little worse.

The Good People focused their energies on weaving their cloth. The small swaths Eddie had first noticed had with the passage of time grown into sheets. Everyone's sheet grew at the same rate, and they all wove the fabric in the same way, with one hand, not watching. Eddie could not tell what they wove the stuff from.

Gradually the sheets began to resemble garments—specifically, cowls, but for full-sized people.

"Who are those robes for?" Eddie asked when he saw what shape the cloth pieces had taken. No one answered. Then again, that reaction was never uncommon here.

Another question nobody ever answered was "What day is this?", though Eddie had asked repeatedly at first. None of the Good People knew a Wednesday from a Saturday or cared to learn.

This subject occupied Eddie anew each time he left the hearthside to collect yimcha. One warm night as he arrived at the vine-covered slopes it occurred to Eddie why his lack of timekeeping troubled him: The weather had not grown any colder in the time he had spent hidden inside the ash grove. *Does time move more slowly at the fire?*

Eddie took his jacket off and spread it on the ground. The stink that arose off his own body made him raise his face away from himself.

Something darted across the edge of his vision, something dark and fast—a bat, hunting insects above the high reeds. *I've been living in that clearing for months, it feels like. By now all the bats should already have found a dead tree full of bugs and hibernated.*

He caught sight of his left arm.

In the moonlight his wound appeared black and his skin gray-white. By now this sight had jarred him on several occasions, but tonight he found it plainly unbelievable: The gangrene had eaten an armband clear around his forearm, to the...was that *bone* there, at his limb's core?

"No fucking way," Eddie said softly, without meaning to speak.

Impossible, yet his left hand still worked. With the fingers of his right hand Eddie examined the gap. That light-colored rod still joining his lower arm to his body wasn't bone, though it felt harder than human skin to the touch.

Eddie loaded several pounds of pods into his jacket, and hoisted it into a sling over his back, as he always did. But as he walked he could not pry his eyes from the hideous gouge around his forearm. When he reached the entrance to the glade again, he stopped, and checked himself under the distant streetlamp.

It hasn't looked anywhere near this bad till now. Eddie dumped the yimcha onto the ground beside an ash tree. Then he went up to the fence, where the light was better. And then, for the first time since the night he killed Liam Coogan, Eddie left the Corridor altogether and walked right onto Colden Street.

He stayed beneath the streetlamp a long time, staring at his wound, until he noticed himself shivering. It had not become cold; he had a chill because he was starving.

Rapidly his situation came clear to him: He had not eaten or bathed in weeks, and his arm was about to fall off. He put his jacket on and started moving briskly toward Main Street. Someplace with food should be open there, whatever time it might be.

On his way to Main Street Eddie saw no one. The houses he passed seemed both taller and farther recessed from the street than normal, though Eddie didn't know any specific house along Colden Street or Kissena Boulevard well enough to pinpoint just how its roof or foundation had changed. Presently a suspicion took shape in his mind that an artist had painted the houses and alleys on canvas backdrops to either side of him. Then at last Kissena met Main. Yet here too Eddie detected the surest of brushstrokes limning where the sky met the uppermost stories of the empty department stores.

An all-night coffee shop upstairs from the subway terminal had a rack of donuts in the window. Eddie stared from the Boston cream to the crullers to the eclairs, his mouth squeezing his dry salivary glands to drool. His throat cracked.

FOUR FOR A DOLLAR, the sign told him.

"Shit!" Eddie said. He had no money, had not thought of it. Maybe they would feed him at the hospital, if he went to the emergency room. They'd damned sure treat him... *Oh*. Eddie stared at a passing taxi. *They'll amputate my arm. Then jail.*

He walked down the stairs to the subway station. The clock said 3:13. The lady in the toll booth ignored him. A middle-aged man in a CPO jacket, obviously on his way home from working a late shift, came out through the turnstile.

"Excuse me, sir," Eddie said.

The man acted stunned by Eddie's raggedness.

"I'm really hungry, could you spare some change?" Eddie asked.

Without a moment's thought the guy reached into his pocket and handed Eddie two dollars. He walked away before Eddie could thank him. Not long afterward a black guy on his way into the station gave Eddie fifty cents, and asked whether he'd come from Ireland or England.

It would be at least three or four more years until homeless beggars would overrun the subway and commuters would adopt the daily habit of shaking one's head from side to side without making eye contact.

A transit cop came up the staircase at the terminal's far end, and Eddie split before he had to answer any questions.

Upstairs the countergirl in the coffee shop winced when Eddie came in. He could not tell whether his appearance or his odor offended her.

"Let me have some donuts," he said, holding the money up.

"Okay," she said, stifling her gag reflex. "What kind?"

She wanted him out of there quickly. She even poured him a cup of coffee and didn't charge him. She handled his money as though she feared infection from touching it.

Eddie couldn't care how he smelled or looked. When he left the coffee shop he searched for the nearest doorway or alley, and found a cement step at the side entrance of an Oriental grocery. Leaning against the steel gate that the owners locked over the door at night, he took a big sip of coffee.

It burned him, but not from the heat. The liquid hit his mouth with the flavor of room-temperature gasoline. His nose and throat and even his eyes closed while he choked.

So he bit into a donut, a glazed donut, the first one he pulled out of the bag. A second later he spat it out, and tried another, a filled one. He spat that out too.

He entered the coffee shop about three minutes after he had left. The countergirl moved quickly toward the cash register. "That coffee tasted like shit," he told her. "Why did you give me fucked up coffee?"

"I can't help you," the girl said.

"You can't sell donuts like this," Eddie said. "Taste this." He held the box up to her.

She shook her head, very nervously. *Does she know me?* "No, thanks," she said.

"Look, I don't have a lot more money," he said. "You have to—"

"The police will be here in a second," she blurted. "You better get out of here."

It took a second or two for Eddie to comprehend: She had rung the alarm. "Hey, I didn't threaten you or anything."

"I'm telling you, the cops are coming," she said. "If you're not out of here, they'll *take* you out."

Eddie accepted her at her word, and fled the shop as fast as he could run. The police had to have some kind of bulletin out for him, if even just as a missing person. And they'd put him in a hospital, especially once they saw his arm. And the doctors would cut his arm off.

The cops arrived at the coffee shop before Eddie cleared the block, but they did not see him. He crouched among an immense pile of black plastic garbage bags, in front of an apartment building. The cops entered the shop. Eddie crept away and rounded the corner.

Wearily he trudged back across Queensborough Heights to the Farm. His joints ached, and as he shivered he tried to eat another donut but chucked the box away in disgust. When he reached Colden Street he wondered suddenly if sugar might be the wrong thing to eat after starvation. Maybe he needed rice, or bread.

The sky had lightened, just barely, so he entered the Farm and recollected the yimcha pods he had dumped outside the ash grove, and carried them in to the clearing.

"Bring us any donuts, did ye?" Gareth greeted him.

Several of them around the fire guffawed. Their laughter no longer held the creepy power it used to, back when Eddie feared this place. His imagination might have amplified their jeers back then. They sounded apathetic lately, although just this moment they seemed pissed off that they nearly had to cart their own yimcha in here.

"Ye went outside to do a job," Brayson said. "Ye don't scoot off for a walk midway through."

Eddie shrugged. "If you saw me cut out, then you saw where I left this shit," he said.

"Don't go walking off again," Brayson warned him.

Very quickly Brayson turned his attention to something in his pocket, which gave Eddie the impression that Brayson wanted to end the matter while still in authority. Brayson seemed to Eddie a great deal older than, say, Gareth—not more mature; rather, more antiquated. Eddie had come to infer comparative ages from many of them, now that he considered it.

Brayson didn't spend much time staring into the fire, either, unlike the others. Eddie never observed what he did instead, but Brayson stayed in the clearing.

"So I was in the fire?" Eddie asked Gareth, snapping a piece from a pod as he squatted beside the hearth.

Without looking Gareth nodded.

"Donuts tasted horrible," he said. "I was starving, though."

"Ye cannot eat that shite no more," Gareth informed him.

"Why not?"

No one answered, Eddie sat back, watched the fire.

♥ ♥ ♥

Eddie awoke from a dream of Marypat (he'd had them for years while she was Desmond's wife, but it didn't happen often nowadays) to find the entire glade bustling.

"No, ye don't know what yer talking about," some loudmouth complained. "Ye give the alert over nothing."

"Been here a sight longer than yerself," Brayson reminded him.

Good People Eddie had never seen before had crowded into the clearing, to watch the fire avidly. No one paid Eddie the slightest glance.

"I tell ye, it's set to happen," Brayson said.

"Look at it," Gareth said to the other man. "Can ye not see it's different?"

He meant the fire. Eddie sat up, rubbing his eyes, and looked at the flames. They did indeed appear changed, coated by a pale film.

The loudmouth seemed greatly outnumbered, whatever his contention. If an altered fire foretold some greater portent, most of those present believed this event imminent. The prospect excited them.

They shed their tattered robes.

Eddie doubted his senses. The Good People stood naked all around him, compact and misshapen. He studied the finely wrinkled skin that covered their thighs and knees, their genitals, their buttocks, every inch of them mapped with that reptilian pattern.

"Eddie," Gareth said, in a tone Eddie himself might have employed speaking to Jabberwocky. "Ye go get the yimcha for us, and ye wait here until we get back. Understand me? Ye don't go noplace."

Eddie nodded, clearing his throat, and croaked, "Where are you going?" *And aren't you going to put your clothes back on first?*

No one answered him. They had their eyes locked on the fire, on that odd caul coating the flames. It had a pronounced blue tint, now that Eddie stared at it.

Inside his mouth he ran his tongue over his teeth, which felt thick with plaque. The disrobed Good People waiting around him were mesmerized by the fire. For once Eddie wanted to avoid it.

"Sure as hell, I can feel it," Brayson said.

Many in the assembly murmured agreement.

They stayed that way for a long time. Eddie had four yimcha that he had not eaten, that lay on the ground beside him. He couldn't even imagine eating one. His stomach would spin.

The loudmouth—he seemed young—held two pods in his hand. Now that the crowd had ceased paying attention to him, he allowed these to drop to the earth and surrendered his attention to the flames. All at once Eddie grasped it: They had to fight the urge to eat the yimcha, because they didn't want to see the pictures in the fire right now. They wished to watch the fire itself.

"That's it," Brayson said, triumphantly.

The caul atop the flames turned green. Just as suddenly it went yellow, then orange, then red. The red deepened past brown, to the verge of black.

And then a pit opened in the hearth. The ground did not rumble; the soil did not rupture. The fire itself became a trapdoor.

Gleefully Brayson stepped over the hearthstones and dropped from sight. Gareth quickly followed him. So did several others, and then everybody else.

The Good People marched into the hole in an orderly but rapid fashion. So many of them pursued one another down so quickly that Eddie assumed they would all land in a heap wherever they hit.

❦ ❦ ❦

The exodus into the fire lasted a long time, and by the end they got pushy. Violence flared in spurts but dissolved fast. Everyone just wanted to get down the hole.

In the end the naked crowd thinned and the last few seemed to dash directly from the woods into the pit.

Then the flames resumed, with no trace of that pale film upon them. Eddie coughed and rubbed his eyes, as though the fire's return were the incredible part of what he had just witnessed.

The fire crackled and mewled, traceless, untouched. He squinted at it. Faint pictures flickered into view, and out again.

His appetite no longer mattered. He didn't eat yimcha for sustenance, anyway, or at least not for the same kind of sustenance that food had once given him. Once he woke fully he realized yimcha couldn't really turn his stomach when his stomach had been empty so long.

So he snapped himself nearly one-third of a pod and chewed it. *Fuck yourself, Gareth. I'll pick the pods when I fucking feel like it.* Syrupy resin from the crushed husk reached his taste buds. The bad flavor had become a signal to him, a warm greeting. For half a second this signal reminded Eddie of the way he would taste junk when he injected it; just before the rush hit his head, he always felt the drug sweep across his tongue.

No point remembering those days, he quickly told himself. The picture inside the fire came into focus.

Inside the flames Eddie saw a verdant meadow, lit soft blue-white by a full moon. Naked people pranced across the greenery, tackled each other, humped on the grass. These people stood full size, all different ages, though almost all were adults. More were male than female. They drank crude cups of something, probably wine. Eddie heard them whoop and howl.

An older man marched cheerfully across the field, surveying the festivity. Without hearing him speak, Eddie recognized this older man as Brayson. Not long after that Eddie also spotted Gareth rolling on the ground with a blonde woman. Gareth appeared middle-aged.

"Nice party," Eddie said, to no one.

Brayson hollered at everyone about a ceremony. His voice sounded odd.

That went on for a long time. When Eddie ran out of yimcha he climbed to his feet and wandered down the passage to the Farm. As soon as he reached the night outside the grove, his own stench nauseated him. *I need a shower.* It was warm enough that he could wash himself at a water tap. Instead he went directly to the yimcha and harvested a jacketful of pods.

His arm looked worse than ever. The chasm had widened. Eddie did not want to carry his load back to the clearing yet, because having to see his forearm under the streetlamp would wig him.

So he piled the yimcha beside the land wall, put his jacket on and hiked into the Corridor, away from the Farm. The horse trail felt quiet tonight. He spotted a rabbit crossing the path ahead of him. The improvement in his night vision amazed him.

At the soccer field Eddie observed a couple fucking on the bleachers, close to the end he had walled up. A flash from the dream he'd had earlier, the dream of Marypat, darted through his mind. He left the soccer field.

Outside on Roosevelt Avenue Eddie grasped fully how wretched he appeared. Drivers stared without slowing as they passed. Through tremendous focus of will Eddie resisted the need to check out his wound, yet he did squeeze his jacket sleeve and felt the empty gap. It made him shudder.

When he followed the street out of the Corridor altogether, a rich, warm fragrance beckoned to him. *Some kind of plant, that smells like.* It grew stronger and stronger, until he arrived in front of a small white building with large windows: Bella Chica's, the pizzeria.

Pizza didn't smell the way he remembered. It didn't used to seem so herbal to him. It was oregano that he noticed most now.

Through the wide windows he watched customers eat. There weren't very many. In his pocket Eddie still had some change, but even if he had enough for a slice, they would chase him out of the shop once they caught wind of him.

He walked around the corner, and up the back alley behind the pizzeria. A dumpster stood beside their back door. Eddie lifted the lid and peeked inside. *Hah!* He fished one of several pizza boxes from the top of the trash. It contained dry, brittle pizza, probably left over from closing last night.

Eddie tried to eat it anyway. He sank his teeth into the hard crust and heard a brutal crunch toward the back of his mouth. When he spat out the stale dough, half of one molar accompanied it.

Eddie cursed softly, and stroked his fractured tooth with his tongue. The tooth had broken razor-sharp. Already Eddie thought he tasted blood on his tongue.

Eddie checked the other boxes inside the dumpster. Empty. He returned to Roosevelt Avenue, to the front of the pizzeria. He could wait until closing, and they would have to throw out tonight's leftovers. *Yeah, but what kind of leftovers will they have? More stale shit?*

Eddie paused, thinking. Scheming.

He memorized the phone number on the pizzeria's sign. Then he left, and went to locate a payphone.

He found no phone before the Corridor started, and knew that he would reach the next one on the far side. Patiently he traveled. In his sense of mission he had lost his anxiety about stalking the streets plainly visible. As he crossed the Corridor it meant nothing to him, even when he passed the soccer field just in time to hear that girl whimper in orgasm on the bleachers.

When he reached the other side, he first made certain he could read the number on the payphone. Then he dialed the pizza place.

"Hello, Bella Chica's," a guy answered. In the background Eddie heard plates colliding, kitchen noise.

"Yeah, I want to order a pie," Eddie said.

"Too late, sir, we don't deliver past—"

"No, I'll come pick it up," he said.

"Okay, we could do that," the guy agreed. "What would you like?"

"A large pie," he said. "Onions, anchovies and pepperoni."

The guy wrote it down. "All right, sir," he said. "That'll be about half an hour. We'll be closing in forty-five minutes, so don't come late, all right?"

"Sure," Eddie said.

"So what's the name, sir?"

"Collins," Eddie said.

"And your phone number?"

Eddie recited the number off the dial, thanked the guy and hung up. He waited beside the phone. A minute passed, and another.

The phone rang.

"Hello?" Eddie answered.

"Hi, this is Bella Chica Pizza," the guy said. "Did you order a large pie, onions, anchovies, pepperoni?"

"I sure did," Eddie told him. "I'm coming down to pick it up."

"Okay, we're just confirming," the guy explained.

"Confirming?"

"Kids play jokes, you know? They send pies to each other's houses and whatnot," the pizza man said. "I get stuck paying for it. We got to make sure an order's legit, is all."

"Oh," Eddie replied, as though this were a profound revelation. "I wondered why you needed my phone number when I'm coming down to get the pie."

"Yeah, I'm real sorry if it's an inconvenience," the guy said.

"No, not at all," Eddie said. "Well, I'll be down there in half an hour."

"See you then."

Eddie listened to the guy hang up, and did the same. *Smooth as babyshit.* If by chance anybody came to Bella Chica's for a pie during the last fifteen minutes the pizzeria was open, they would certainly not accept this anchovy-onion thing. An hour from now, there would be a fresh pie in that dumpster.

In an approaching car, someone yelled, "Desmond, no!"

Eddie turned and jumped away from the phone.

The Coogans' Impala breached the curb and missed him by inches. Kelly hollered at Desmond from the passenger seat.

Eddie charged through the brush into the Corridor. He ran down a dirt path that led to the horse trail. Behind him as he fled he heard Desmond maneuvering his car to follow, with Kelly's shouts all but lost in noise.

Then the Impala came flying down the horse trail. *Shit, he drives like a motherfuck now.* Eddie left the path but kept moving in the same direction. He had to get farther into the Corridor, to the Farm. To the clearing. To the fire.

Desmond's high beams cut the dark into day along the path. When the car turned a slight bend and the headlights nearly shone on Eddie, he held still against a tree. The lights passed him, and so did the car. Eddie watched the tail lights sail away into the growth, hunting him.

A quarter-mile up the path the car halted.

He knows I'm in here. Eddie wiped sweat from his head. *They know they had me between there and the start of the trail. Do I run?*

He drew several deep breaths, watching the car reverse slowly toward him. A feeble ray of light played upon the trees and ragweed, and Eddie realized that Kelly had some kind of flashlight trained out the window, searching for Eddie in the brush.

The amount of energy Eddie had summoned without warning impressed him. He calmed his heartbeat, waiting for the car to pass him again, and lay flat on the ground when it did. Kelly's light did not penetrate anywhere near him. The Impala passed backward, toward where the path met the street. As he rose to his feet Eddie nearly forgot to dodge the headlights, since they were in the back now.

Once again under cover of darkness, Eddie continued his journey toward the Farm. He stayed off the main path, even after it fed onto the horse trail. As he hiked Eddie checked over his shoulder to chart his pursuers' progress back behind him. At one point they seemed to think they had spotted him off the road, but instead they flushed an animal—a large rabbit, most likely—from the reeds.

"Good luck, fellas," Eddie said out loud, moving onward. He wanted to put as much distance as possible between himself and them by the time they realized he had slipped ahead of them. *If they even get that.* They had no reason to suspect where he was headed. They might assume he left the Corridor entirely before they doubled back.

Eddie made good time alongside the horse trail. When he looked back, the Impala sat in the spot where it had entered the Corridor, back by the payphone.

Though he reached the vicinity of the Farm quickly, Eddie did not want to return to the fireside just yet. He knew time would turn weird on him once he did, would speed up or elapse or whatever happened when he sat by the fire. His pizza would be fossilized by the time he escaped the ash grove again.

Fuck them, telling me to wait for them. I'm not their servant. Eddie sat on a stump beside the trail, gazing up at the stars. *When was the last time I smoked pot?* he wondered.

A cloud bank hid the moon for many minutes. Wind combed the reeds. A bird shrieked mournfully from a distant tree. Eddie watched the heavens for a long, long time.

"How long is it now?" Eddie asked no one. "It's got to be an hour since I called Bella Chica's."

He got up and walked toward the soccer field, but in fact Eddie did not want to take the same route to the pizza shop this time. Crossing the soccer field meant walking Roosevelt Avenue out in the open for several blocks, with Desmond and Kelly cruising the streets to catch him.

So Eddie covered more of the distance inside the Corridor, and then picked his way from the path through the undergrowth to the street. He emerged on a sleeping suburban block of Underhill Road, which followed the Corridor's perimeter perpendicular from Roosevelt.

A car turned the corner behind him. He froze for an instant.

It wasn't Desmond. *He's not going to come up here looking for me. They saw me down there at the other end. By now, they probably both doubt they ever saw me at all.*

Eddie set off to pick up his pizza.

SIXTEEN

Bella Chica's had closed for the night. Not a single car remained parked anywhere on the block. Eddie surveyed the strip carefully from one corner, ready to bolt at the first sign of an Impala.

Then he crept around the corner and up the back alley to the dumpster. He could smell the oregano from forty feet away, and the aroma of onions nearly overpowered him.

What if the pizza guys know this trick? Eddie halted in his tracks, picked anxiously at his scalp. *They're waiting by the back door with the lights out, to see who shows up and raids their garbage. Wiseasses must pull this every week.*

Moonlight filled the alley. An overhang kept Bella Chica's back door in shadow.

I could just swear I'm a runaway and I smelled the pizza.

Beside a trashcan farther down the alley, a rat poked at a crumpled paper sack.

"Oh, bullshit," Eddie scolded himself, and opened the dumpster. The pizza lay in a damaged box with the name COLLINS printed on it in black magic marker. A huge grease stain had smeared the phone number.

Eddie removed the box and opened it. Two slices had disappeared from the pie. "Shit, how much fucking onion did they *put* on this?" he asked out loud.

He stuffed half a slice into his mouth, chewed, and spat the dough against the dumpster. *It hurts.* Tiny clumps of cheese and onion seared his gums. He could not expel them from his mouth fast enough, especially since he had slit his tongue open repeatedly on his broken molar and did not want to touch it with his filthy fingers.

"I can't eat this anymore," Eddie conceded at length, spitting pizza at the pavement. "I can't eat."

Tight with frustration, he slapped the remaining pizza onto the building. It spattered the white bricks. A bit of red sauce stained his fingers.

Headlights.

When Eddie turned around, Desmond's car had already entered the alley. Now it bore down on him. The punctured muffler's report reverberated off the walls. The passage filled with noise.

Eddie took off. Behind him he heard a great scrape, and he turned around to see that Desmond had wedged the Impala between the dumpster and the brick wall. The car could follow no farther.

Desmond climbed out the driver's side window. Eddie kept going. If they pursued on foot, he could outrun them. Eddie O'Kane had grown mighty light on his feet.

"Don't!" Kelly bellowed, back by the car. "I said *don't!*"

When he reached the sidewalk Eddie glanced backward; Desmond had a twenty-foot lead on Kelly, who was still clambering across the car's hood to come join the chase.

As Eddie rounded the corner out of the alley, he realized that Kelly was not shouting at him but at Desmond. Escape had seized Eddie's full attention. He had not listened.

Desmond said nothing, just moved forward. He emerged from the alley in the steady gait of a track runner, yet did not spot Eddie's flight down the overgrown driveway of a brick tudor house two doors away. In the shadows Eddie halted and watched Desmond book past.

"Put the gun back in your pocket," Kelly said. "Without me you wouldn't have thought of coming here—you wouldn't have even answered the payphone."

That's how they knew to wait for me here: The pizzeria must have called when I didn't show to pick up the pie. Kelly should make Detective.

Kelly stalked across the mouth of the driveway, across Eddie's narrow field of vision. As he did he lowered his voice. Eddie could not hear either of them until Kelly erupted, "I came here with you, now put the fucking gun away! I don't need to get arrested! *Your* old man ain't a cop, and *you* won't get your balls busted over it!"

Eddie followed the driveway to a cement yard. He crossed the yard and padded down the other side of a two-car garage. One back yard away to his left ran the pizzeria's back alley. A redwood fence separated the rear of this yard from the rear of the neighbor's around the block.

Eddie scaled the fence easily. From its peak he surveyed the neighbor's grounds.

A very loud and agile Doberman leaped at him from the other side.

Eddie smashed his forehead off the fence as he fell. The blow to his skull was too severe for the pain to sink in right away, so he rolled on the concrete, palms pressed to his brow. He hissed as the pain flooded across his cranium.

Desmond and Kelly arrived calmly, just as Eddie climbed to his feet. Eddie did not see Desmond's pistol anywhere.

"Okay, Eddie," Desmond said.

"Go away, Desmond," Eddie replied.

"You shot my brother, Eddie," Desmond told him.

"Why? Because some psychic says so?"

"Witnesses identified you," Desmond said. "They saw everything."

"Nobody who wasn't retarded," Eddie sneered, and then realized what he had just said.

Kelly called, quite loudly, to any neighbor in earshot, "All right, somebody call the police. We caught a wanted criminal out here."

"Can't go to jail, Kelly," Eddie said. "They'll amputate my arm."

"Tough shit," Desmond said.

"What's wrong with your arm?" Kelly asked.

Desmond and Kelly kept their distance from him, in large part due to Eddie's current hygiene.

"Desmond shot me, a while back," Eddie began.

"Last fall," Desmond corrected him. "Stop trying to sound Irish."

Eddie unfurled the sleeve of his jacket. Both Kelly and Desmond grimaced when they saw the wound eaten clear through Eddie's muscle and flesh.

"You got to go to a doctor with that," Kelly told Eddie. "You'll lose your arm if you don't. That's—man, that's the worst gash I ever saw."

"Nobody's taking my arm off." With a clumsy nonchalance Eddie cataloged all the potential weapons in reach: a trowel neat the azalea, a four-by-six around the planter. A spade leaned against the fence to his right. *Rocks?*

"Eddie, you're going to jail," Desmond said.

"I said, I can't," he reminded them. "You don't know what's going on, all right? You can't possibly understand what I'm talking about."

"We don't have to," Kelly said, before hollering again, "Will somebody please call the police?"

"Guys, I'm..." Eddie began, and stopped. What he found himself saying stunned him; he had not thought of it previously. "I'm becoming something else. You have to back off. It's really easy for me to, like, lash out. I can't explain it, you'd think I'm crazy."

"No," Desmond disagreed, gritting his teeth. "I don't think you're crazy at all. And acting nuts isn't going to let you walk away with—with killing an innocent fucking *child*—"

Overcome, Desmond in one movement pulled the pistol from his pocket and fired at Eddie, who took the bullet in the thigh but did not fall. The report echoed off the brick houses around them.

"Oh," Kelly said, almost reverently.

Desmond hesitated, his hand wavering between aiming and putting the pistol back into his pocket.

"Man, you can't see there's something wrong with him?" Kelly asked Desmond. "Don't shoot him. Desmond, he's lost his mind. Just smell him—he's got to be living under a bush."

That gave Desmond pause. He brought the hand with the gun down to his side.

Eddie limped sideways, as if testing the damage to his leg. *It fucking hurts, you fat prick.*

"Hey, somebody?" Kelly yelled. "Call the police!" Then, to Desmond, he said, "You should get out of here with that gun, man. That's assault with a deadly weapon, could get you years—"

Eddie grabbed the handle of the spade and swung it. He missed Desmond's face entirely and connected with Kelly's head. Kelly collapsed and met the earth as dead weight.

Desmond brought the gun back up and shot Eddie point-blank in the chest, and then again. Eddie felt the second bullet exit from his back.

Each second stretched. Both Desmond and Eddie stood still, expecting Eddie to drop. Instead he stumbled forward, and Desmond put a round through his arm.

Stop fucking shooting me! Eddie speared the shovel blade-first through Desmond's sternum.

Desmond dropped his gun. The spade stuck out at a right angle from his chest. He staggered backward, and as he lost his fight against gravity his face filled with moonlight. Blood gushed from Desmond's mouth, formed a black beard on his chin.

Eddie watched his best friend connect with the concrete and cease to breathe. Then he knelt over Kelly, whose head had changed shape from the blow Eddie had dealt it. Already Kelly's shattered left temple had swollen to resemble a balloon. What looked like blood pooling in Kelly's eye socket was in fact the start of a massive hemorrhage beneath his skin.

If any inhabitants of nearby houses had heard Desmond fire the pistol four times, they gave no sign of it. No windows opened, no curtains parted. Not a single light blinked on.

Eddie didn't care, either way. He stayed on his knees, staring hard at the corpses around him—well, in Kelly's case, a near-corpse—and tried to recall how it felt to cry. Inside himself he sensed only a deep and airless void, an envious longing for a soul that might take ill at his own deeds.

Eddie squatted there in that stranger's yard for hours, wishing he had not gotten so practiced at murder. The moon sank. The sky lightened.

❦ ❦ ❦

The sun did not rise. Eddie finally got to his feet. He yanked the spade from Desmond's chest and used it to smash both of Desmond's knees, then Kelly's. *Let's see ye come haunt me now.*

He saw with numb disgust that ants had discovered Desmond's blood. They circled the shore of the red lake filling his puncture wound. Desmond's eyes lay open, and a few scouts now explored there as well.

Eddie limped out the driveway to the street. His boot soles scratched the sidewalk as he walked. The bullet in his thigh hurt worse than his arm or the chest wounds. Every time his weight leaned on it, bolts of pain speared up his leg as high as his stomach.

Nobody saw Eddie drag himself back to the Corridor. The streets sat empty. The gray firmament hung bleak and heavy upon Queensborough Heights, a sunless morning that would never end.

As he crossed the soccer field, Eddie stopped and examined himself. *Why ain't there any blood on me clothes?* Through the hole in the leg of his jeans he checked where the bullet had opened him. The slit gaped when he stretched the skin, but no blood came out.

His chest wounds, too, were dry. And his forearm—Eddie took his jacket off to examine it. The flesh from the gap all the way to his hand seemed gamey. A small flap of skin hung over the edge of the rotted chasm. Eddie grabbed this flap and tugged.

His arm ripped—not just the skin but the meat, all the way down to that bonelike rod inside. Eddie peeled it all the way up and over his hand. His flesh came away in a large rubbery glove.

Eddie had uncovered another arm, much smaller. His true arm.

The moist surface of his new skin withered upon contact with the air. Rapidly Eddie's true hide shriveled into a serpentine pattern he knew quite well.

A groove marked the spot where Desmond's shot had pierced him. Above that, the flesh that led to Eddie's elbow—and the rest of his body—appeared spoiled, too. Shortly it would turn rancid. He needed to shed his skin.

Eddie left his denim jacket on the grass and headed for the horse trail, for the Farm. A weird energy propelled him, which might have been starvation or a drug effect, and might have been something else. The sky had grown so bright it clouded his vision. He did not see the men in cowls almost until he reached them.

www.ingramcontent.com/pod-product-compliance
Lightning Source LLC
Chambersburg PA
CBHW010334150726

47988CB00022BA/3497